TO YOUR PEOPLE YOU ARE DEAD

Anghara slowly raised her head. The bright emissary was watching her, but the spark of pity in its eyes had dimmed. "They will mourn your family, and they will mourn you, even though you still live. You must take on a new identity and leave the Southern Isles. Cairn Caille is barred to you."

Anghara's face was grey as old parchment. Her gaze lit on one of the shards from the shattered timepiece that lay upon the floor. It caught the morning light and winked back a rainbow flicker of purplish bluc; it was the shade that her people had always associated with death. It was also, by a terrible irony, the color of her own eyes. She looked up from the shard of glass and met the emissary's gaze. Her eyes were haunted, and she said:

"I shall be called Indigo."

Other Tor Books by Louise Cooper

The Initiate: Book I in the Time Master trilogy
The Outcast: Book II in the Time Master trilogy
The Master: Book III in the Time Master trilogy
Mirage

BOOK·ONE·OF·INDIGO

LOUISE·COOPER

A TOM DOHERTY ASSOCIATES BOOK
NEW YORK

This is a work of fiction. All the characters and events portrayed in this book are fictitious, and any resemblance to real people or events is purely coincidental.

NEMESIS

A different version of this novel under the same title has been published in the United Kingdom by Unwin Hyman (Publishers) Ltd.

A TOR Book
Published by Tom Doherty Associates, Inc.
49 West 24 Street
New York, NY 10010

Cover art by Robert Gould

ISBN: 0-812-53401-8

Library of Congress Catalog Card Number: 88-51638

First edition: June 1989

Printed in the United States of America

0 9 8 7 6 5 4 3 2

Earth felt the wound, and Nature from her seat
Sighing through all her Works gave sign of woe
That all was lost

Milton: Paradise Lost

For the great cats, the great apes, the wolves, the bears, and all other creatures whose "humanity" puts humanity to shame.

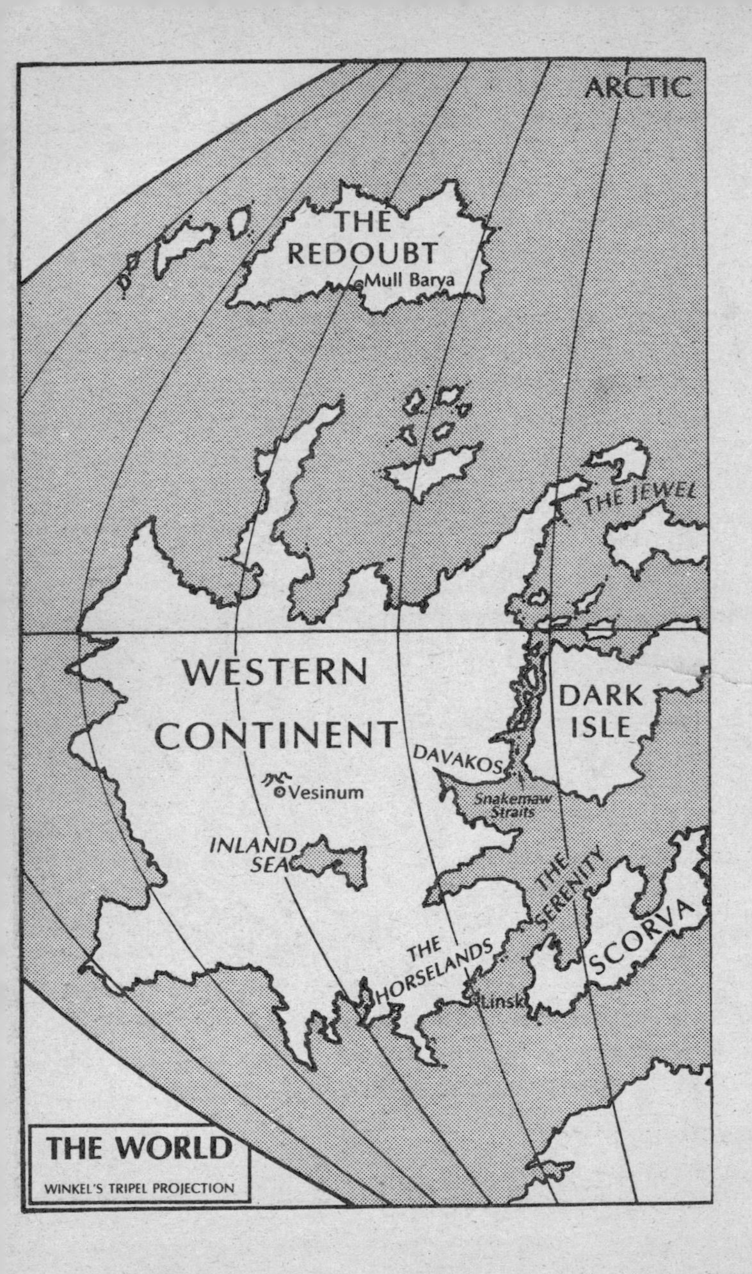
ARCTIC
THE REDOUBT
Mull Barya
THE JEWEL
WESTERN CONTINENT
DARK ISLE
DAVAKOS
Vesinum
Snakemaw Straits
INLAND SEA
THE SERENITY
SCORVA
THE HORSELANDS
Linsk
THE WORLD
WINKEL'S TRIPEL PROJECTION

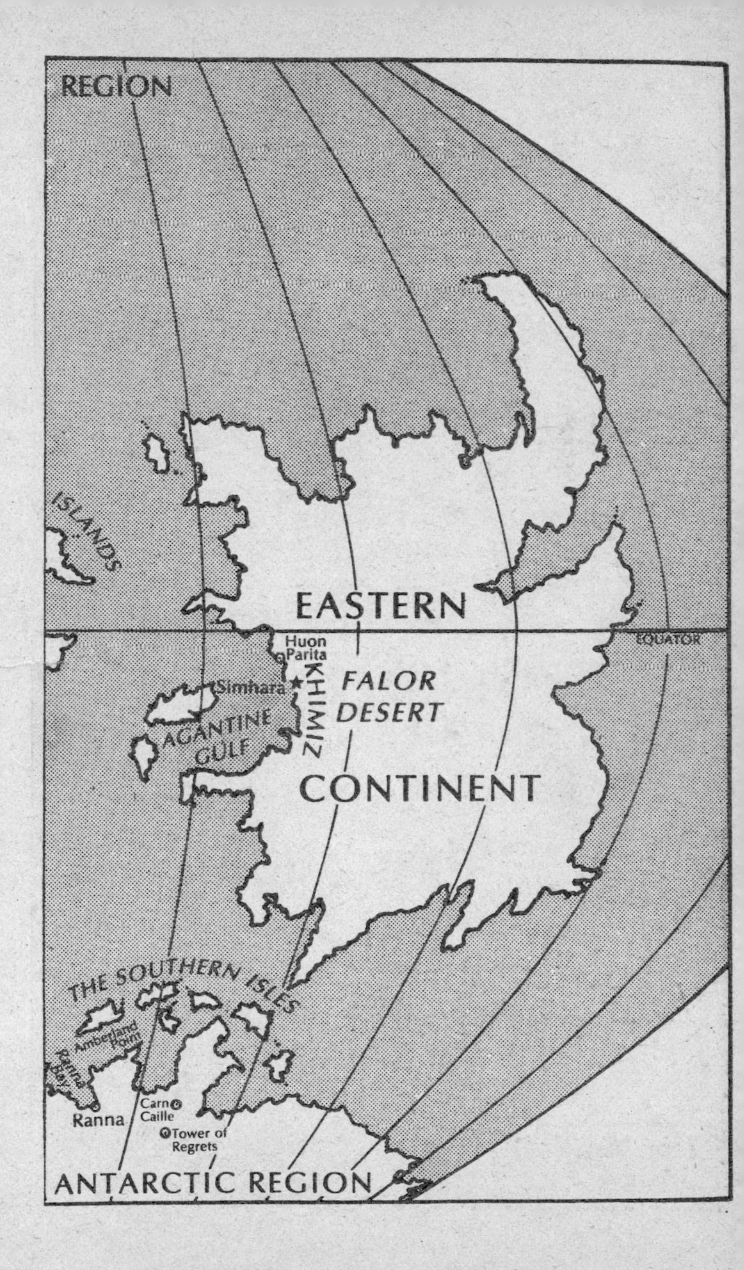
REGION
ISLANDS
EASTERN
EQUATOR
Huon
Parita
Simhara
KHIMIZ
FALOR
DESERT
AGANTINE
GULF
CONTINENT
THE SOUTHERN ISLES
Amberland
Point
Ranna
Bay
Ranna
Carn
Caille
Tower of
Regrets
ANTARCTIC REGION

·PROLOGUE·

The legend of the Tower of Regrets: Cushmagar the harper's telling.

There was a time, a time and a time, before we who live now under the sun and the sky came to count time. Before the brown hare ran and played on the southern tundra, before the great gray wolf came to the forests, before the winding of the hunter's horn sounded among the summer trees. An ancient time and an ill time, when things that should not be walked upon the land, when long day became long night, when summer clothed itself in winter, and that which should be north was south, while that which should be south was north. Then did the Earth our Mother cry out, for her children had been moved to great evil against her. They had taken their fill of her bounty and then they had taken more than was their need or their birthright. They stripped her beauty from her flesh, then they devoured even her very flesh, until she was a thing of bare bone. In the lonely night she wept for her wounds that would not heal, and she cried for her children to restore to her that which they had stolen; but her children heard her not. Her children laughed and sang and told tales of their own prowess, and in their boastful revels they heard not the cries of the Earth our Mother.

And so for long and long did the Earth languish in her pain and her shame. She granted the gift of life to her children, and her children took all she gave and more, while repaying nothing in fee. And the Earth cried, and still her children heard her not.

But in that time of evil, while our Mother Earth writhed in pain, there came a man, a good man among ill men. A man of the islands, son of the sea, brother of the storm, a man whose heart was moved to outrage at the vilification of Mother Earth by the vampire-children who suckled at her desiccated breast. This man's name we know not, but his memory will be forever lauded in our songs and in our stories; for he it was, he and no other, who cried out against his fellows. He it was who stood alone as the champion for whom our mother cried. And he it was on whom she bestowed her greatest blessing, and on whom she laid her greatest burden.

For there came a time when the Earth could sustain her grief no longer. Wrath filled her at last, where before she had felt only pain. This wrath fell upon her children who had so abused her, and she rose up to take her vengeance on the perpetrators of evil. But even in her rage she was moved to pity for the man of the islands; and one night as he slept upon his bed the Earth spoke to him with the voice of the murmuring sea, and the voice of the sweet summer breeze, and the voice of the singing bird. She sent a bright creature to stand at the foot of his bed, and that creature spoke to the man of the islands with all those voices and with the voice of the Earth herself. And the bright creature said:

"Man of the islands, you have championed the Earth our Mother, but yours has been a lonely voice and alone amid chaos. Now I come to speak to you with the voice of our Mother, and I tell you this: the children of the Earth have betrayed their nurturer's trust, and the time is at hand when they must pay the price for that betrayal. Our Mother's wrath is roused, and only the greatest of sacrifices will slake her thirst for vengeance."

And the man of the islands cried out in distress and he said to the bright creature, "How can this terrible thing be averted?" And the bright creature spoke sternly, saying: "It cannot be averted. Man must answer for what he has done, for if he does not, then the evil will continue and the Earth our Mother will die. Do not plead, man of the islands, for your fellows. Listen, instead, to the message I bring to you from Mother Earth, for by that and that alone may your race be saved."

The man of the islands fell silent; for though he knew that he slept, he was wise enough to know, too, that the bright creature spoke a deeper truth than that of any dream. And though his heart was heavy with dread, he listened as he was bidden.

And the bright creature spoke again, and it spoke these words. "Man of the islands, the Earth is moved to wrath, and her wrath will not be contained. No word or deed can sway her. She will raise her hand against her children, and there will be great destruction and great suffering. But her vengeance is not infinite. And when it is done, new life will burgeon again through all her lands. Man will raise his head from the dust of destruction, and he will see about him the leaves springing anew on the trees, and he will see about him the shy, wild creatures sniffing the sweet air, and he will know that the world is reborn.

"But for this rebirth, man of the islands, there will be a price. Man has learned great magic, but his magic has outgrown him and the master has become the servant. If he is to live on when the Earth our Mother is done with her vengeance, then he must exchange his great magic for a smaller magic and an older magic. He must relinquish the power and the strength by which he has striven to achieve ascendancy over our Mother, and he must become again what he was so long ago: a child of the Earth and bound to the earth and at one with the Earth. This, man may hope for—but only if you, man of the islands and son of the sea, will take upon your shoulders the final burden of the Mother's champion."

The bright creature paused then and it smiled with infinite pity, for it had seen the great grief that overcame the man of the islands, and the great fear that lurked unspoken in his heart. It waited and it waited while the man wrung his hands in turmoil; but at last there came an answer.

The man of the islands raised his eyes, and he said: "What must I do?"

And the creature smiled again, for it knew, as the Earth our Mother knew, that this son of the sea was worthy of her trust. It smiled, and it said:

"Go you to the farthest reaches of your land, to the great tundra that borders on the icebound polar wastes. Build there a tower, a single tower without windows and without embellishment, and with one single door. Build it of stone dug from the tundra, and build it so strong that no hand might sunder it. When it is made, go alone to its door at evening, and enter in, and close and bar the door at your back. Await the sun's setting,

and with that setting will come the vengeance of our Mother Earth. You will hear such things as no mortal creature has ever heard; you will hear the crying and the pleading and the dying of your fellow men, and your heart will be torn asunder with grief. But you must harden your heart, and you must turn your thoughts from their suffering. On no account must you open the door, for if you do, you will sign the death warrant of the human race. This will be your greatest test, and you must not shirk it. When all is over, and our Mother's thirst is slaked, then and only then will you see me again. And I will come to you, and I will tell you what you must do." Again it paused, and yet again it smiled. "No more will I say to you now, son of the sea. But if you would see your people live and learn and prosper, do not fail!"

And with these words the bright creature was no more to be seen.

The man of the islands did not sleep that night. And when morning broke and the sun stood up in the sky, he rose from his bed and he went out into the world and he saw it with new eyes. Now, the magic of man in those days was indeed of a greater order than the magic of our times. His spells could chain the elements, stop the seas in their courses, bind the gales in their raging. He could move upon and above and under the Earth, and in his traveling he was as swift as thought. He was master of his fellow creatures, lord of the air, king of the water. He knew no fear, and he knew no taboo. No door was closed to him.

But the glory and triumph of man was at an end. This he knew, this son of the sea, as he looked into the eye of the sun and heard again the words of the bright creature, the messenger of Mother Earth. Man's reign was done. But man might live, and learn, and prosper.

And the key to his living lay in the hands of that man of the islands, that son of the sea.

His heart was heavy and his shadow lay long before him as he turned his face to the great tundra. But his steps did not falter, for he knew what he must do. He was a lion and he was a wolf; he knew he would not fail. And so he came to the tundra and he found the place where he must build. How he built and how he toiled we do not know; such ways as were his ways are lost to us. But he built, and the tower without windows grew alone on the plain, and the tower had no embellishments and but one door. And when the tower was done, he stood before the door at evening and he opened the door and went in, and he barred the door behind him, so that he was alone in the windowless dark. And as he stood in that bleak and lonely place the tears came hard and fast for those he had left behind. And then the moment came when the sun set below the far horizon.

What the man of the islands heard on that endless night, and what images his mind conjured, we cannot know and dare not ask. We sing of his torment, and our harps and our pipes cry the laments of his agony, but still we cannot know, and still we dare not ask. For on that night the seas rose up against the land, and the land was torn asunder, and the fish of the sea perished for want of water in which to swim and the birds of the air perished for want of air in which to fly and the beasts of the land perished for want of earth on which to run. But the tower on the tundra did not fall. And man, in his thousands and in his millions and in his tens of millions, cried out to the screaming skies, but the skies paid no heed to man, and man perished with the fish and with the birds and with the beasts. But still the tower on the tundra did not fall.

All through that long and dreadful night the man of

the islands crouched within the tower that he had built. And at last there came a moment when all sound and all motion ceased. A strange and deathly quiet descended upon the world, and beyond the tower walls, where the man could not see, the dark receded and the first gold arch of a new morning showed itself above the far horizon. In the quiet the man wept, for he knew that all he had known and all he had loved was no more. Mother Earth's vengeance was complete, and her new life was the death of his old ways.

And then in the depth of his sadness there came a light within the tower, and the man looked up, and in the light he saw the bright creature, messenger of the Earth, standing before him. And the creature smiled with pity on the man and spoke, as it had spoken before in his dream.

"Man of the islands, son of the sea, the day of your race is done and the world is clean again. The time has come for you to open the door, which you barred as the sun set, and walk out into the new world.

"Much has changed, my friend. The land you knew is no more. Summer and winter have changed their places; that which was north is now south, and the great magic which man once wielded is lost to him forever. But with that magic and those works has also gone the evil which was man's creation and with which he scourged the Earth and brought about his own downfall. I will speak to you one last time, you man, you survivor, you champion, and I will speak to you of the burden which the Earth our Mother now sets upon your shoulders."

The man of the islands could not answer: his soul was too full for words to form upon his tongue. The bright creature touched his brow so that he raised his eyes, and when he looked he saw that the creature's countenance was filled with pity and with sadness and with joy all at once.

And the creature spoke one last time, and it said, "Man of the islands and son of the sea, to this task does the Earth our Mother now bind you, and this task shall endure for all your days and the days of your children and your children's children and all who follow you through the march of time. The moment has come for you to walk forth into the world, and when you cross the threshold you must bolt and bar the door behind you, and never again may you set your face toward this tower. Return to your home among the islands, where you shall prosper under the sun and the rain and the wind, and do not return to this place, no matter how great the temptation. And when you wed and a son is born to you and that son grows to be a man after his father's image, you shall tell him the tale of the Earth our Mother and her vengeance on the children who betrayed her. And the burden which you have borne shall pass to him and to his heirs; they shall guard the tower, and no human eye will gaze upon its door and no human tread shall sully the earth around it.

"This tower will endure, man of the islands. It will stand as a symbol of the folly of your kind, and as a warning to the multitudes yet unborn. If you would see your people live and grow, then let these stones lie on in solitude, and let no hand be set upon them.

"Man of the islands, son of the sea, this is the burden that the Earth our Mother lays upon you, and this is the trust she places in your heart. Do not fail her."

And the man of the islands looked up once more, and where before the bright creature had stood there was now an emptiness and a sighing and a firefly glow that faded into dark. And the creature's words rang anew in his troubled mind as he stepped with slow steps to the door of the tower he had built, and as his hands raised the bar and lifted the latch, his heart was heavy with the dread of what he might see when he went forth from that place.

The door opened at his bidding, and his eyes gazed upon the light of day and the orb of the sun that rode in the sky. And though the world about him was changed and changed, and though the trees he had known were no more and the rivers he had known were no more and the seas he had known were no more, yet the land was the land he knew and the land to which he had been born. As he gazed and as he wondered at the land so strange and so familiar, there came to him from out of the south a white bear of the snows, and treading in the bear's footsteps came the gray wolf of the tundra, and behind the wolf came the hunting cat of the forest, and after the cat came the innocent brown hare, and all the small things that ran and hopped and crawled upon the land followed in their wake. And the man of the islands looked upon these creatures, and he knew that the Earth our Mother had placed the heritage of their kind and his kind in his hands. And he bowed his head and tears fell from his eyes, and in his heart he swore a silent oath that such a great task and such a great trust should never be found wanting, and that mankind would not forget.

And so the man of the islands bolted and barred the door behind him, and he turned his face from the tower and he set his steps across the plain to make a new home and a new place from the ruins of the old. And the creatures of the Earth withdrew to their domains, to the snow and to the tundra and to the forest, and the tower stood alone and alone.

What became of the man of the islands, the son of the sea, we do not know and cannot say; for his was a time, a time and a time, before we who live now under the sun and the sky came to count time. But the tower he built with his own hands endures still upon the empty plain, and in our time we turn our faces from that place, as we must forever do.

You who sit at my side by the fire, you whose restless ghosts walk in the shadows of my dreams, you children yet unborn, I speak to you as that bright creature spoke so long ago. If you would see your people live and prosper, then let those ancient stones lie on in solitude. For this is the burden that the Earth our Mother has set upon us all, and this is the trust she places in our hearts. We must not fail her.

·CHAPTER·I·

Queen Imogen laid a hand lightly on her husband's arm and said: "Well? What do you truly think?"

Twenty-three years of marriage had taught Kalig, king of the Southern Isles, to recognize every nuance of his consort's moods and reactions, and he detected the pleasure in her voice although she tried to sound neutral. He smiled, and pulled his gaze from the finished painting to look affectionately at her.

"I think," he replied, "that we might tell Master Breym we're pleased with his work."

Imogen laughed and clasped her hands together, moving away from him and crossing the room until she was close to the painting. The summer evening light slanted through the window behind her, framing her with a gold aura in which dust motes danced lazily, and for a moment the years slipped away from her and she looked young again.

"Not too near," Kalig advised. "Or you'll see nothing but the paint, and lose the image."

"With my eyes as they are, it'll be a blessing if I can see that!" But she stepped back nonetheless, allowing him to take hold of her hand. "Seriously, my love. *Are* you pleased?"

"I'm delighted; and I'll make sure Master Breym is very well rewarded."

Imogen nodded her agreement. "The first portrait of us all as a family," she said with satisfaction. "And the first in all the Southern Isles to be painted in this new style."

Kalig didn't know which pleased him more: the painting itself, or his wife's obvious delight in it. His decision to employ the talented but unorthodox Breym to capture the likenesses of the royal family of Carn Caille had been largely at Imogen's urging; he himself had had doubts, though he admitted willingly that his knowledge of art was to say the least limited. But his wife's instinct had been true. The likenesses were superb; so lifelike that it was easy to imagine them moving and stretching their arms and stepping down from the linen-covered board into the room. And the pigments Breym had used were restful on the eye; colors softer yet somehow richer than the harsh tints favored by most artists, lending the portrait a subtlety he'd never encountered in a painting before.

The portrait depicted himself, tall, his auburn hair graying now, dressed in the court robes he wore for the most formal ceremonial occasions, standing in the great hall of Carn Caille with sunlight slanting in at the window much as it slanted in this window now. At his side, Imogen was a graceful figure in a gray-and-white gown, dignity and serenity personified; while on low stools before their parents sat their son and heir, Prince Kirra, and their daughter, Princess Anghara.

Breym had captured twenty-one-year-old Kirra's innate mischief in the tilt of his head and the faintly insouciant way in which his hands rested on his thighs, while Anghara, by complete contrast, sat with her face half shadowed by the curtain of her tawny hair, her violet eyes cast down in a look of troubled contemplation. Kalig felt a swell of pride in the portrait. In years to come, when he had been succeeded by a dozen generations, his descendants would still gaze on this picture, and they would take the same pleasure and pride in their ancestors as he took now.

Reluctantly, Imogen tore her gaze from the painting. "We should send for the children," she said. "And Imyssa—I promised her she would see the portrait as soon as it was ready."

Kalig laughed. "Just so long as she doesn't start looking for omens in the pigment."

"Oh, let her. At her age we can afford to indulge her a little." She stepped forward again, drawing him with her, and peered at the board, screwing up her shortsighted eyes to see better. "Of course, there's now one family member missing. Once Anghara weds, we'll have to think about another commission for Master Breym, to include Fenran. If we'd known a year ago, when the portrait was begun—"

"Then we'd have waited, and by the time it was finished Kirra would have found a wife. Then another wait, until there were grandchildren to be added to the picture." Kalig squeezed her hand. "If we left it much longer, Master Breym would have had to include our death-masks!"

Imogen frowned to show him that his joke was in bad taste, but otherwise let it pass. "Nonetheless, it might be as well to retain him for a while," she insisted. "The marriage is only a month away, and—"

He silenced her with another squeeze, then lifted her

fingers to his lips and kissed them. "Whatever you wish, my love, we shall do. I'm well aware that we're notoriously short of works of art at Carn Caille, and I know how eager you are to bring a little culture into our barbarous southern lives! For as long as my coffers can afford it, you shall have whatever you want!"

The gentle ribbing was a reminder of the days, long ago, when Imogen had come from her home in the eastern continent to become Kalig's queen. Like most marriages in the aristocracy, it had been a pragmatically arranged match, designed to unite a wealthy merchant principality with the military power of the Southern Isles. The pragmatism had worked, giving much-needed security to the east and equally desirable prosperity to the fierce but impoverished south: and, against the odds, the unlikely pairing of the unsophisticated heir to Carn Caille, whose world revolved around hunting, riding and fighting, and the educated nobleman's daughter accustomed to artistic pursuits and the elegant life of a city had, after an uncertain start, proved to be a love-match. Kalig and Imogen had learned from each other, his exuberant love of life trading with her gentility; and now, many years on, the greatest compliment they could pay their daughter was to hope that her marriage would prove as happy as their own.

Imogen's family, they knew, disapproved of the outlandish notion that Anghara should be allowed a husband of her own choosing. Kalig had laughed their disapproval off with the comment that no power on, under or above the earth could ever persuade the princess to acquiesce to an arranged match, while Imogen, more diplomatically, had assured her relations that the Northman Fenran came of an indisputably noble family, had proved himself in the service of Carn Caille and would make an eminently suitable consort for their daughter. Thanks to her tact, doubts had been largely assuaged; and there would be a good contingent of eastern representatives at the nuptial celebrations in the autumn.

It was, Imogen reflected, a good deal easier to settle her daughter's future than it would be when it came to Kirra's marriage. As he was Kalig's heir—though not, she prayed daily, for a good many years yet—a pragmatic alliance would be necessary to safeguard the Southern Isles' future prosperity, and she had spent many an intriguing hour with Imyssa, who had been nurse to both children since their birth, listing the names and qualities of highborn girls from all parts of the great sprawl of the world who might be considered as a worthy future queen. Kirra looked on his mother's deliberations with huge amusement, which for Imogen was a relief; the young prince was twenty times more tractable than his sister and would accept his parents' choice happily so long as the girl in question had a pretty face and an equable temper. Sometimes Imogen awoke in the night sweating at the thought of the troubles that would have been heaped upon her had Kirra's and Anghara's personalities been reversed.

Kalig's voice broke in on her reverie. "My love, much as I admire Breym's work, we'll find ourselves rooted to the floor if we stand her gazing on it for much longer. The light's fading, I'm hungry—"

"You're always hungry!"

"—and before I retire tonight, I must speak to Fenran about the hunting rights in the western forest. There's been some dispute among the small landowners over . . ." Kalig's voice trailed off as Imogen laid a hand on his arm and patted it.

"Fenran is out riding with Anghara, and I doubt if we'll see hide or hair of them before dusk." she said placidly. "There's plenty of time to settle hunting rights; the season isn't under way yet. Tonight, my dear husband and lord, you and I will dine privately in our chambers, and I'll sing your favorite songs for you, and we shall retire early." Mischief and affection glinted in her eyes. "Business can wait until tomorrow."

For a few moments Kalig gazed at her; then his face broke into a slow, broad smile. He said nothing, but lifted her fingers to his lips again and kissed them. Then, with a last satisfied glance at the portrait, he let her lead him from the room.

As Kalig and Imogen were making their unhurried way to their private quarters, Princess Anghara Kaligsdaughter was reining in her iron-gray mare at the top of the escarpment that marked the southernmost edge of the forestlands. From this vantage point the view was breathtaking. To the north the trees began to take hold, gradually at first, then growing denser, until they merged into a sea of unbroken blue-green; while southward from the escarpment's feet the land was empty and flat to a hazy horizon, broken only by the contours of rock outcrops and the occasional patch of stunted and scrubby vegetation. In the right weather and with the light at a certain angle it was just possible to glimpse the edge of the vast southern tundra that ended only when it met the implacable glaciers of the polar region. Today, that distant pale shimmer wasn't visible; the sun was too low (though during the short summers it barely dipped beyond the curve of the world), and its mellow orange-gold light made all distances nothing more than an indistinct blur.

The barren plains, and the tundra and glaciers beyond, were part of Kalig's kingdom, but no one had ever ventured far into those southern wastes. Indeed, the landmark that stood at the limit of human exploration was just visible from the scarp as a long shadow fingering the landscape almost directly ahead; a sharp and isolated rectangle of darkness among the smaller and less distinct silhouettes of the scrub. A single stone tower, its door barred to any trespass by an edict that had been old when Kalig's nine-times-great-grandfather had fought his way to rulership in Carn Caille. The edict was harshly simple: the tower must never, *never* be opened, or even approached. The reasons for that irrevocable law were hidden in the uncountable past, surviving only in the cryptic forms of ballad and folklore: only the tower itself remained, solitary, threatening, obscure.

Anghara shivered as a light wind sprang up and chilled her arms. Such an old place, its origins long forgotten. Yet the ruling house of Carn Caille had lived for centuries with its unspoken threat, and might do so for centuries yet to come.

"A silver penny for your daydreams." The voice at her side, warm, quizzical and faintly teasing, brought the princess out of her reverie. She turned and saw that Fenran had ridden up the escarpment to join her, reining in his horse and sitting easily back in the saddle while his gray eyes lazily assessed her.

"You gave up the hunt too soon," he said. "I told you—patience has its virtues!" And he gestured before him, drawing her attention to the small, furry corpse that dangled over his saddle pommel.

She laughed. "A hare? Fenran, your prowess is unlimited! A whole *hare*—I'm in awe!"

"It's more than you managed, woman!" Fenran made a mock swipe at her with his free hand, then patted the dead creature. "Imyssa will appreciate it, even if you don't. And when she's jugged it, and added her herbs to it, and muttered her incantations over the cooking pot, I'll see that you don't get the smallest taste of the result!" He grinned at her. "Seriously, though . . ."

"Seriously?"

"It's getting late. Any creature with half a grain of sense is in its lair or burrow by now, and we should be going. If the shadows grow much longer, Imyssa and your mother will start to fret."

Anghara sighed. She was reluctant to abandon the long, bright day for the walls of Carn Caille, and up here on the escarpment, the old feeling had her in its grip again, the fearful, exciting, insatiable feeling that had assailed her so often since she was a very little girl and had looked out across the southern plains for the first time. The imperative feeling of wanting to *know* . . . Fenran saw something of it reflected in her face, and his own expression tightened into a frown. He followed her gaze to the faraway shadow on the plain and said: "You're not still thinking of the Tower of Regrets?"

Angry with herself for being too transparent, Anghara shrugged. "There's no harm to be had in thinking."

"Oh, but there is. Or there could be, if the thoughts get too strong a grip." He leaned over and squeezed her arm. "Forget about it, my little she-wolf; it's safer. The horses are tired, and your future lord and master is hungry. Let it rest, and let's go home."

It wasn't in Anghara's nature to allow herself to be maneuvered, or to obey anyone—her father included—for no better reason than a sense of duty. But in the time they had known each other Fenran had learned his own ways of handling her mercurial character and stubborn temper, and something in his voice both mollified and persuaded her. She smiled faintly at him and, with only a small show of reluctance, urged her mare forward to follow him down the slope.

* * *

"Come on now, my poppet—just look at the hour! Come you back to your bed, and get your sleep!"

Anghara turned from her window to where Imyssa hovered like a plump, mothering hen. The old nurse had been fussing with the bedcovers, smoothing the underblanket, twitching at the goose-down-filled quilt until it was rigidly straight, plumping the pillows; now, with no more to occupy her hands, she bobbed about like a small boat in the girl's wake.

Anghara sighed irritably. "I *can't* sleep, Imyssa; I'm not tired, and I don't want to go back to bed. Just go away, and leave me be."

Imyssa regarded her, blue eyes sharp in their sheaf of wrinkles. "You're fretting again, and don't think I don't know why."

"You don't," Anghara retorted. "Witch you may be, but you can't read my thoughts; and they're none of your concern."

"Oho, they're not! D'you think I don't know you just as well as I know the lines on my own hands, when I delivered you from your mother's body and nursed you from infant to grown woman?" Imyssa folded her arms. "I don't need my Craft to tell me what's amiss with you!" She took a pace nearer to the princess. "I know where you've been, and I know what you've seen today; and I say to you, put it out of your mind and away, in the dark places where it belongs!"

The trouble with Imyssa, Anghara thought, was that her wise-woman's skills *did* allow her to read minds, or at least inclinations, too well. She hunched her shoulders moodily and turned back to the window, gazing out at the dark jumble of Carn Caille. There was no moon tonight, but the sky reflected the sullen fires of the sun a bare few degrees below the horizon, and the courtyard and the ancient keep that marked the stronghold's boundaries were clearly visible. Beyond

Carn Caille, over the turf-grown hills and past the crowding trees of the forest, were the plain and the tundra and the Tower of Regrets. . . .

Imyssa's voice broke in on her again. "Forget about that place, my own one. It's not a burden you'll ever have to bear; it's for your brother to take up when the Earth our Mother finally gathers the king to Her embrace; though may She grant it's many years yet." Now there was more than a hint of reprimand in her voice, and something that Anghara thought smacked of dread. "Take heed of my advice, for I *know*," Imyssa added darkly.

Anger rose afresh in Anghara. "What do you know?" she demanded. "Tell me that, Imyssa—just what do you know of the Tower of Regrets?"

Imyssa pursed her mouth. "Nothing, save for the law that no one has ever broken—and I don't question it. Better creatures than you have obeyed that law since time began, and if you want to be wise you'll follow their example!"

Her voice was suddenly so emphatic that Anghara was taken aback. Only a very few times in her life had she heard Imyssa speak so fiercely; the old woman's nature was too mild and too fond for such an ugly edge, and its manifestation now was unnerving. Guilt came hard on the heels of chagrin; she hadn't intended to upset Imyssa or take out her ill mood on her, and suddenly she regretted her outburst.

The nurse saw the fiery light of defiance slowly fade from Anghara's gaze and, anxious not to dwell on an unpleasant subject, she turned to a low table near the bed. On the table stood a timepiece: an ornate and complex device of delicate, blown-glass bulbs and tubes in a silver filigree frame. Colored liquid flowed through the glass in an intricate pattern, filtering slowly into the bulbs and filling them, one for each hour that passed. When twelve hours had passed, the structure could be rotated within its frame and the entire process would begin again. The timepiece had been a birthday gift to Anghara from Queen Imogen's family, who set great store by such inventions, but the princess privately shared Kalig's view that it was a frippery plaything and the hour could be told as easily, and a good deal more conveniently, by looking at the sky.

Imyssa now tapped the filigree frame with a light fingernail, and the timepiece gave off a faint, sweet, ringing sound. "Look at the hour!" she said, thankful for a new topic to divert them both. "There's a feast tomorrow to celebrate the start of the new hunting season, and you're to play for the king's guests. What sort of state will you be in if you don't get your sleep?"

"I'll be well enough." But Anghara's resentment was fading, and there was a tinge of affection in her voice. "*Please*, dear Imyssa—leave me be now."

The old woman frowned. "Well . . . then I'll mix you a draught to settle you." She eyed her charge. "Something to put paid to those stormy thoughts in your head."

It would be easier to appease her, and perhaps even the artificial peace of a draught would be better than the torment of unfulfillment. Anghara nodded. "Very well."

Satisfied, Imyssa bustled through the low door that separated Anghara's bedchamber from her own. As she prepared a sleeping-potion from the collection of herbs which she kept in a small satchel and carried everywhere with her, her voice, affectionately chiding, carried through the open doorway, interspersed with the rhythmic thump of a small mortar and pestle.

"You should by now be well able to do this for yourself, my poppet, instead of relying on old Imyssa to do it for you! The bones and spirits of my grand-dams know I've tried to teach you my skills since you could barely toddle, and they know, too, that you've got the talent in you as surely as any wise woman ever born! But no; you've never knuckled down to your studies like a dutiful girl. Too busy riding and hunting and running with the boys . . . I don't wonder your poor mother the queen nigh on despairs of you sometimes!" There was the sound of liquid being poured, then a silver spoon rattled briskly and noisily in a pottery cup.

"Mother doesn't despair of me," Anghara contradicted. "She accepts me as I am, Imyssa, dear. Besides, what use will witch-skills be to me when I'm wed?"

"What use?" Imyssa's voice grew louder and she appeared in the doorway with the potion in her hand. "Whatever use you can think of, and I could name you a hundred without pausing for breath! You can scry, you can foretell the weather, you have a way with horses and dogs that's the envy of every man in Carn Caille; and don't think I haven't seen you using those little tricks I taught you to bend someone to your will without them any the wiser! Then there's—"

"Yes, yes," Anghara interrupted hastily, aware that Imyssa could and would fulfill her promise to name a hundred different possibilities if she weren't forestalled. "But I won't *need* them." She smiled. "It doesn't take magic to persuade Fenran to my way of thinking."

The nurse snorted derisively but, aware that Anghara needed sleep more than she needed a debate, made no further comment, only held out the cup. "There, now. Drink, and get you to bed." And under her breath she muttered, "Won't need them, indeed!"

Anghara drank the draught, which was in honey-sweetened cider and tasted soothingly good, and made no protest as Imyssa pulled the tapestried curtain over her window and turned down the wick of her lamp until it was a barely glowing pinpoint. She let the old nurse chivy her into bed, and as the covers were pulled up over her shoulders Imyssa said, more gently, "Don't you fret, my little one. You've happier things to think on than old legends. Good night, poppet."

Imyssa smelled pleasantly of fresh leaves and honey and the pressed essence of downland flowers, scents which carried memories of childhood; and Anghara reached out and squeezed her wrinkled hand before the lamp was extinguished and the room sank into the shimmering half darkness of a southern summer night.

·CHAPTER·II·

To mark his pleasure at their impending marriage, King Kalig had granted Fenran and Anghara the rare honor of leading the dancing at the feast which heralded the start of the hunting season. Watching them walk out on the floor together, to the applause of the assembled company, Kalig sat back in his chair and smiled, proud of the picture they presented and well content with life at large.

Formal dancing was another of the innovations which Queen Imogen had brought to the untutored court at Carn Caille. It numbered among her favorite recreations, and when she married she had been determined not to be deprived of it. Persuading Kalig and his nobles to refine the chaotically rumbustious cavorting that sometimes accompanied the court's more drunken revels had taken a great deal of patience and tenacity; but finally a happy compromise was reached by introducing some set steps and an element of grace into the best of the old country dances. The "new entertainment" became surprisingly popular, and Imogen had discovered an unexpected ally in Fenran, who had taken great pleasure in music and dancing in his own father's household.

Watching the couple as they stepped and spun down the length of the great, raftered hall, Imogen thought how splendid a pairing they made. Anghara scorned the convention of braiding her hair and wore it as it suited her best: loosed and flowing over her shoulders like a tawny waterfall, setting off the uncomplicated lines of her tightly cut green gown. She was as tall and slender and graceful as a young willow; a credit to her royal house. And Fenran made the perfect complement, the picture of elegant sobriety in gray and black, yet with a wit in his eyes and a strong, self-willed, perhaps even faintly reckless look to his tanned face that offset his apparent austerity. The marriage between these two promised to be stronger even than Imogen had initially hoped, for beneath the hot fires of passion that burned in them now was a firm core of compatibility and like thinking which would keep the fires burning when old age turned passion into no more than a fond memory.

Strange, Imogen thought, how such an insignificant event as Fenran's arrival at Carn Caille a little over two years ago could have flowered, against all likelihood, into something that would change all their lives. Although these days he was reluctant to speak of his earlier life, Fenran had been born the second—or third, Imogen couldn't remember which—son of Earl Bray of the Redoubt, a large island right across the world in the far north. A family quarrel had resulted in Fenran's leaving his homeland at the age of eighteen; since then he had wandered the world selling his brain or his sinew to anyone who cared to employ them. He had arrived in the Southern Isles as a temporary crewman on a cargo ship from the east, and a quirk of chance had brought him to Carn Caille when a foreman of the train designated to bring the cargo from Ranna Port to Kalig's court went sick with a fever and Fenran took his place. Liking what he saw of the uncompromising but open-handed south, Fenran had set out to ingratiate himself and prove himself in the king's service, and by round-about means it hadn't been long before he was established as a warden of the vast game forests abutting Kalig's stronghold.

Kalig kept a firm hand on the tiller of his realm and little escaped his attention, so the special diplomacy of his new warden in dealing with territorial disputes among the foresters soon came to his notice. Interviewing Fenran, he was impressed with the young man's frankness and intelligence, and Fenran had found himself promoted to the king's direct service, with his own accommodation at Carn Caille and a place at the table of the royal household. And Anghara, on first meeting her father's new right-hand man, had recognized in him a sharp mind and a ready wit, a sense of independence and courage that matched her own. Their pairing was, Imogen thought with satisfaction, all she could have hoped for her daughter.

A familiar touch on her arm broke her reverie, and she turned her head to see Kalig leaning slightly forward in his chair. He was smiling at her, his eyebrows raised in quizzical invitation, and all around the higher tables people were watching them expectantly. Taking her cue, Imogen rose gracefully to her feet and let Kalig's fingers twine with hers. They bowed to each other amid applause; then he was leading her from the table to follow Anghara and Fenran into the swirl of the dance.

* * *

The dancing continued for two hours before Kalig finally called a halt. Cups were refilled, mostly with beer or cider or mead, though some of the more adventurous guests were developing a taste for the wines imported from the east; and then people began to call for Anghara to sing and play for them.

She was at the high table, seated between Fenran and her brother, Prince Kirra. Kirra, a year younger than Anghara, had hair a good few shades lighter, almost sandy; freckles bridged his nose and when he smiled he showed a crooked front tooth. But the last traces of adolescence were rapidly giving way to a breadth and stature that promised to rival his father's. Kirra was a hunter, a rider, a fighter; and people who knew him predicted that, when Kalig eventually joined his ancestors, Kirra's reign would be anything but uneventful.

Now Kirra leaned across to tug affectionately at a lock of Anghara's hair. "Come on, sister—don't be shy!" He ignored Fenran's snort of suppressed laughter at such an idea. "Your harp's tuned and ready, so you've no excuse for disappointing us."

From her cushioned chair Queen Imogen smiled at her daughter. "Sing us one of the old ballads, Anghara. Something sweet and sad."

Anghara looked at Fenran, who traced his forefinger slowly along her hand. "What about the Song of the White Bird?" he suggested softly.

Her eyes lit warmly; as always, he had judged her mood and what would suit her the best. A servant stepped deferentially forward with her small, polished wood lap-harp, and the assembled company rumbled approval and thumped the tables as she stepped out and took the traditional minstrel's place at Kalig's feet.

At the first clear notes of the harp, liquid and yet as sharply bright as the sound of breaking icicles, the guests fell silent. Anghara closed her eyes as she played the introduction to the ballad, then began to sing in a voice that was husky but unfailingly true, with a vibrato which carried an almost chilling edge. The song told of a great white seabird that came out of the north and flew across the southern ice in search of morning. The folktale from which the ballad came was one of the oldest in the Southern Isles, and much of its original sense had been lost. No one understood the symbolism of the white-winged seeker sailing endlessly above the great glaciers and calling to the sun that never rose; but the song was beautiful, filled with haunting images of great sadness and loss and longing. As Anghara sang, Queen Imogen surreptitiously brushed her fingers across her cheeks, and when the whole company joined in the lilting yet melancholy chorus, even Kalig could be seen blinking more rapidly than normal.

There was a great deal more table-thumping when the ballad was done, and Anghara was pressed to sing another. Judging the tenor of her audience, she chose a shorter but equally poignant song, then, to rest her voice, played a fisherman's chantey on the harp alone. This was greeted with cheers of approval and, the drink now beginning to take effect, with demands for the island work-songs in which everyone could join. The musicians who had played for the dancing added their instruments to Anghara's harp, and the company roared its way through songs of stormy seas, ferocious battles, old feuds and lost loves. After an hour or so the tone of the songs started to shift subtly as some of the bolder—or drunker—men present introduced a bawdier element, and Imogen, seeing that Kalig was too embarrassed to join in as he might have done without her restraining influence, smiled faintly and rose from her seat, indicating that she had decided to retire. Taking their cue from her, many of the other women also rose, and Imogen looked quizzically at her daughter.

"Aren't you tired, my love?"

Anghara smiled up at her. "Not yet, Mother. I'll stay on a while."

"Very well. But remember, a woman needs her rest. Not too late, now."

"Yes, Mother." The princess's smile broadened affectionately.

Kalig stood up and kissed his wife—a gesture that was greeted with shouts of approval from the rowdier tables—-and the queen left the hall at the head of a small procession of ladies. As a page closed the door behind them, Anghara rose from her place at the king's feet, setting her harp aside, and rejoined Fenran at the high table. Tonight was the first time she had played in some while and her fingertips were sore from the harp strings; she had done enough and it was time for the paid minstrels to take over. Besides, she wanted to be free to concentrate on the entertainment which would follow when the singing was done.

The diehards in the hall had already launched into an alehouse favorite, a complicated and highly dubious rant about a mermaid and a well-endowed sailor; others were losing their inhibitions and joining in, and Prince Kirra, to Anghara's left, was singing lustily. Fenran refilled Anghara's cup, then slipped an arm around her shoulders and drew her close to him.

"Isn't this song too much for your tender ears, love?" he teased.

She screwed up her face at him. "I learned *this* ballad from Kirra when I was eight and he was seven!" she retorted, then laughed. "Mind, we'll have to make sure that it doesn't creep in at our wedding festivities, or my fine relations from the east will have seizures."

"You should sing the Song of the White Bird at the

celebrations,'' Fenran told her. ''I'd challenge anyone, Easterner or no, not to be moved by that.''

''I can't sing at my own wedding; Mother would never allow it.''

He smiled, a private, secret smile. ''Then you must sing it for me. Afterward, when we're alone. . . .''

Any reply Anghara might have made was eclipsed by a roar that almost lifted the hall roof as the ballad came to an end. In the lull that followed, King Kalig thumped his fist on the table for silence, setting knives and plates rattling.

''Cushmagar!'' the king roared. ''Bring in Cushmagar!''

Those feasters close enough to hear took up the shout, and Anghara smiled, adding her call to theirs. ''Cushmagar! Cushmagar!''

In response to the shouting, the doors at the far end of the hall were pushed open from without. A blast of cold air stirred up the overheated atmosphere and set the great fire smoking, and it heralded the entrance of an elderly man who shuffled slowly across the threshold, supported on the arm of a young servant boy. Behind the pair came two more servants who between them manhandled a harp four times the size of Anghara's, maneuvering it as carefully as if it were made of glass. The cheers that greeted their arrival were deafening; even Kalig was on his feet and applauding as the small procession made its slow way up the center aisle of the hall toward the high table.

''Cushmagar! Cushmagar!'' The old man smiled a shy smile, bowing his head to right and left as he acknowledged the approbation. His young assistant glanced up at Kalig, received a gesture of assent and guided his charge toward the reserved place at his king's feet.

Cushmagar the harper lowered himself with grave

dignity onto the heaped cushions and waited for his great harp to be placed before him. He was a wiry man, all limb and sinew without a scrap of spare flesh, and with his shock of hair, white but still abundant despite his years, he resembled nothing so much as an ancient, gnarled but still thriving blackthorn tree. Ten years ago cataracts in both eyes had robbed Cushmagar of his sight, but his remaining senses, perhaps in part to compensate for the loss, were still uncannily keen. Every man, woman and child in the Southern Isles knew of Cushmagar and honored his name. He was the king's own harper, the bard of bards; and in his knowledge of the folklore and myth of the far south he had no equal.

The harp was set gently down before the old man, and as Cushmagar flexed his fingers Anghara felt a deep-rooted thrill course through her. This was the moment she had awaited with the greatest anticipation of all: the high point of the traditional hunting season feast when the temporal, corporeal world of eating and drinking and carousing stood aside for a while and gave way to the world of magic and mystery, things which the hand could not touch but which pulsed and flowed in the deep caverns of ancestral memory. The princess held her breath, not wanting to break the spell as a profound silence cloaked the hall. Cushmagar smiled. His fingers touched the harp strings and a ripple of sound spilled from the instrument, conjuring up the murmur of sweet water over stones, the whisper of unhuman voices deep among summer trees. Then a shimmering cascade of notes shattered the expectant hush, flooding like a great tide into the hall. A deep, involuntary sigh issued from the assembled company, counterpointing the music's surging power, and Anghara closed her eyes, giving herself up to the rushing lament of the sea that flowed from the ancient harper's fingers.

This was the most time-honored moment of the celebrations, the moment when tribute was given to the implacable forces of nature to which every living creature owed fealty. It had always been the duty of the highest harper to offer the tribute in his own way, and Anghara believed that no man had ever matched or would ever rival Cushmagar in his invocation of that fealty. The ancient bard was inspired by something beyond the reach of ordinary mortals. His harp flung open the hall doors and brought in the great vista of the world: the towering cliffs and rolling sea-straits of the scattered islands; the dappled, reflective peace of the forest tracts; the wild beauty of the southern tundra; the haunted, echoing emptiness of the vast ice plains beyond. Listening, rapt, Anghara found time to feel deeply grateful that her time and Cushmagar's had overlapped; and grateful, too, for the great privilege of having had him for her teacher. Her skills would never come close to his, but he had nurtured her talent and shown her how to conjure her best, and it was a boon she could never repay.

She felt Fenran's fingers come to rest lightly on hers as Cushmagar's dedication continued, and knew that he shared the thrall of the music. They sat, hands linked but neither moving a muscle, until, after a time which no listener in the hall could have judged, the last rippling notes merged into a poignant chord that hung heavy in the warm air before dying away. For a few moments the gathering was utterly silent. Then a gradual swell of sound, murmuring, growing ever stronger, surged on the harp's final echoes as a hundred men and women released the sighing breaths they had held while the spell was on them.

Cushmagar raised his blind eyes toward the king's table and smiled again, a small and faintly self-deprecating smile that quite deliberately broke the enchantment and brought back the real world. The ceremony was not quite over, but what followed would be mundane: the traditional and expected acknowledgment of his skills. The magic was done.

Kalig stood up, and at this signal the entire company rose to its feet. With great deliberation the king took a plate of beaten pewter and began to heap it with delicacies from his table. When it was full almost to overflowing, he poured mead into a cup, then left his place and walked with formal dignity to where Cushmagar sat. Standing before the old harper, Kalig bowed low and set plate and cup at the man's feet as though making an offering to a deity. Approval rumbled through the hall; then massed voices took up again the shout they'd made at the harper's entrance.

"Cushmagar! Cushmagar! Cushmagar!"

Still smiling, still as diffident as ever, Cushmagar waited for his young page to run forward and put the mead-cup into one of his hands whilst guiding the other to the plate. He drank deeply, then bit into the roasted leg of a fowl with teeth that were strong and sharp. Everyone watched as he chewed and swallowed; then he set the victuals down and his gusty sigh of satisfaction rose to the rafters.

There was cheering of a more general nature as Kalig returned to his chair, and it carried an unmistakable element of relief. The ritual had been conducted and all was well; the harper's music had driven away the dismal ghosts that might otherwise have haunted the steps of the hunters in this new season; the king had offered the proper reward to the harper, and the harper had not found it wanting. All was well—and now the lighter side of Cushmagar's work could begin.

"A story, Cushmagar!" Prince Kirra leaned eagerly forward in his seat, gesturing with his wine-cup though the old man couldn't see him. "Tell us a tale to light our way to bed tonight!"

Cushmagar chuckled, and his fingers stroked the harp, wringing a thin, shivering moan from the strings. "What manner of tale, royal prince?" His voice was a baritone which age had barely diminished. "A fable of the sea? Or of the forests? Or—"

"No," Anghara interrupted without realizing what she was doing, and as Cushmagar turned his head in the direction from which her voice had come, confusion filled her. She met the old man's sightless gaze and had the discomfiting feeling that, despite his blindness, he saw her as well as he had ever done before he was afflicted. And then she knew what it was that drove her, and what she had to hear.

"My princess." Cushmagar's voice filled with affection. "My little singer of songs and fighter of battles. Have you loosed your hair tonight, little singer? And is your harp well strung and the wood polished and fed with beeswax, as I taught you?"

Anghara smiled, biting back the emotion that the old man's reminiscence conjured up. "Yes and yes, Cushmagar."

The harper nodded approval. "Then you've earned a tale. What would you hear?"

"Tell me of the Tower of Regrets, Cushmagar. That is the story I would hear tonight."

Her brother whispered warningly: "Anghara—" Beside her, she felt Fenran shift uncomfortably, and from his chair Kalig frowned. But their disapproval didn't shake her: if Cushmagar was willing, no one would gainsay him. It was a long time, a very long time, since that oldest of stories had been told in the hall of Carn Caille, and the retelling was overdue. She wanted to hear it—she *had* to hear it, tonight.

Cushmagar deliberated for a long time. Then at last he looked up at her again.

"Very well. Let it be as my princess wishes." He raised a crooked forefinger, exhorting his listeners to silence. "Here begins the legend of the Tower of Regrets."

His hands touched the harp, and the harp cried, mournfully, like the fabled call of the White Bird of Morning, lost and lonely and desolate. A shiver ran through Anghara's veins and her hand tightened involuntarily in Fenran's; when she glanced at him she saw that his dark brows were drawn together and his face tense. The harp's moaning cry still hung in the air, and over it came Cushmagar's voice, slipping now into the lilting, lyrical chant of the formal storyteller.

The story was the oldest of the thousands of mythic tales that wove their way through the history of the Southern Isles. As a child, Anghara had lain in her bed on lamplit winter evenings and listened, enraptured, to Imyssa crooning the legend of Mother Earth's pain and betrayal in the form of simple, melancholy lullabies; asleep, she had dreamed of the Son of the Sea and his lonely burden; but the old harper's telling of this strange tale tore at her in a way no other could do. His voice conjured up images that were at once terrible and beautiful, while his hands wrung a majestic counterpoint from the harp strings that fired those images into vivid life. The sea, the gale, the cruelty of man, the torment of the great Earth herself, all marched through Anghara's mind as, still holding tightly to Fenran's hand, she closed her eyes and lost herself in Cushmagar's storytelling.

He would never teach her words of the myth, or the music that illuminated it. However hard she pleaded or cajoled, he would never tell her. "Every harper must sing his own songs, little princess," he would say, "and this is not a song for you." Then he would pat her hand and chide her for neglecting her practice piece, firmly changing the topic. . . .

She pushed the involuntary memory of those lost days out of her mind. The tale was almost done, and the harper's music building toward a dizzying, rippling climax before falling away to the final, sweet and infinitely sad cadence that shivered in the hot, smoky air. The notes hung silver, shimmering, creating a strange harmony as Cushmagar uttered the final words of the myth in a single slow, whispered breath.

There was no applause to break the silence that descended on the hall. To shout, stamp or thump the tables would have been too crude a tribute to the old master, who sat, head bowed, at the king's feet, his hands now resting passively in his lap. Anghara's eyelids fluttered involuntarily and opened; through the haze that filled the hall from fire and candles she saw her father, a shadow among shadows, rise slowly from his chair and take a step toward the old man.

"Cushmagar." Kalig's voice was distorted with emotion. "You do Carn Caille an honor it can never justly repay. What gift can we give you in return for your genius?"

Cushmagar raised his sightless eyes and smiled. "None, my lord. I have a roof to my head and clothes to my back; I am amply fed, and I have a captive audience to indulge and flatter my ramblings. I assure you, my lord, *that* is the heart's desire of any harper!"

There was laughter, and Anghara realized that Cushmagar was deliberately and deftly manipulating the prevailing mood in the hall, as if he sensed danger in the aftermath of his story. And though he joined in the laughter readily enough, anyone who knew Kalig well would have seen the sudden rush of relief that overtook the unease in his eyes.

Someone called: "Let's have a riddle song, Cushmagar!" The harper chuckled, and struck a discord on the harp that brought a chorus of groans. Then he played a quick, skittish tune that introduced an old court favorite which demanded a good deal of audience participation in the form of questions and answers. Cups and knives hammered the tables in wholehearted approval, and as the company roared into the first verse Anghara sat back, suppressing a cold shiver of distaste. She didn't want to sit listening to children's songs, not in the wake of Cushmagar's earlier performance; it seemed a travesty. She wanted to hold on to the mood that gripped her, not lose it. If there were ghosts in the harper's tale, she didn't want to banish them.

And so, pleading tiredness, she made her excuses and rose to go. Fenran kissed her hand—in public, he could do no more than that as yet—and she stepped around the table, bending toward old Cushmagar and whispering her thanks and a fond good-night in his ear even as he played. Her touch alerted him; he took one hand from the harp strings and gripped her wrist.

"Have a care, little princess!" His voice was nearly inaudible against the background of noisily enthusiastic singing, and his words were for her ears alone. "Don't travel too fast, or too far. Remember that, my singer of songs—for all our sakes!" And he released her, swinging back into the rhythm of the cheerful song so quickly that she wondered momentarily if she had imagined the whole incident.

But she hadn't imagined it: and neither had the brief exchange escaped her father's notice. As Anghara moved to his side to kiss him, Kalig stared hard at her and she thought he might say something; but he thought better of it. He took her hand, squeezed it, paused—then patted her fingers gently and, shaking his head, turned away as she left the long hall.

* * *

The heavy doors closed at Anghara's back, and the sounds of the revels were shut out. From the hall the main wing of Carn Caille's great fortress stretched away to either side; the princess paused to take a deep breath of the clearer air, then turned left toward the stairs that led to the women's quarters and her own bedchamber. Somewhere in the distance a loose shutter was rattling with a hollow, uneven rhythm; a cold wind had found its way in and swirled through the passages; Anghara felt it tugging at the hem of her skirt and chilling her ankles as she walked, and stray gusts hooted dismally in the old stone building's highest towers. It was late, and only a few torches still burned along the walls. They guttered, uneasy in the drafts, and the gloomy atmosphere made her think of other days, other lives, the many generations of her ancestors who had walked within these walls and whose shoulders had borne the burden of the Tower of Regrets and its secret, as Kalig's bore it now. The images wouldn't leave her; once, she stopped and looked back, almost expecting to see the shadows gathering and forming familiar shapes behind her. The passage was deserted . . . but still the images remained, and strongest of all was Cushmagar's haunting evocation of the ancient and lonely tower out on the tundra. *They* had known its secret, those ancient kings and queens who had ruled down the ages in Carn Caille. Her father knew it, and one day her brother, Kirra, would learn it, too; but she would never be allowed that privilege. The mystery of the Tower of Regrets was forever barred to all but the reigning monarch; and yet for as long as she could remember, that mystery had held Anghara in a thrall from which she neither could nor wished to escape. Fear, fascination, longing, the frustration of knowing that her curiosity could never be sated; they all melded together into an ache so strong that at times it was a physical pain. On occasions such as tonight the ache had made her rash and foolish; to ask a harper for the story of the Tower of Regrets at such a celebration was a flagrant breach of protocol, and only Cushmagar's willingness to comply had prevented Kalig from voicing his disapproval. The incident would not be forgotten.

Anghara sighed. It was too late to regret what she had done, but she wouldn't sleep easily tonight. She walked on, and tried to dispel the cold *frisson* that assailed her as though a legion of ghosts followed in her wake.

·CHAPTER·III·

The first full hunt of the new season left Carn Caille next morning—and it left behind an irritable and frustrated Anghara. She had slept badly, plagued by fragmented and ugly dreams, and when Imyssa brought her breakfast tray at the usual hour she also brought word from Queen Imogen, commanding her daughter to attend her for a fitting of her wedding gown.

"Today?" Anghara protested. "I can't, Imyssa! It's the first hunt of the season!"

"Then you'll simply have to miss it, won't you, poppet?" the old nurse said placidly. "There'll be plenty more."

"Don't be so complacent!" Anghara fired back. "The first hunt of the season may mean nothing to you, but it does to *me*! Mother could easily choose another day—"

"That she couldn't, because the seamstress's sister has been taken ill and left her shorthanded, so your mother can't change her plans just to suit your whims. You may say what you please, my girl, but you'll obey your mother the queen and there'll be no arguments." Imyssa gave her charge a long look, then added tartly, "Besides, after what you did at the revels last night—"

Anghara frowned angrily. "You weren't at the revels. How would you know what happened?"

"I know what I know," Imyssa retorted. "And I'd have thought better of you. Have you learned nothing in all these years? Have all my teachings simply fluttered through your head and out the other side? Asking Cushmagar for that ballad!"

So that was it. A subtle form of punishment to show her parents' disapproval of her breach of protocol, and a gentle warning not to do it again. Anghara hunched her shoulders and scowled. "Why should everyone make such a fuss about it? Cushmagar's played it time and time again; it's nothing new."

"Not at a hunt feast, he hasn't. It's a wonder to me he didn't refuse it and cast a bad omen on the whole season!"

"But he didn't refuse."

"Maybe not. But he could have." Imyssa paused, then sighed and moved toward the bed. She pushed aside the untouched breakfast tray and sat down, reaching out to take the girl's hands.

"Poppet, you must forget those things. Forget the old stories and the old secrets. They're not for you. You'll never need to bear your father's burden, that's for your brother to carry; so put it away and out of your mind, because it doesn't belong there." She saw Anghara about to protest and shook her head. "Now, don't you try to pretend you don't understand what I mean. Imyssa's a wise old bird. She knows what's in her little chick's thoughts."

Something in the nurse's tone made Anghara feel as though a sliver of ice had slipped between her ribs. She tugged her hands free, suddenly distressed and a little unnerved.

"You shouldn't know, Imyssa. You *shouldn't* know what I'm thinking, what I'm feeling . . ."

"But I do, my pet, because I see with more than my eyes." Imyssa tapped her forehead, and her face looked suddenly drawn and old. "And I see beyond you, into a future that frightens me. I see a danger that you don't know and can't know, because although you've got the power, you won't use it. Use it now, child—use it now, for all our sakes; put your trust in old Imyssa, and *forget* these things!"

Her words went home like a breath of icy south wind, and Anghara looked at her again. "What danger do you see?" she whispered.

"That I can't say. Maybe a wiser woman than I could tell you, but I haven't the skill to see any clearer. But you've a lifetime's happiness before you, my little one—and if you want to hold to that happiness, don't think on the Tower of Regrets."

Anghara shuddered suddenly, involuntarily. "I dreamed about it last night. About the tower."

"Then that only bears out what I'm saying. It isn't right that you should have such dreams. That old place must be shunned and forgotten, and if you go against that, you go against the Earth herself."

For a moment the girl seemed to be looking through Imyssa and beyond her, into a realm only she could see, and the dread in her face made the old nurse shiver. Imyssa turned her own face to the window, where streaks of thin, high cloud made patterns against the morning sky, and silently mouthed a protective invocation. The charm calmed her mind; after a few moments she was able to turn back to Anghara and present a placid face.

"Eat," she said. "And then dress yourself. It won't do to keep your mother the queen waiting."

She waited until, slowly and with some reluctance, Anghara began her breakfast before moving away quietly to her own adjoining room.

And so Anghara watched the hunt ride out, trying to curb her frustration, but with little success. When the hunters were gathered in the courtyard, Fenran leaned down from his horse—a tall, dark brown mare that she herself had selected for him—and kissed her upturned, angry face.

"Don't fret, love." His smile was both loving and wickedly amused. "We'll hunt again tomorrow—just the two of us. And meanwhile I'll bring you back the choicest kill."

"If you catch anything bigger than a hare!" she retorted. Fenran laughed, and the princess's anger relented. She slapped the mare's rump, setting the animal sidestepping restlessly.

"Good hunting, my love. Let the Earth Mother bring you back safely."

The cavalcade made an impressive sight as it rode out under the arch of the ancient fortress keep and into the bright morning. Kalig led the hunters, resplendent on his heavy bay gelding, with the senior hounds, huge, shaggy and gray, streaming through the gap to either side of him. Behind him was Kirra, riding abreast with Dreyfer the houndmaster, then Fenran beside the chief of Kalig's forest wardens, the remainder of the hound pack swirling and belling in a torrent around their mounts' legs. Behind the dogs rode the lesser nobles, guests and servants, and Anghara felt a sharp twinge of irritation as she saw a good sprinkling of women among their number. She'd had new riding clothes made for this occasion, had planned her strategy, the game she would pursue . . . and now her plans were ashes.

The last of the riders passed through the arch, and the sounds of hooves and voices and baying hounds were muffled beyond the solid granite walls of Carn Caille. Somewhere above Anghara's head a shutter banged noisily and pointedly: Imyssa, tidying the princess's room and issuing a timely reminder of her duty. Anghara sighed and with a last, regretful look at the sky's hard blue invitation turned and walked back into the great hall.

She found her mother in the antechamber that led off the great hall, and which the family had in recent years made a part of its private domain. Sunlight streamed in through the tall window, highlighting the new portrait which dominated the opposite wall. Imogen sat on a padded couch, surrounded by partly unrolled bolts of cloth, while Middigane the seamstress squatted on a low stool at her feet.

Middigane was a plump little robin of a woman with blue eyes and hair that was still jet-black despite her advancing years. She was an outer Islander, a shipmaster's widow who had returned to her girlhood trade when her husband was drowned in a spring storm, and despite the inconveniences of transporting her from her home to Carn Caille whenever a consultation was needed, the queen had insisted on securing her services for Anghara's wedding gown. Imogen had discovered Middigane's talents some years earlier, and declared that she was the only seamstress in the Southern Isles who could begin to match the skills of her more sophisticated eastern counterparts. Her only regret was that Middigane staunchly refused to leave her own island for a permanent pension at Carn Caille; but, knowing Middigane, Anghara privately believed that her refusal stemmed from an interest in the more virile men of her locality, which she would find hard to indulge under the queen's eye.

As the princess entered, Middigane rose and bobbed her curtsy. Anghara kissed Imogen, and the queen studied her shortsightedly but critically.

"You've lost more weight, Anghara. How many times have I told you, you don't eat enough? Middigane, I suspect we'll have to bring the waist of the gown in a little further."

Middigane dived into her rolls of cloth and shook out Anghara's wedding dress. As yet it consisted of little more than underskirt and bodice, but the completed gown would be a fantastic concoction of pearl-gray silk overlaid with silver lace, and finished with a vast train onto which Middigane planned to stitch a myriad tiny opals. Anghara would have greatly preferred something far simpler, but Imogen wouldn't hear of such an idea: she was determined that the marriage of her only daughter should be an occasion of the utmost splendor and solemnity, and she intended to show the visiting dignitaries from her homeland that Carn Caille could match any eastern panoply. There had been a few skirmishes between mother and daughter, but Imogen had her way, and Anghara was resigned to the prospect of a wedding accompanied by full ceremonial.

With Middigane fussing and bobbing at her elbow, she wriggled out of her clothes and climbed into the gown, then stepped up onto the low stool to allow the seamstress to get to work with her pinning and stitching. Imogen picked up some embroidery she'd set aside and, smoothing the fabric over the frame, said:

"Anghara, your father and I were not pleased by your behavior at the revels last night."

Anghara looked around, drawing a squeak of protest from Middigane, and her cheeks flushed angrily. "Mother—"

"No; I want you to hear me, child." Imogen looked up, and her normally placid eyes were harder than usual. "Your rashness in speaking as you did to Cushmagar could have blighted the entire hunting season. As it is, no harm was done; but I would prefer to think that you will *never* consider acting so foolishly again."

Anghara was well aware that Middigane was listening intently; though, in the way of highborn Easterners, Queen Imogen had no scruples about speaking her mind in the presence of inferiors. Now the tale of Anghara's misdeeds would doubtless be spread around the outer isles the moment Middigane set foot on her home ground again, and the princess felt like a child of five admonished before her sniggering peers.

She turned her head away angrily. "As you said, Mother, no harm was done."

"That isn't the point. I want your assurance, Anghara."

She clenched her teeth. "You have it." And she winced as Middigane, distracted, made a clumsy movement and stabbed her with a pin. "Woman, be more careful!"

"Anghara." Imogen's voice was ice, and, knowing the tone and her mother's rare but implacable temper, Anghara subsided. The queen waited until the fire had gone out of her look, then rose to her feet.

"I will leave you in Middigane's capable hands," she said. "When she has no more need of you, you may attend me in my dressing-chamber, and we'll look at the jewelry you're to wear for your nuptials." She exchanged a kind and faintly long-suffering smile with the little seamstress, then turned her back on her daughter and left the room.

Anghara looked out of the window at the bright day. She thought of the hunt, of Fenran, of the baying of hounds and the heady excitement of the chase. At her feet Middigane hummed tunelessly through a mouthful of pins; the princess fidgeted from one foot to the other and resisted the temptation to step on the little woman's hand and pretend it was an accident. A month, she thought. Only a month.

Her sigh was a faint breath in the sunlit room.

Queen Imogen made no further reference to the previous night's episode when Anghara attended her in her room later that day; nonetheless, the residual tension in the atmosphere between mother and daughter was palpable, and discomforting. For two hours the princess sat at Imogen's side, dutifully examining the bewildering array of necklaces, coronets, bracelets, rings, that Imogen, with impeccable taste, had selected for her to choose from. She couldn't concentrate; the fact that she was missing the hunt still rankled, and—though she didn't dare say as much to her mother—she had very little interest in the proceedings. What Imogen advised, she would wear. She longed only to be away from the stifling walls of Carn Caille and out in the bright sun.

At last, though, the ordeal was over. Anghara left her mother's chambers and hastened back through the corridors of the old fortress toward her own room, anxious to be rid of her formal court clothes and to make the best of what remained of the day before the hunt returned. There would be another feast tonight, though on a lesser scale than yesterday's celebrations; before it began she needed the chance to be alone for a while, to nurse her wounded feelings and improve her temper so that the evening's revels wouldn't be marred.

Imyssa, thankfully, was not about when Anghara

reached her bedchamber. She scrambled out of her gown, leaving it carelessly crumpled on the bed, and changed into shirt, jerkin, trousers and long boots. Imogen didn't approve of her wearing such garb, but the rough-and-ready lifestyle of Carn Caille was a strong enough argument in itself to overcome the queen's protests: any woman who didn't sometimes follow the men in her manner of dress would find the scope of her activities severely restricted. Anghara finished dressing and, as an afterthought, thrust her favorite broad-bladed knife into its sheath at her belt. She hadn't yet decided what she would do to cheer herself, but an idea was beginning to tug at her mind, and if she chose to follow it the knife would prove useful.

She caught her hair at the nape of her neck, so that it hung down her back like a horse's tail, and skimmed down the servants' stairway in the direction of the stables.

Someone—she suspected Fenran's hand in it—had had the good grace to ensure that Sleeth, her own mare, hadn't carried another rider on the hunt. In the mellow gloom of the stable the animal greeted her with a good deal of eager whickering; she'd sensed the excitement in the air that morning and couldn't understand why she had been left behind. Anghara spent some minutes energetically brushing the mare's coat; it was a task she enjoyed despite the fact that there was a plethora of grooms to do it for her, and by the time she had finished she felt internally cleaner and calmer. Sleeth was restless, anxious for exercise, and through the window Anghara squinted at the sun. She judged that it would be two hours, perhaps three, before the hunters returned to Carn Caille. Time enough for her to enjoy a long and invigorating ride, and perhaps—she grinned to herself—bring Fenran back a surprise he hadn't bargained for.

There was no one about when she led the saddled mare into the courtyard, which meant no one to ask where she meant to go, or to insist that a servant accompany her. The courtyard basked in orange-gold light, long shadows reaching out from the keep and the main hall; the day had a chill, heralding the approach of autumn, but there was no sign of the fine weather breaking. Anghara would need no escort. She hauled herself up into Sleeth's saddle and turned the excited mare's head toward the gateway.

Later, the princess told herself that it had been nothing more than chance which brought her to the escarpment on the tundra's edge. She had avoided the area of the hunt and fully intended to take a route through the northern reaches of the forest where the wild pigs of the region were so fond of rooting. The pigs were small but ferocious; if she succeeded in killing one and brought it back to Carn Caille, the joke would be on Fenran and her father.

But somehow matters hadn't worked out as Anghara had planned. With the uncanny perversity of their kind the pig herds had chosen to spurn their customary scavenging-grounds, and the largest game she had seen all afternoon was a vivid-tailed cock pheasant that took off at her approach, wings whirring among the leaves as it squawked its guttural alarm call. At last, bored with searching for quarry that wasn't to be found, she had allowed Sleeth to pick her own path through the trees; and when the edge of the forest appeared ahead and the slope of the long scarp showed beyond the thinning branches, there had seemed no reason why she shouldn't ride on just a little farther, to the top of the ridge. For the sake of the view, she told herself. Nothing more.

Yet when she reached the crown of the escarpment

and sat gazing out across the bare plain, the dissatisfaction and the unformed longing came back so strongly that it was like a physical pain within her. She couldn't count the number of times she had ridden to this place and looked on this view. But this time, it wasn't enough. Something was alive and awake in her, tearing at her mind with savage claws, and in its wake came memories of the dreams that had plagued her through the night and the thought of Cushmagar playing his harp in the great hall. She could hear his voice again, the words of the ancient ballad, the rippling, shivering music that throbbed like the blood in her veins, a deep-rooted and vital part of her and her world and her heritage.

With sudden chagrin she realized that her vision was blurred by tears. Angrily she blinked them away, wiping her face with her sleeve. She had no cause to cry; she wasn't a child now, and the day's disappointments were too insignificant to warrant such a reaction.

But the day's disappointments had nothing to do with it. They might have been a catalyst, but no more. Anghara was crying for something else, something she couldn't name or identify, a hunger that haunted her but which she couldn't assuage.

Sleeth grew restless, and the princess gathered in the reins, looking out again at the plain below her. This escarpment marked the boundary of her experience; she'd never ventured beyond it onto that wide wasteland, for although Kalig had never expressly forbidden her to do so, there was a tacit understanding at Carn Caille that the plain should remain untrammeled.

But Kalig had never expressly forbidden it. . . .

Almost without conscious awareness, she had turned the mare's head and was guiding her along the edge of the scarp. Half a mile or so ahead the ridge began to drop away, sloping quite gently downward until the sharp cliff merged into a litter of scrub and scree where, once, a small river had flowed to link plain and forest. It was said that this undulating east-west line had once marked the boundary of the polar ice, but the Earth Mother had decreed that the great glaciers should retreat southward and loose their grip on the land, that it might be fertile. Superstition darkly foretold a day when the sun would fail and the distant ice ramparts would march back from their exile to claim the plains again, but few people believed such a thing could ever be. The sun continued to shine undimmed; the Earth Mother's hand filled the forests and the farms with new life each spring; the world turned as it had always done.

As it had always done. . . . Again Cushmagar's voice echoed in Anghara's mind. *There was a time, a time and a time, before we who live now under the sun and the sky came to count time. . . .* A world beyond her reach, beyond her comprehension. When things that should not be walked on the land. And the one barrier between that long-forgotten world and the world Anghara knew stood out there on the plain, a brooding, solitary shadow, a lonely sentinel. The Tower of Regrets.

Sleeth snorted and stopped. Looking between the mare's alertly pricked ears, Anghara saw that they had reached the place where the escarpment dipped away. Below them lay a small, sheltered valley where the vanished river had cut a gentle V into the land. It was lush with ungrazed grass, its sides clothed in bramble and hawthorn; even from here she could see the dark shine of ripe berries among the bronzing leaves. Her heart began to pound.

"On, Sleeth." She chirruped to the mare reassuringly. "On down." She meant to pick berries, she told herself. Nothing more.

The valley bottom was a peaceful place. The wind

had dropped away completely, and the small vale basked in warmth. As soon as Anghara had dismounted and released her, Sleeth began to graze, snatching eagerly at the abundant grass, and Anghara sat down on a small, turf-topped knoll, elbows resting on her knees as she looked down the length of the valley to where it widened out onto the plain. From here she had a very different perspective of the landscape; she was almost on a level with the plain, and at closer quarters it looked far more tangible than ever it had done from the top of the escarpment. And accessible. A mere fifty paces, and she could step onto that scrubby ground and walk among the stunted bushes. A mere half hour, and she could ride four, maybe five miles toward the distant tundra.

And toward the Tower of Regrets.

The thought crept up on her without forewarning, and a cold shiver of shock that she could have considered such an idea made her skin crawl. The taboos inbred in her, crooned in babyhood by Imyssa, drummed into her forming mind by her tutor, reinforced in every rite and ceremonial by which Carn Caille marked the changing seasons and the turning years, were too old, too strong, to be overthrown. The tower was barred to all humanity; a prohibition which could never be lifted.

But surely it could do no harm to ride a little closer. . . .

She turned her head and saw that Sleeth was watching her. The mare had paused in her grazing, and in her eyes was an uncanny intelligence, a silent warning, as though she knew what was in her mistress's mind and sought to caution her. Or was her own conscience attributing supernatural powers to the animal in an attempt to find an outside focus? Anghara wondered. Some people held that beasts understood human thoughts and emotions with a sure telepathic instinct, and Anghara found herself unnerved by the clear message in Sleeth's look. Oh, yes; the mare *knew* what she was thinking—and abruptly, reacting to the momentary stab of fear, she was angry. Her father's censure, her mother's subtle punishment, Imyssa's scolding, were all combined, or so it seemed to her, behind Sleeth's accusing gaze.

She would not be so treated! She was no longer a child, she was a woman; her elders considered her mature enough to marry and order her own household, yet they chided her and lectured her and bound her about with *Thou shalt* and *Thou shalt not* as though she were no more than five years old. She would not suffer much meaningless strictures, such humiliations, any longer!

The anger was like strong mead in her brain, and Anghara acted on it without a moment's thought. She wanted to grasp the anger and savor it before it had a chance to abate; she wanted to strike back at her parents, at Imyssa, even at old Cushmagar, for the slights she imagined they paid her. In a single, rapid movement, she sprang to her feet and strode toward Sleeth. The mare was startled and reared away as she snatched at the trailing reins; with far more force than was necessary, Anghara wrenched her head around, cursing volubly. Sleeth whinnied, frightened now and fighting back.

Anghara had never used a whip on Sleeth. She carried a lightweight switch with a short, plaited thong simply because it was a part of riding regalia, but its only function had been to flick flies from the mare's ears and withers. But now her anger was at such a peak she couldn't contain it. The mare was blameless, and a rational part of Anghara's mind knew it, but she was no longer willing to give any ground to reason. The animal was the focus of her fury, the imagined condemnation an intolerable insult. She lashed out, and the switch cracked through the air to slash against the velvet skin of Sleeth's neck.

Sleeth uttered a terrible sound that was half snort and half scream. She flung her head up, eyes rolling and showing the whites, and stood shivering violently, all four legs splayed and rigid. Anghara's conscience twisted inside her but she ignored it. Her mouth set into a tight, ugly line and she pulled herself into the saddle, gathering the reins viciously short. She touched the switch against the mare's neck again, a warning of what to expect as the price of disobedience, and, very briefly, looked back over her shoulder at the still, peaceful valley. It was an obscene contrast to her mood.

She hauled the mare's head around until she was facing along the ancient stream bed toward the plain, then slammed her heels hard into the animal's flanks and drove her forward.

·CHAPTER·IV·

The sounds of the returning hunt approaching Carn Caille could be heard when the great tide of riders and hounds were still half a mile away. In her chambers, where she had been resting before the evening feast, Queen Imogen heard the distant baying, the eager, repeated winding of the horns, and smiled indulgently. A good hunt, she suspected; the participants, jubilant with success and buoyed up by much mutual congratulation, had already begun to celebrate.

She rose from her couch and rang a small handbell to summon her tiring-woman. She only needed to change her gown and dress her hair to be ready to greet Kalig, but she wanted to take her time and be sure that she looked her best.

As she sat down in front of her looking-glass while the servant began to brush the long, fair coils of her hair, Imogen felt a faint twinge of regret that she had not allowed Anghara to ride with the hunt. Kalig had agreed with her that the ban was a suitable punishment for their daughter's wanton indiscretion, but Imogen had the feeling that without her influence he would have let the matter pass. It was, after all, the last of such great hunts before Anghara's wedding; by next year, with the Earth Mother's blessing, the princess would be in no condition for such frivolities and would have other and more important preoccupations. Though she had never understood her daughter's passion for what she herself considered unfeminine pursuits, Imogen nonetheless felt a little guilty that she had deprived Anghara of what could well be her last chance to enjoy them.

Ah well, she thought; there was nothing to be gained from regretting. One couldn't turn back the sun's march. There would be other hunts before the wedding, and Anghara would get over her disappointment soon enough.

Below her window the courtyard suddenly erupted with joyful noise and, craning her head a little, Imogen saw the first horsemen come clattering through the great arch. Kalig was in the lead, windblown, vividly red-cheeked from the sharp air, laughing; Kirra and Fenran not a length behind him. Her family, she thought with quiet, satisfied pride. And later tonight Anghara would unbend and come out of her sulk, so that the picture could be completed.

The world was good.

"She isn't in her chambers." Prince Kirra walked cheerfully into Fenran's room without knocking and made his announcement with undisguised glee. "Imyssa says she hasn't seen her since this morning, when she went—with very bad grace, I gather—to answer Mother's summons." He flung his lanky frame into a carved chair, which creaked a protest, and helped himself to a cup of ale from the flask on Fenran's table. "Ahh . . ." He swallowed, wiped his mouth and grinned. "Better! I'm as parched as a desert."

Fenran's gray eyes regarded him with tolerant amusement as he briskly toweled himself. His first action after any hard day was to immerse himself in a tub of hot water and wash away the sweat and grime of his exertions: this apparent addiction to bathing baffled Kalig but had Imogen's firm approval, and Fenran thought privately that the queen would have been pleasantly surprised by the civilized nature of life in the Redoubt, his northern homeland.

Aloud, he said to Kirra: "Anghara will show her face when she's a mind to. She'll appear in time for the feast, take my word."

Kirra laughed. "You're an optimist, Fenran! Either that, or you don't know my sister as well as you like to believe." He refilled his cup. "Don't ever say, when you're old and enfeebled and she's drained all the fight from you, that I didn't warn you of the kind of spitfire you'd be taking on as a wife!"

Fenran chuckled as an image of Anghara in a temper arose in his inner vision. "I know it well enough, Kirra. And I wouldn't want her any other way."

Kirra got up, nursing his ale, and strolled across to the window. The sun was lowering but still hung above the fortress's perimeter wall; though the year was waning, daylight was still almost perpetual in these latitudes.

"If *I* know Anghara," he said, subtly implying that Fenran didn't, "she isn't even in Carn Caille. She'll have exploded from here like a hurricane the moment Mother dismissed her, and she'll be away licking her wounds at one of her favorite haunts."

Fenran would have laughed with him, but, without warning, something like a cold hand touched his mind.

He didn't understand the feeling, but momentarily, it unnerved him.

He said: "Have you checked the stables?"

Kirra didn't notice the abrupt change in his voice. "Stables?" he repeated blankly. "No. Why?"

"If Anghara left the fortress, she'll have taken Sleeth."

"Oh, I see." Kirra paused, then frowned. "I thought I saw Sleeth among the horses on the hunt today."

"No. I made sure she stayed behind."

"Did you?" Kirra looked around and grinned pityingly. "You shouldn't indulge Anghara so, Fenran. You're only storing up trouble for yourself!"

Fenran found suddenly that he had to bite his tongue as Kirra's unrelenting banter started to grate. Though he couldn't pinpoint any rational cause, he was worried; it was an instinct that had come out of nowhere, and he had learned to put a good deal of faith in his instincts.

"Kirra," he said, and this time there could be no mistaking the edge to his tone, "I think we should find her, without delay."

The younger man stared at him. For a moment Fenran thought the prince would dismiss what he'd said with another jocular remark, but Kirra had enough sensitivity to realize that this time banter wouldn't do, and his demeanor changed.

"What is it, Fenran?" he asked. "What's wrong?"

Fenran shook his head. "I can't explain it to myself, let alone to anyone else. Imyssa would call it a sixth sense."

"Imyssa's a wise bird, despite her shortcomings."

"I know." Fenran hesitated, then: "Kirra, will you do something for me? As a friend?"

"Of course."

The Northman's eyes met his in quick gratitude. "Search for Anghara. Round up a few servants, if need be, and comb Carn Caille until she's found."

Kirra's eyes narrowed. "You haven't encountered any ill omens, have you? After what Anghara did last night—"

"No, no, nothing like that. As I said, I can't explain it. All I can do is ask you to indulge me in this."

Kirra was growing more uneasy with every moment; he had a healthy respect for the supernatural, and the thought that the normally practical Fenran might have had a Sight disturbed him. "I'll do what you ask, Fenran." He started toward the door. "And perhaps I'd best alert Father—"

"No." Fenran shook his head emphatically. "Not yet; I don't want to alarm the king without good cause. Let's keep it between ourselves for the time being." He forced a smile. "Doubtless I'm worrying for no reason. I'll finish dressing and join you in a few minutes."

"Very well." Kirra continued to look searchingly at him for a few moments longer, as if hoping to find some unvoiced explanation in his face. Then he opened the door, and his footsteps diminished along the stone floor of the passage.

In her room, Imyssa slept fitfully in a chair. One of the hazards of old age was a tendency to doze off at unlikely moments; she should by now have been helping Anghara to prepare for the evening's feasting. But Anghara wasn't there.

If the old nurse had been awake, and had looked out of her window to where the sky was slowly turning to a livid orange, she might have seen the cormorant as it flew over the great keep of Carn Caille. A solitary black silhouette against the fiery heaven, a rare bird on this coast, a bird whose sighting meant a dark portent. Had she seen it, Imyssa would have run to her runes and her herbs and cast a scrying spell to determine the meaning of the cormorant's appearance. But she didn't see it. Instead, in her shapeless dreams she twitched as though palsied, and her wrinkled eyelids fluttered in an unconsciously fearful and unhappy spasm.

Anghara opened her eyes to find herself staring at a piece of shale a few inches from her face. Her rib cage and right arm were sore; when, with an involuntary reflex, her legs moved, she found that she was lying facedown on dry, sere earth, her head twisted at an awkward angle. Something rustled behind her; startled, she jerked away from it before realizing that it was nothing more than a stunted bush, and that she'd tangled one foot in its withering and desiccated branches.

The bush had broken her fall. . . .

She hauled herself up onto her elbows and for a moment thought she might be sick. Her head spun, and when she explored her skull with tentative fingers, the gentlest pressure on her left temple sent pain knifing through her.

She *ached.* Her clothes were scuffed, there was sandy soil in her hair and the palms of her hands were grazed; somewhere, dimly, she remembered stretching her arms out in a futile attempt to stop herself from hitting the ground too hard when Sleeth—

One fragment of memory triggered the rest, and angry chagrin filled her. She hadn't fallen from a horse in years, and Sleeth's nature had always been predictable.

Only Sleeth hadn't been willful or temperamental. She had been *terrified.*

Anghara had had nothing but trouble with the mare

as she rode across the plain. Sleeth jinked at shadows, seeing phantoms and enemies behind each gnarled bush and in the contours of every boulder. Sidestepping, snorting, shaking her head in an effort to loose her rider's hold on the reins, she had become more and more unreliable with every yard they covered. But the princess's anger refused to abate. Ferociously she controlled Sleeth, forcing her on, and the mare's reluctance only served to reinforce her own determination. But finally—and Anghara couldn't remember how much time had passed, or how far they had traveled, before it happened—Sleeth's nerve had broken. A shrieking whinny, a fit of uncontrollable bucking, and the princess had been flung from the saddle, pitching ignominiously over Sleeth's withers to be knocked unconscious on the hard ground.

She shouldn't have been so foolhardy. The anger that had gnawed at her throughout the day was in ashes now, and she bitterly regretted her pigheadedness. *Leave well alone,* Imyssa had said; and Imyssa was right. She'd brought herself nothing but trouble by her insistence on riding into this forsaken wilderness. Now for all she knew, Sleeth had bolted for home, leaving her alone, lost in this vast, hostile stretch of nowhere.

Moving slowly, gingerly, the princess sat up and rubbed at her eyes. The lashes were encrusted with sand and grit and she couldn't focus properly. She wondered how long she had lain here. Through her watering eyes she could see that the sky was still bright, but the warmth of the day had given way to a deep, unfriendly chill. Something moved a short distance away, but it was a blur; she rubbed her eyes again, and at last the world clarified.

Sleeth hadn't bolted. Instead, she stood some twenty yards from where Anghara sat. The mare's head was down and she had a dull, defeated air: she watched Anghara uneasily and made no attempt to approach.

"Sleeth. Come up, girl. Come up." Anghara's voice sounded unsteady; the fall had left her in poor control of her faculties. Sleeth tossed her head nervously but didn't move.

"Sleeth!"

Still Sleeth refused to obey, though now Anghara realized that the mare was torn between the conflicting demands of the orders to which she had been trained and her own innate fear. She wanted to come to her mistress but couldn't. She didn't dare.

The last shocking fragment of scattered memory fell into place, and the princess understood why the animal was so afraid.

Sleeth stood in sunlight, but Anghara herself was in shadow. A long shadow, hard-edged and alien. She knew what it was before she summoned the courage to turn her head: she had seen it grow from a faraway speck as she forced the unwilling mare on across the plain, taking form, developing solidity, becoming three-dimensional, until finally it was no longer a shade from her imagination but a looming, tangible reality.

The Tower of Regrets.

A wave of nausea washed through her and her stomach contracted. She forced the spasm down, trying to convince herself that her terror was irrational and had no sane cause. But it wouldn't release its grip. The legend was too old, the place too long abandoned; and the words of Cushmagar's ballad rang like an eerie echo in her mind. *No human eye will gaze upon its door and no human tread shall sully the earth around it.* Taboo. A forbidden place. An inner voice screamed at her to get up, run to Sleeth, ride north with all the speed she could force from the mare and never once look back.

Her fingers scrabbled in the thin soil as she pulled herself into a crouch, poised to obey that urging. . . .

And before she could stop it something else, something dark, primal, beyond her control, made her turn her head.

Her involuntary intake of breath was a sharp sound against the silent backdrop. Not thirty yards away,the Tower of Regrets reached up into the sky, blotting out the lowering sun. The great wall that faced her was in silhouette, and from it the tower's shadow reached out like a giant, malignant finger to touch her. She could almost believe that the shadow had enfolded her in an unclean embrace, that even if she moved out of its clutches she would carry its taint with her into the sunlight. Feeling as though serpents moved in her blood, she stared, transfixed with the crawling enormity of her trangression, at the great monolith.

It had been built foursquare, a rectangular pattern that was alien to the gentle curves of Southern Isles architecture. And though the ages had weathered it and softened its contours, something about that unnatural, hard-edged shape filled Anghara with repugnance. It was cold, faceless, the blank and forbidding stone facade unrelieved by a single window or even the smallest embellishment. It dwarfed her, like a giant, predatory animal, seeming to drain the life and the strength from her bones, and she had the terrible sensation—illusion, she told herself, *illusion*—that if she didn't escape its influence she would freeze to the spot on which she stood, and take root like the twisted bushes in this awful place.

Sleeth gave a sharp neigh. The tower's spell shattered, and Anghara's head whipped around. She saw the mare standing alert, head high now as though she'd heard some sound beyond the range of Anghara's ears.

She felt the horse's fear, and again the urge to flee filled her.

But she couldn't. Not now, now that she was so close. Slowly, she turned to look again at the Tower of Regrets and took a grip on her unsettled imagination. It was a tower, nothing more; a structure built by hands as human as those of the artisans who had raised Carn Caille. Stone and mortar, vulnerable to the elements. It had no supernatural power, it housed no demons save those her own nightmares had created. And she wanted to exorcise those demons, once and for all.

She had taken a pace toward the tower before she realized what she was doing, and only Sleeth's shrill, distressed cry made her halt again.

"No," she said aloud, not knowing whether she spoke to herself or to the mare. The empty plain carried the word away flatly and without echo. She didn't dare approach the tower. She *must not* approach it: it was wrong, forbidden. . . .

But if she did not learn, know, understand, the demons of her dreams would haunt her for the rest of her life. She would never have such an opportunity again!

Shades of Kalig, Imogen, Imyssa, Cushmagar, even Fenran, rose like accusers before her inner eye. *Let those ancient stones lie on in solitude.* The legend must not be sullied. The Earth Mother's trust must not be broken. The long chain of her ancestors had kept faith; she must hold to their example, hold to it for her life. . . .

And the Tower of Regrets beckoned, as though it had waited, through all these centuries, only for her.

Anghara pressed the back of one hand against her mouth and made a small, inarticulate noise. She couldn't think clearly: it was as though the tower had an independent sentience and had reached out to touch her, bind her . . . She had stumbled forward as the thought shuddered in her head, and now the great, flat wall reared before her; she was no more than ten paces from it.

She could see the door, a low, modest rectangle in the tower wall. The man of the islands, whose hand had set it in the stone, had not been tall. One minute, Anghara thought, one minute only, and she could see what he had seen, know what he had known. And the ghosts which had dogged her since childhood would be destroyed forever. One minute. No more. She would not step over the threshold. She would look, once, and then she would leave this place and never return. Just one minute. Just a single look.

The sun was flaring on the horizon, hurling titanic, angry crimson spears across the sky. Dark would come within the hour, but Anghara neither knew nor cared. The sheer wall of the Tower of Regrets was before her, though she couldn't remember walking those last few, crucial steps. The door was precisely the same height as she was.

She reached out and laid her hand on the ancient, petrified wood.

"The feast's about to begin," Kirra said. "We can't delay it much longer, Fenran. We'll have to tell Father."

Fenran nodded unhappily. They were on the wall that flanked the great keep of Carn Caille. The sun, touching the horizon now, colored their faces and tinged the old stone blocks a stark blood-red. Fenran was trying not to see portents in the ominous light.

Any trace of levity was long gone from Kirra's manner. It had taken the two young men only minutes to discover that Sleeth was indeed missing from the stables, and a discreet but swift search of the fortress had revealed no sign of Anghara. At first Fenran had managed to accept Kirra's assurance that the princess was simply out riding and would be back well before the light began to fade, but as time passed and the great arch still failed to ring to the sound of hooves, his nagging sixth sense grew stronger and more urgent.

Hoping against hope that this time he would see something where before there had been nothing, he turned yet again to stare out from the fortress, shading his eyes against the sunset's glare. The landscape was still and empty; there was no sign of a distant rider moving toward Carn Caille.

"Fenran." Kirra touched his arm. "We can't delay."

The Northman nodded, unable to express the foreboding that now felt like a vicious predator eating him from within. He couldn't look directly at Kirra; he simply turned toward the steep stairs that led down to the courtyard, and in silence the two began to descend.

And when the tower was done, he stood before the door at evening and he opened the door and went in, and he barred the door behind him, so that he was alone in the windowless dark.

Cushmagar's voice whispered in Anghara's mind as, with only the faintest of shuddering protests, the door of the Tower of Regrets swung gently open to the pressure of her hand.

So easy . . . She had expected locks, bars, bolts; but there were none. Only a simple latch that lifted to the touch, and ancient hinges that murmured wordlessly as they moved for the first time in untold centuries.

A deep-hued shaft of light from the waning sun fell across the threshold, across a bare earth floor from which dust motes rose in languid spirals at the sudden movement of air. Anghara's throat closed, the muscles tightening until she could no longer draw breath, and she stared, mute, immobile, at what the door and the dying sunlight had revealed.

It was such a simple place. A single, unfurnished chamber, naked earth and naked stone, silent, untrammeled, empty; and the suffocating tension which had built up within her drained away into a sensation of bewildered disappointment. This was the focus of Carn Caille's most ancient and revered legend, source of a terror and a superstition that was etched upon the souls of every inhabitant of the Southern Isles. And yet this forbidden place, within whose walls the fate of the world had once resided, contained *nothing*.

Anghara's right foot slid with a shuffling sound on the dry soil, but the fear that had gripped her earlier was gone. She felt cheated: despite her resolution to do nothing more than look into the tower, pique and curiosity were mingling to propel her forward, just a little way over the threshold. A dark shape lurched across the floor, momentarily blocking the ingress of the light, and she balked before realizing that it was nothing more than her own shadow.

Fear of shadows was a child's nightmare. And if the Tower of Regrets held no greater terror than shadows, then the legend was a lie. The princess drew breath, tasting the stale, musty but unthreatening air, and the last of her doubts faded. She looked back to where Sleeth still stood and watched her anxiously, then stepped into the room beyond the door. Two paces, three, four; now she could see the far wall, as featureless as the rest, and judged that she must be roughly in the chamber's center. She stopped and, pivoting slowly, gazed around her. She felt no awe, only a peculiar, numb emptiness that was emphasized by the physical emptiness of the tower. A long way above her head she sensed rather than saw the ancient rafters that held the roof in place; no birds nested there as they did in the rafters of Carn Caille. The Tower of Regrets was utterly lifeless.

But not entirely empty. Anghara's eyes were adjusting to the dimness now, and as she turned again, she saw something in the farthest corner, directly opposite the door but beyond the reach of the intruding light. She thought at first that it must be a trick of shadow, but no: it was solid, real, and it gleamed with a peculiar dull sheen.

Her heartbeats altered abruptly to a staggered, thumping pulse of excitement, and again she looked quickly over her shoulder. The light was fading rapidly, but she still had half an hour or more before the sun sank below the horizon for the brief, late summer night. One look, one swift investigation to satisfy the curiosity that ate at her, and she could be away with the last of the sunset to guide her back to the river valley.

She set her back to the door and approached the dark corner, queasy with anticipation now and not knowing what to expect. Then she stopped again, and stared.

The thing she had glimpsed, the thing that shone faintly in the gloom, was a chest. In shape and size it resembled nothing more remarkable than the chest in her own bedchamber, in which clean linen was stored between scattered layers of aromatic herbs. But as she dropped to her knees and studied it more closely, Anghara realized that it was made of a substance that had never been seen in Carn Caille. She thought it must be a metal of some form, but no metal she knew had such a sheen; the faint glow that burnished its surface was utterly uniform yet gave off no reflection, no matter the angle from which she studied it. Its color was not quite silver, not quite bronze, not quite a steely blue-gray; it seemed to have no hinges, and try as she might, Anghara could see no dividing line between casket and lid. The chest bore no decoration, but in the very center of its front surface a single square of the same bizarre material stood out in slight relief. A catch? If so, its design was as alien as the rest of this strange artifact, and Anghara couldn't imagine how it might work.

For a few minutes she stared at the chest, her thoughts rioting. If, as the legend claimed, no one had set foot in this tower since the day of the Earth Mother's vengeance, then this strange metallic casket could have belonged only to one man—the nameless Man of the Islands, Son of the Sea, who had built the tower and kept vigil throughout that terrible night. Why he had brought it here only to abandon it when he emerged from the tower into the new world, Anghara couldn't imagine; but the thought of what the chest might contain made her giddy with excitement. Here could lie the answers to a myriad mysteries about that long-lost age; buried truths which historians, scholars, bards and seers would give all they possessed and more to understand. A treasure trove of knowledge, only waiting to be uncovered. And she had uncovered it. . . .

But how to open the chest? With the excitement mounting feverishly within her, Anghara had no further thought for the wisdom of what she was doing. The old taboo was shattered, the Tower of Regrets' spell broken. All that mattered was to learn its final secret.

Her hands moved swiftly but uncertainly over the surface of the chest. The metal—if indeed it was metal—felt strange to the touch, almost as if she were running her palms over a sheet of petrified liquid. She found the sensation faintly repellent, but continued until she had covered every inch of the surface. There were no seams, and she sat back on her heels, irritated by her defeat. Her only other hope lay in the small, raised panel, and gingerly she reached out toward it.

A last relic of caution and superstition had made her avoid touching it before, but if the chest could be opened, then this was the only possible way. Unaware that she was biting her lip—a childhood quirk which she hadn't exhibited in years—Anghara pressed the tips of her fingers against the small square.

She couldn't be sure if it was her imagination, but she thought she heard a faint, whistling hiss, like air escaping. What *wasn't* imagination was the foul stench that assailed her nostrils. It lasted only a moment, but it was strong enough and vile enough to make her jerk back, gagging and clapping a hand to her mouth. And as she rocked on her heels, a thin dark line appeared along the front of the chest. It widened rapidly, and she realized with a shock that, silently, without any further prompting, the previously invisible lid of the casket was rising.

It lifted in one smooth movement to stand vertically, revealing the chest's gaping interior. For a moment Anghara was transfixed, stunned both by the simplicity of her discovery and by the alien nature of the catch; then she lunged forward, gripping the smooth metallic edges to peer inside.

Her gasp of anger, frustration and disbelief echoed hollowly in the chamber as the princess stared into the chest. It contained *nothing*. Not one relic or clue; not even a trace of dust to show where something had rotted away. The chest was completely empty.

Anghara drew back and got to her feet, sick and breathless with the sense of having been cheated. She had been so *close*. She had broken every law, every taboo to come to the Tower of Regrets, and the tower had deceived her. Bereft, she turned and took a step toward the door, making no attempt to quell her rising fury. The legend was a lie after all. The Man of the Islands had left no legacy. There was nothing here to fear—there was *nothing* here! She wanted to leave this loathsome place; she wanted to get away from the plain and its childish, foolish superstitions and go back to the comfort of Carn Caille and her own people. Tears of furious disappointment stung her eyes, blurring the brighter rectangle of the doorway, and she stumbled toward the open air.

A cloud passed across the sun, and the light dimmed. Behind her, something uttered a soft, satisfied sigh.

·CHAPTER·V·

The nape of Anghara's neck tingled as though lightning had struck a bare few feet from where she stood, and cold sweat broke out on her body. Her back was toward the strange metal chest, and she dared not turn, dared not look over her shoulder. She had imagined the sound, she told herself as her pulse hammered suffocatingly. She was alone in the tower. There could be no one behind her.

No further sound came. The silence was horrible, and at last Anghara could endure it no longer: her fear of the unknown was greater than the fear of any revelation. Forcing her feet to obey her and move, she turned around.

Between her and the empty chest stood a child. It was silver-haired, clad only in a simple gray tabard and haloed by an uneasy, phantasmic aura. And it was regarding her with silver eyes that were utterly devoid of any compassion or humanity. The eyes transfixed Anghara; she desperately wanted to look away, but she was held fast, staring into the twin vortices like a rabbit hypnotized by a deadly snake. In them she saw a depth of cruelty beyond her ability to comprehend, a terrible and hideous intelligence that mocked the paralyzing fear within her.

She tried to speak, but her throat was locked and her voice had turned to dust. She tried to move, but her feet were rooted to the tower floor. And the fear was turning to terror now, held back only by a perilously flimsy barrier that was on the brink of giving way.

The child continued to regard Anghara with quiet, implacable malice. Then it smiled. Its teeth were cat's teeth, small, sharp, feral: the grimace transformed its entire face into something monstrously evil—and, like an invisible fist punching her in the stomach, the barrier between Anghara and blind panic snapped.

Her own voice ricocheted in shrill echoes through the Tower of Regrets as she screamed, giving way to the black tidal wave of horror that swept over her. Her paralysis shattered and she flung herself toward the door, cannoned into the lintel and rebounded, spinning off balance from the tower to fall painfully on her shoulder. Unable to find the coordination to get to her feet, she crawled and scrabbled on all fours toward where Sleeth had been, desperately crying the mare's name. The furious red glare of sunset bathed her, *but it would be gone, it would soon be gone, and she would die, everything would die—*

The ground beneath her seemed to move sideways without warning, as though the world's very dimensions had abruptly shifted out of kilter. Anghara sprawled, struggled to recover, and this time was swaying on her feet when the vibration began. A rumbling, as of a titanic but faraway storm . . . The earth shook, and at her back a vast shadow reared up, a cloud of darkness blotting out the failing day. The tower was shaking, great stones grinding together, mortar cracking, beams splintering—

"Sleeth!" Anghara staggered forward, fell to her knees, dragged herself upright again. Ahead of her in the red-shot gloom a shape moved, lurching across her path: her hands clawed out and she reeled against the mare's side, fingers tangling in a stirrup strap. Sleeth danced fearfully, head flung up and eyes rolling; she towed Anghara with her as the princess struggled to catch the saddle pommel and gather the reins, then stamped on her mistress's foot as Anghara vainly strove to restrain her. The pain momentarily eclipsed Anghara's panic; her hand tightened on a handful of Sleeth's mane and she called on all her strength in a frantic effort, hauling herself up and scissoring her legs across the mare's back. Sleeth bucked and took off at a gallop, stirrups and reins flying while the princess clung precariously to her neck; at last she managed to catch a rein as it whiplashed past her, and hauled grimly, keening a shrill command and steadying Sleeth's wild and erratic flight.

A single *crack* split the air above them with a vast voice, and Sleeth shrieked, slewing sideways and almost falling on her haunches. As the mare's hooves scrabbled for purchase in the dust Anghara's head snapped around, and what she saw was imprinted indelibly and forever in her memory.

The Tower of Regrets was falling. It had split from roof to foundation, like a log severed by a woodsman's axe. And from its crumbling ruins a roiling cloud of what looked like dense black smoke was rising, funneling skyward and already towering far above her. But it wasn't smoke. There were forms in the darkness, twisted things, howling things with insensate eyes, clawing hands, black wings that beat the air and churned the dark stuff that gave them birth into new and more monstrous shapes. A legion of unhuman horrors, phantoms, nightmares, erupting into the world from which they had been barred for countless centuries.

The tower gave a final sigh, a chillingly mortal sound, and began to cave in on itself. The roiling darkness gathered strength, pulsing into the sky, spreading like a black canopy.

And suddenly Anghara knew where it was bound.

She gathered the reins—her whip was lost—and lashed Sleeth's flank. The mare sprang forward, ears flat to her head, and Anghara crouched over her neck like some demon rider on the Wild Hunt, screaming as she drove her mount toward the distant escarpment. Sleeth raced with the speed and desperation of the damned, as though she knew and shared the terror in her mistress's mind. And Anghara sobbed in despair for what she had done, as the dark horror unleashed from the shattered tower came boiling and storming in their wake.

"You should have told me before." Kalig kept his voice low so as not to alert Imogen, who was in conversation with one of her ladies and thus far unaware of Kirra's news.

"I'm sorry, Father. We saw no point in alarming you—or angering you—without good cause."

"*Angering* me?" Kalig glanced toward the conspicuously empty space at the high table, where Anghara should have been sitting. The feast had just begun, and servants bearing dishes were scurrying the length and breadth of the great hall. Near the hearth a harper, a lute-player and a piper had struck up an air; beside them stood Cushmagar's great harp, but the old bard had not yet put in an appearance. "I was angry enough to begin with, thinking that your sister was deliberately shunning the feast through a fit of temper. But this . . ." Kalig shook his head. "You should have told me."

"My lord, I must take full responsibility for our silence," Fenran put in. The Northman's face had an unhealthy pallor, made starker by contrast with the hall's warm light. "Prince Kirra wanted to inform you immediately, but I insisted that we wait." He hunched his shoulders and stared unhappily at the floor. "I now think that was a very foolish mistake."

The king regarded him for a moment or two, his expression giving nothing away. Then he said: "Wise or foolish, it's done and can't be undone now. But I don't want to waste any more time. Kirra—leave the hall discreetly; don't alert your mother. Find guard-captain Creagin, and tell him what you've told me. He's the best man to organize a search for Anghara."

Fenran said: "May I have your leave to go with Prince Kirra, sir?"

"Yes, go, Fenran. I'll join you as soon as—" And Kalig stopped as there was a sudden flurry of untoward activity by the hall door.

As though the king's utterance of his name had conjured him from his post, Creagin came in. He glanced quickly around at the company, then without a word of explanation to anyone strode briskly up the central aisle toward the high table.

Fenran and Kirra exchanged a glance, trepidation in both their faces, and Kalig stepped forward to intercept the captain.

"Beg pardon for the intrusion, my lord." Creagin, stocky and swarthy and a full head shorter than any of the other three men, made an abrupt bow but dispensed with any other niceties. "There's something odd afoot to the south. Thought I'd better bring word rather than wait till we know more."

Fenran felt his stomach constrict, and Queen Imogen looked up from her conversation with a curious frown.

"What manner of oddness, Creagin?" Kalig asked.

"Don't rightly know, sir. The sentry who first set eyes on it thought it was weather, but—"

"Weather?" Kirra interjected.

"Yes, sir. Bad weather, but unusual bad. Black clouds the like of which I've never seen before, only it isn't clouds." Creagin shifted uncomfortably from one foot to the other: a military man, he understood only that which had a logical foundation, and trying to explain this obviously wasn't at all to his liking. "I don't rightly know what it is—but it's coming up from the south so fast, I reckon it won't be long before we're in the midst of it."

The thoughts of his three listeners instantly turned the same way, though none of them could have explained why. Now Fenran was feeling distinctly sick . . .

"Very well," Kalig said tersely. "We'd best investigate. Lead the way, Creagin, if you please."

He stopped to reassure Imogen, who had overheard only part of the exchange, then followed Creagin, Fenran and Kirra toward the door at the far end of the hall. They were passing the hearth when a terrible discord rang out, instantly silencing every other sound. The musicians who had been standing near Cushmagar's harp jumped back—one only just avoided falling into the fire—and several of those around the hearth made hex-signs before their faces in alarm.

Kalig turned his head in time to see the strings of Cushmagar's harp still vibrating as the hideous clash of notes it had uttered slowly died away. *The harp had cried out, with no hand to touch it. . . .* A cold, superstitious dread filled the king.

"Quickly!" he said, his voice harsh with fear. "Get to the keep!"

Men rose and followed him as he hastened after his three companions. No one hesitated or called for an explanation: all knew that when a bard's harp spoke of its own volition, it was a dire omen. Behind him, Kalig heard Imogen's calm voice calling her agitated ladies to order, but he could spare no time to look back at her. Creagin and the others were running now, more joining them; amid the hubbub someone shouted for Cushmagar to be fetched. Kalig raced through the chill, dimly lit passage beyond the great hall, and as he went he drew his sword in an automatic reflex. It wasn't his heaviest double-handed war blade, but in an emergency it would have to do. Fenran and Kirra, he saw with relief, were also armed, and others, following the unwritten rule that ensured battle-readiness at the smallest provocation, were peeling off toward the armory to fetch more weapons.

Torches guttered and danced in their brackets as the running men agitated the air. Then Kalig burst out into the courtyard on Kirra's heels, and onto a chaotic and shocking scene.

The sun had set, but the courtyard was alive with flickering lights that darted hither and thither and turned the darkness into a shadowy nightmare. Men were running while sergeants bellowed orders; one group pounded up the steps to the ramparts while sentries shouted and gesticulated. Kalig didn't pause, but headed straight for the stairs, calling Kirra and Fenran to follow. They took the steps two at a time and emerged breathless onto the narrow battlement surrounding Carn Caille. And there, roiling out of the night toward them, was a vast, spreading cloud of darkness. How far it extended, how fast it moved, they couldn't tell; but it had blotted out the last dim fires of the sun below the horizon, and no one could doubt that it was heading directly for the fortress. In its dense heart forks of lightning crackled, but lightning of an order no one had ever seen before: silver and purple and scarlet. And on the rising wind that the monstrous phenomenon forced before it came eldritch and hideous sounds—a shrieking, howling, wailing cacophony that assaulted their ears with the glee of a thousand laughing demons.

"Father!" Kirra gripped Kalig's arm. "That thing has no earthly origin!"

Kalig knew that as well as any man. Swords couldn't prevail against such a horror. And surely no witchcraft known in Carn Caille could hope to combat it.

"Sir!" A man's hoarse voice; at the far end of the rampart a sentry was gesturing frantically. "Sir, on the sward! Perhaps a quarter mile away—there's a horseman!"

"What?" Fenran, making the connection before anyone else, spun about to look, and by the terrible glare of the erupting lightning in the heart of the manifestation he saw the tiny, forlorn figures of a horse and rider galloping desperately for the fortress gates. A tremendous flash lit up the sky and he had a momentary impression of the horse's color, the rider's long, flying hair—

"My lord!" he yelled above the racket. "It's Anghara!"

Kalig swore in shock, and for a moment was paralyzed. *Anghara would never reach the keep in time. That howling, demonic horror would overtake her, swamp her—*

"Open the gates!" he bellowed, his voice carrying

like a bull-roarer. "Open the gates for the Princess Anghara!"

Fenran was already away, leaping down the steps toward the ground, pelting for the great archway under the keep. He added his strength to that of the men struggling to haul the huge wooden gates back on their hinges, and as at last they grated open he tried to rush through.

"No, sir!" A powerfully built sergeant dragged him back, shouting in his ear. "You can't do anything—she's almost here!"

And out of the thundering darkness came Sleeth, a demon-horse with mad eyes and foaming mouth, ears flat to her head, galloping under the stone arch to slide to a rearing, whinnying halt in the courtyard. Anghara slithered out of the saddle. Fenran caught her before she could fall and she dropped to all fours, hair sweat-plastered on her skull and panting like a wolf.

"Warn them!" The voice that grated from her throat was a guttural, unhuman snarl. Fenran took hold of her arms and tried to pull her upright. For a moment she fought him—then her head came up and eyes that were utterly dead stared at him through the wet curtain of her hair. She drew her lips back from her teeth in a dreadful rictus, and he knew that she was insane.

"The tower . . ." Her hands clamped on his shoulders like talons. "Earth Mother help us all . . . *the Tower of Regrets has fallen*!"

"Anghara!" It was Kalig, who had at last caught up with Fenran. "My child, what—" And he stopped, looking in horror at her face.

"My lord, she says—" Fenran swallowed something in his throat that was trying to stop him from forcing the words out. "She says the Tower of Regrets has fallen!"

Even in the torchlit darkness he could see the color

draining from the king's face. Kalig's fist clenched and he brought his knuckles up hard against his mouth. "*The Mother preserve us*! Then that—that thing out there—" He looked again at Anghara, and suddenly every muscle in his body tensed and strained as his stunned mind groped for and found an inkling of the truth. His hand shot out and he snatched a handful of the princess's hair, his voice shattering Fenran with its despairing ferocity.

"What have you done to us?"

"Father—" Sanity returned to Anghara's eyes, and with it full knowledge of the horror she had wrought. The howl of the approaching monstrosity dinned in Fenran's ears, but Kalig and his daughter were oblivious of it, locked like a grim tableau, both frozen by realization. Fenran caught the king's arm, wrenching him aside.

"Sir, there's no time for recrimination now! Whatever's been unleashed, it's almost upon us!"

Even as he spoke, the shrieking, wailing voices rose to a crescendo, counterpointed by warning yells from the men on the ramparts. A huge, furnace-hot breath blew across the courtyard—and as Fenran looked up in shock, the leading edge of the giant wing of darkness came boiling over the battlements, erupting into a thousand howling, phantasmic forms that bore down like a tide. Human screams mingled with their insensate and demonic shrieking, and doll-like figures fell flailing and cartwheeling from the walls as the phantom legion unleashed from the Tower of Regrets poured over the walls. Winged monstrosities, flapping, aborted horrors, things with the heads and tails of serpents, great gaping mouths filled with fangs like knives, talons and claws and mutated hands, scales, hair, white and leprous skin—every nightmare ever conjured, every demon ever dreamed, was falling on the unprepared defenders of Carn Caille. Fenran's reeling senses saw something explode out of the chaos toward him—bird and snake and horse and something else unnameable, it beat twisted, distorted wings and swung a grotesquely huge head that was almost nothing but a mindless mouth toward him. He couldn't move: he was transfixed, unable to believe what his eyes told him—then a sword blade flashed across his vision and the thing sheered off, its neck cut almost through and a foul white fluid pumping from it.

"Rally!" King Kalig stumbled past Fenran, carried onward by the force of the blow he had struck, and his roar battered against the cacophony that swamped the courtyard. *"Carn Caille! Rally to your captains!"*

His cry snapped the Northman out of his paralysis and Fenran swung around, in time to see one of the gate-sergeants falling under the onslaught of two white, gibbering creatures with hideously bloated torsos and spindle legs. The man's death-cry as his throat was torn open churned Fenran's stomach, and he realized that, supernatural or no, demonic or no, these were no phantoms, but appallingly, physically *real*.

Kalig was gone into the mayhem, still shouting, and his captains were striving to obey his order and form their men into some semblance of fighting ranks. More people now came spilling from the fortress; not only warriors, but courtiers, councillors, stewards, grooms, artisans, every man—and not a few women—capable of wielding a weapon. The scene was one of hellish chaos, black shapes of men and monsters battling across the courtyard, torches flaring in feral pinpoints, humans and things that were not human screaming with bloodlust or pain or rage—there was no time for coherent thought or reasoning: everything was stripped down to a grim, raw battle for survival.

Fenran swung around and realized that Anghara still

crouched immobile on the flagstones. She was weaponless, and it was as though she was unaware of the carnage around her, had blotted it from her consciousness.

"Anghara!" He caught hold of her, dragged her toward him. "We've got to fight! As you love life, *listen* to me!"

Her mouth opened, but if she uttered any sound it was lost in the din of battle. A wild-eyed warrior skittered past, struggling to fend off something that jumped and snapped and giggled; the thing lunged and the warrior's head rolled from his shoulders, his attacker bounding over the corpse and away. Fenran snatched the fallen man's sword and tried to thrust it into Anghara's hand, his voice rising toward hysteria.

"*Fight*, woman! Damn you, *wake up*!"

She shook her head, her hair stinging his eyes, and though she took the sword hilt, her grip was slack and useless.

"Anghara!" Knowing no other way to rouse her, Fenran smashed the back of his hand across her face. She recoiled—and the intelligence jolted back into her eyes, and with it fury.

"You—" The word choked off as murderous reality struck home, and her voice became a lost wail. "Fenran . . . !"

"Fight!" he yelled again. "For Carn Caille, for our lives! *Fight!*"

A huge, misshapen ghoul slid from among a knot of decimated warriors and propelled itself on winged limbs toward them, like a hideous parody of a grounded bat. Anghara shrieked, and her sword came up at the same moment as Fenran's in a defensive swing. She struck the monstrosity between the eyes, he slashed its torso: it gibbered and weaved away, hopping, but with no visible injury.

"To your right!" Anghara yelled, and Fenran lashed out at a horror resembling a sickly white and bloated corpse. Behind it came more, embattled with a detachment under Creagin, whose face was covered with his own blood but who was fighting like a madman. An appalling maelstrom of clashing sounds battered their ears: battle-cries, howls of agony or terror—somewhere Prince Kirra was yelling, calling men to his side—and above all, the bloodlusting, mindless shrieks of the unleashed hellish legion. And now there were new noises to add to the chaos: the piercing screams of unprotected women. Anghara, momentarily unassailed, had time to turn her head, and she saw that the demon horde had overcome the few men who strove to hold the main door to Carn Caille, and were streaming through into the fortress. Lightning danced in the lower windows, and she thought of the great hall, the feast, Queen Imogen—

"*Mother!*" She turned, breaking from Fenran's side, and was away across the courtyard before he realized what she was doing. Something black and festering gibbered across her path and her nostrils filled with the stench of corruption, but she evaded it, racing on.

At the door, bodies of the makeshift guard were piled bloody and broken across the threshold, and eyeless, fanged shapes tore at their flesh. Anghara kicked corpses from her path, unable to think of anything but her mother's peril, and was almost through the carnage to the interior when a hand jerked her back.

"No, Anghara!" Fenran spun her against him, struggling with her as she fought to break free. He was the stronger, and he hauled her bodily away as a hot and terrible light began to glow inside the building. *Fire*—the great hall was ablaze, flames leaping in the windows; a wall of heat swept along the corridor and out of the door, scorching Fenran's face and singeing tendrils of his hair as he dragged Anghara clear. Screams echoed from within the walls, and the sounds of running feet; then some seven or eight women appeared at the entrance, with Imogen in their midst.

The queen's gown was on fire, and her ladies beat ineffectually at the flames, their cries ringing across the courtyard. Horrified, Fenran released Anghara and ran toward Imogen, thinking to drag her clear—but before he could reach her, a winged shape so black that it defied sanity plummeted from somewhere above his head and fell on the shrieking women. The physical force of the air it displaced buffeted Fenran and Anghara backward; the princess had a momentary image of two eyes like burning coals where the phantom's head must be—then a fireball erupted from the middle of the group of women, a white-hot blast that sent Anghara skidding across the courtyard, tangling with Fenran as they both crashed to the flagstones. She heard Imogen's last cry, a barely human screech of unimaginable torment; then heat seared her unprotected back as the black phantom took to the air again, yelling its delight and triumph and grazing her spine with a trailing wingtip.

"*Mother!!*" Anghara howled like an animal and rolled over, hands clawing at the flagstones as she tried to writhe toward the blazing funeral pyre of Imogen and her attendants. She neither saw nor heard the approach of the scaled, feathered half-bird, half-snake that burst suddenly from the melee at her back and came hopping, flapping, lurching toward her; even when Fenran yelled a warning, her mind was locked on the charred, distorted corpses collapsing into embers before her. But when the thing opened a beak as long as she was tall and uttered its raucous challenge, she twisted around, and her jaw dropped as she saw it closing for the kill.

Fenran answered the challenge with the high, ululating call of a Redoubt warrior. He was on his feet again, gripping his sword two-handed and raising it above his head as he interposed his body between Anghara and death. Recovering her wits, the princess scrabbled to reach her own sword, and as her fingers clamped on the hilt she saw Fenran's blade shear down at the gaping beak.

Sparks flew as steel met bone—and Fenran's blade shattered, leaving him with the broken hilt in his hand while shards of metal cartwheeled into the churning air. He staggered back, unprotected. Crying his name, Anghara sprang, but she was too late. The serpent's head turned, the beak snapped shut—and the monstrosity gored Fenran through, smashing ribs and breastbone to rip into his heart.

Fenran's mouth opened, face muscles straining almost beyond endurance, but instead of a scream, blood exploded from his throat. His body jerked wildly like a fish on a spear, and the demon tossed its head, once, flinging Fenran's ruined corpse into the air. As it began to fall the creature sprang skyward, catching the body before it could hit the ground. For a single moment the monstrosity hovered, and as she stared into its eyes Anghara saw ghastly intelligence, mockery, evil—the silver eyes of the phantom child in the Tower of Regrets. Then it launched itself up, wings beating, Fenran's corpse dangling from its talons.

Anghara watched it rise. She was on her feet, but her mind and body were frozen far, far beyond her reach. She felt nothing but a detached bewilderment, and was oblivious of the horrors around her. Fenran was dead. Fenran, her lover, her betrothed. Dead. Slain by a demon that was even now rising, rising into the sky, its unhuman laughter ringing like the cry of a nightmare seabird. Behind her, her mother's body was smoldering ashes. And the legions of hell were killing, killing, killing. . . .

It wasn't real. In a moment she would wake up in her bed and find Imyssa ready with kind words and a soothing potion and a candle to banish the shadows. It was a dream. A dream. A—

The scream began as an uncontrollable bubbling deep down in her lungs. It rose, gathering strength as realization took form and substance, as Anghara's senses opened to the sights and sounds and stenches of carnage, and a thin whine, the miserable protest of a whipped dog, issued from her throat. The whine became a cry, the cry a wail, and suddenly the wail erupted into a shriek of grief and despair that cut through the roiling chaos like a banshee's howling.

Anghara fell to her knees, blinded by tears as the scream went on and on, tearing her larynx. She didn't see the grisly forms and warped shadows of the demon horde sweeping toward the center of the courtyard; didn't hear the clash of a thousand wings or feel the hot whirlwind as they gathered and merged and spun; was unaware of the moment when they lifted into the shouting air, a living tornado, and arrowed upward into the night. All she knew was the sound of her own screaming voice, until the final dam within her broke and she fell forward, the sword clattering from her jerking hand as she sprawled unconscious onto flagstones soaked with Fenran's blood.

·CHAPTER·VI·

Dawn crept over the ramparts of Carn Caille in a thin and pallid mist as the sun showed its first angry sliver in the east. The fortress was silent. No lamps were lit in the windows; no sentries moved against the slowly lightening sky. Somewhere over the sea a gull was crying mournfully; the light wind, capriciously veering between northwest and northeast, hinted at rain before too long.

She didn't know how many were dead. For perhaps a minute, perhaps an hour, she had sat where she had been since consciousness returned, hands limp and useless in her lap, head turning slowly first this way, then that, empty eyes taking in the scene about her.

Men and women of her father's court. They had fought with all their formidable skill and strength, and now they lay broken, discarded, cut down like so much wheat in a harvested field. A harvest of blood and souls. And she, Anghara Kaligsdaughter, must sing their funeral dirge, for she alone had brought them to this.

At last—her sense of time was as dead as the corpses littering the courtyard—Anghara rose to her feet. She moved like an old woman, shuffling forward one pace, two, three. She couldn't bring herself to look behind her to the doorway where Imogen and her ladies had burned, but progressed with a dull lassitude until she stood before the first of several knots of bodies, and stared down at the tangled limbs and weapons.

Creagin. She hadn't seen him fall, but he was there, one eye gazing into the morning sky, the other an empty socket. Others: she knew their names, but there seemed no point in reciting them. One was no more than nine or ten years old; a groom's apprentice, she recalled.

She moved on. There was Kirra, her brother, heir to Carn Caille. Kirra the prankster, Kirra the good-humored tease, lying in his own blood with his spine half torn from his body.

On again. A litany of names, friends, companions. Horses, stiff-legged and grotesque, their bodies already beginning to bloat. She stood for a long time looking down at one of the dead animals, at its iron-gray coat, the long mane and tail shading from pewter through to white, before realizing with a peculiar, dreamlike detachment that it was Sleeth. She felt sad, but the sadness was remote, as though it originated from a mind that was not her own. She shuffled on across the courtyard.

And at last found Kalig.

She thought at first that he was merely unconscious, for he lay facedown with no apparent sign of injury. The capacity to hope was beyond her, but nevertheless she bent stiffly and turned him over with unsteady hands.

King Kalig, liege of the Southern Isles, her father, had no face. What remained of the front of his skull was so far removed from anything human that it couldn't even revolt her. She let the body fall, and turned around.

Carn Caille lay before her. She started toward it—not the main door; even numbed as she was, she couldn't bring herself to pass what lay there—but a lesser entrance that would bring her via corridors and stairways to her own room. And that was where she wanted to be. She wouldn't find Fenran: Fenran was dead. She had watched him die. She had failed to save him. She would go to her own room, her own bed, and if she could cry, she would cry there where no one, dead or living, could see her. And maybe Imyssa would give her a potion. . . .

Anghara knew she was mad, and the knowledge comforted her. If she was mad, she could surely not be held accountable for her actions, and what she had done would . . .

She stopped and licked her lips as a small inner voice warned her not to pursue that line of thought. Then she moved on again with slow deliberation, counting each step, toward the door. The strengthening sun was touching the ramparts now, and it touched her bent back and the matted strands of her gray hair as she shambled from the courtyard.

Carn Caille without noise, without the light of torches, without the bustle of everyday activity, was a cold and alien place. Anghara passed silent doorways, not pausing to look into the rooms beyond but knowing nonetheless what the doors concealed. Her father's small council chamber. The family's private dining hall. The room where plump little Middigane had sat sewing Anghara's wedding gown that now would not be finished or worn.

The corridor ended and there were stairs. She climbed, reached another passage, began to walk slowly along it. She had encountered no living soul, but the domain of the dead had not extended to these corridors: they were empty and untrammeled.

And at last, her own room. She pushed the door open and stood for a moment on the threshold, dully taking in the familiar furnishings, though they meant nothing to her. The connecting door to Imyssa's smaller room was closed, and for the first time since regaining consciousness the princess felt anguish stir within her. The old nurse was her last link with the world that had been so hideously snatched away from her; if she, too, was dead, there would be nothing left.

She touched the cool, rough wood of the door panel, pushed. "Imyssa . . . ?"

Her voice echoed like a ghost's breath. No one answered her from the room beyond.

"Imyssa!" Her throat was suddenly so constricted that she felt as though she were suffocating.

And a voice—though not Imyssa's voice—answered from behind her.

"Anghara . . . !"

Anghara whirled. There was no one there. Yet she felt a presence, the dim sense of another mind, another soul, reaching out toward her from somewhere close by.

"Anghara . . . help me!"

In the mirror, something moved that wasn't a reflection of the room. Darkness swirled within the glass, shot through with veins of blood-red, and Anghara's back slammed against the wall as she recoiled from it.

"Anghara . . ."

She knew that voice. And now, in the oval of silvered glass on the wall, a figure was materializing. She saw black hair, a face and form she recognized—

"Fenran!" The scream was wrenched past the blockage in her throat and she flung herself toward the mirror, collapsing to her knees before it. He was there within the glass, wreathed in the shifting darkness, and she clawed at the mirror's unyielding surface, striving to break through and touch him. Her fingernails scraped on cold glass, and Fenran's reflection gazed through and beyond her; she seized the mirror's edges, shaking it so violently that it swung on its mounting, calling his name again and again. Then his image began to fade; the darkness swirled away and Anghara was left staring at her own demented face and the image of the room beyond.

She flung the mirror jarringly back against the wall and turned, stumbling and scrabbling across the floor, snatching at her embroidered bedcover, screaming and swearing with a combination of fear and rage as it slithered from the bed and enveloped her. She tore herself free, crawled toward the window, reached up—

And Fenran's face was there again, faint and distorted, in the windowpane.

"No!" Anghara's voice was a savage screech and she swung one arm wildly at the pane. The glass shattered with the impact; blood from her slashed fingers coursed down her arm and a searing, burning sensation fired all the nerves in her hand. She hissed in pain, drawing a breath of the icy dawn air that blew in through the gap, and in the wake of the breath came a wave of blinding redness. She felt herself losing control, felt the building of a suffocating, intolerable pressure inside her; saw the room tilt crazily, heard blood rushing like a tide-race in her ears—

And found herself curled into a fetal huddle against her bed, clutching the ripped coverlet, which was now also smeared with streaks of blood from her fingers. A few feet away lay the shattered fragments of the fragile and intricate timepiece, the precious gift from her mother's people: the silver filigree was twisted into ugly contortions, the colored fluids had soaked into the woven rugs and vanished, and the blown-glass bulbs and tubes were reduced to a hundred thousand tiny shards winking coldly at her from the floor.

She couldn't remember smashing the timepiece, but she knew why she had done it; why she had *had* to do it. And it had achieved nothing. She was still mad. And she still couldn't cry.

Fenran dead. Her father, mother, brother, dead. Imyssa gone. Friends, companions, now nothing more than carrion in the courtyard. The seabirds must already have begun feasting . . . and she still couldn't cry. She was physically alive, but everything else, everything that mattered, had died with them; died because of what she had visited on Carn Caille. And she didn't even have the capacity to feel the agony of her own guilt. There was *nothing* left.

She felt extraordinarily calm. Though tears wouldn't come, and grief and remorse wouldn't come, her mind was nonetheless as still and unruffled as a woodland pool. There was just one more thing left to do, one action that would end the hiatus. She must do it now, with no more delay.

She had lost her sword in the battle, but no matter; it hadn't been her own, and her own would be more fitting for this. Rising, she moved slowly across the room and knelt down beside the old wooden chest that contained her most prized possessions. She lifted the lid—the fleeting memory of that other, stranger chest in the Tower of Regrets was pushed quickly away—and took out the scabbard that contained the slim, polished blade her father had given her to mark her eighteenth year. Withdrawing the sword, she turned it over in her hand, watching it catch the light in the room and reflect it brilliantly. She had cared diligently for this blade, as Kalig had taught her. He would approve of its condition, she thought, and approve of what she meant to do.

She bent her head and took hold of the long mass of her hair, catching it into a single thick bunch. The first deed must be done in one stroke, to show that her intention was true and well founded. Imyssa would have insisted on that. Anghara could hear the old nurse's voice in her head, exhorting her to carry out the deed in the right and proper way. She smiled, and with a single twist of the wrist that held the sword, severed the heavy curtain of her hair. It fell in a silent shower to the floor and she stared at it. *Gray.* Yesterday it had been auburn; today it was gray. She smiled again and stood up, shaking her head so that the shorn remnants flew about her face in a nimbus. Then she took the sword in both hands and reversed it until the wickedly sharp tip was pointed at her heart. Swift, clean: all she had to do was drive the blade home, and it would be over. No regrets, no farewells. Simply retribution and reparation for what she had done.

"No, Anghara Kaligsdaughter."

Anghara jolted, the sword rigid in her hands and her eyes starting with shock. In a split second her mind registered that the voice was calm and unemotional, with no trace of the phantasmic echo that had so frightened her in Fenran's apparition. It was *real.*

She turned her head, and remembered the Man of the Islands and the bright creature which had visited him.

The being that stood within the pale, shimmering aura was beautiful. Whether it was male or female or transcended such considerations she didn't know; its form was an androgynous blend of delicacy and strength. Its statuesque frame was wrapped in a cloak the color of new leaves, and its long hair was the shade of warm forest earth. Milky golden eyes gazed at Anghara; they were filled with sorrow, but utterly pitiless.

The sword fell from the princess's hands, and the clatter it made as it struck the floor was an intrusion on the peculiar quiet that had abruptly descended on the room. She took a step backward, feeling herself beginning to shiver uncontrollably. Then—it seemed the only thing she could do, the only thing she was capable of doing, though it was a desperately inadequate gesture—she dropped to her knees.

"Anghara Kaligsdaughter." The entity looked down at her. "What makes you think that you, too, have a right to die?"

Anghara's teeth chattered. "I—I want . . ." With a terrible effort she took a grip on her unruly tongue and jaw, and whispered, "There is nothing else left . . ."

"You know, then, what you have done?"

The princess squeezed her eyes tightly shut. "Yes . . ." The word was a hiss.

She heard a rustle of movement, sensed the being's proximity as it moved closer. "For centuries past, the blights that once afflicted the Earth our Mother have been chained and confined beyond the reach of man, in the tower built by the hand of that devoted servant enshrined in your legends. Your ancestors have kept faith with the Earth Mother's trust down the years. But not you. You sought knowledge to which you had no claim; you usurped a right that was not yours to command. And now, by your whim, the dark things and the evil things have been released into the world again. What have you to say, Anghara Kaligsdaughter?"

The suffocating sensation was starting to take Anghara over again. She drew breath and had to struggle to drag air into her lungs. "I didn't mean . . ." She stopped, biting her tongue as she realized how pitiful, how inadequate the words were. "If I could only turn back time—"

"You can't. The deed is done."

"But my father and mother—"

"Are dead." the entity's voice was coolly merciless. "Dead, Anghara. That is the truth and you must face it. They were slaughtered by the demons you released with your own hand—and you'll find no refuge from your guilt in madness."

She looked dully at the sword, lying so close to her, yet, it seemed, unreachable. "Nor in death?" she asked.

"Nor in death. To die would be easy for you. You would leave the world behind, leave it to the mercy of what you have unleashed on it. And that, my child, would be a further betrayal of the Mother of us all."

Tears began to trickle down Anghara's pallid cheeks. It was the first breaching of the dam that shock and grief had built within her, and though she welcomed the release it was bitter, bitter wine. *"If I had known . . ."* she whispered brokenly.

"Child, you knew as well as any of your race. The Earth our Mother enforced no choice on you: She granted you the freedom to serve or scorn Her, and it was your own will that caused you to choose the darker path."

Sanity was coming back. Anghara knew it, and the pain of it was almost more than she could bear, for it forced her to see herself for what she truly was. But the bright entity was right: there could be no escape in madness, or in death.

She said, so softly that her voice was no match for the soft moan of the wind insinuating through the shattered windowpane, "What can I do?"

The entity did not answer immediately, and Anghara

wondered if it had heard her entreaty. But when she looked fearfully up at its face, she saw a change in the impassive expression: a glimmer—or did her imagination play her false?—of something that might have been pity.

The bright creature said: "What *would* you do, Anghara Kaligsdaughter? What would you do, to make reparation for your betrayal?"

A deep shudder racked Anghara's frame and she looked away again, unable to meet the dreadful frankness of the emissary's gaze.

"Anything," she said bitterly. "Anything that would bring my family back."

"It is impossible to bring back the dead," the entity replied. "All you can hope to do is expiate your crime."

Anghara looked up through the ragged strands of her shorn hair and whispered, "How?"

"By pledging yourself to rid the world of the evil you have unleashed on it. You cannot die, child: the Earth Mother will not allow it. But She offers you the chance to undo your handiwork.

"When you opened the chest in the Tower of Regrets, you released seven demons into the world. Seven demons which form the quintessence of the evil against which the Earth our Mother rose up so long ago. Even now they are spreading across the land, glorying in their release, and wherever their shadow is cast, humankind will fall prey to their baneful influence." The creature smiled with poignant sadness. "As man is the child of the Earth, so these demons are the children of man: he created them, and used them in his attempt to wrest dominion of the world from the Mother of us all. If left to go their way unchecked, they will bring about man's final downfall; and this time there will be no man of the islands in whom our Mother invests Her trust, for Her trust has been betrayed. If humanity is to survive, the demons must be banished from the Earth. That is the task our Mother sets you, Anghara."

The princess looked down at her bloodstained fists, which she had unknowingly clenched so tightly that the knuckles showed white through the dark red stains. She couldn't speak; the sense of burden was suddenly like the weight of a thousand tons of rock pressing down upon her: a tombstone beneath which she was buried alive, a grave from which the bone-white fingers of the men, women and children who had died for her arrogant curiosity rose to point and accuse. . . .

"The responsibility cannot be shared," the bright entity said. "It is yours alone."

"But . . ." A dam was breaking within Anghara; ghosts filled her head. "I can't hope to achieve such a task." Her voice shook with the beginnings of hysteria. "I can't. *I can't!*"

"Then shirk it, child, and abandon your race to its fate." There was no pity in the emissary's impassive gaze. "That choice is yours to make, if you wish. The Earth our Mother forces nothing upon you, save the responsibility for what you have done. But, one way or the other, you *must* choose. And whichever path you take, death is not an option."

So she would—must—live on, without the hope of oblivion to take away the twin agonies of memory and guilt. Which was better? Anghara asked herself bleakly. To slink away into what small comfort she could find, and live out her days in a desperate and useless effort to forget? Or to pit herself against impossible odds, to face an enemy that could crush her as easily as it had crushed the warriors of Carn Caille, all in a futile quest to expiate her crime? Both roads were a sure way to torment. It would be kinder, surely it would be kinder to the shards of her ravaged mind and body to turn her back on the impossible and accept the lesser pain. . . .

On the verge of giving her answer, and anticipating censure, she looked up at the bright emissary—and paused. The being's expression was as impassive as ever, and she realized that it had no expectations of her; that she was, as she had been told, free to choose. And a voice in her mind said: *You are the daughter of Kalig, king of the Southern Isles! Has your blood run so thin that you cannot match his courage, his fidelity, his steadfastness? Are you such a coward that you cannot face the consequences of your own act of betrayal? What would your father have said—what would Fenran, the son of the Northern Redoubt, the man whom you professed to love yet condemned to death, have said to you now, Anghara?*

The words she had been about to utter curdled in her throat, and she tasted the sour acidity of bile. She had lost all she knew and loved by her own arrogance, but she would not surrender to the final ignominy of cowardice. If nothing else was left to her, she must at least seek the chilly comfort of trying to right the wrong she had done. She owed it to Carn Caille.

She met the emissary's eyes and said: "Tell me what I must do."

She had hoped for some small show of approval, some lessening of the terrible indifference in the being's eyes, but there was nothing. It smiled, but the smile was too remote to have meaning. "Are you sure, Anghara Kaligsdaughter? Once you have pledged yourself to the Earth Mother's service, there can be no turning back."

Anghara bit hard into the sides of her cheeks. "I am sure."

"Very well." And suddenly, to her chagrined surprise, the quality of the emissary's smile changed. For a fleeting moment Anghara saw echoes of peace, pity, an indescribably sad beauty that shone through the cool mask. The smile encompassed earth, sea, sky, the lives and the deaths of every creature that had ever walked the land or swum the waters; it was the sound of Cushmagar's harp, the cry of a seabird, the mourning of the wind, the laughter of revelers, the touch of a loved one. It moved her where all the carnage and the misery she had witnessed had failed; she felt tears welling in her eyes at last—and suddenly the agonizing barriers within her gave way. She turned, dropping to all fours and shaking feverishly as at last the tears which had hitherto refused to fall came streaming down her cheeks. The sounds she made as she wept were unhuman and ugly; the despair of a creature trapped and finally broken as she cried for Carn Caille, for her family, for Fenran, for the destruction she had wrought. And at last there was nothing left but a throat that felt as though a fist had squeezed the life from it, eyes red-rimmed and sore, and an ache that seared her whole body and from which she knew there could be no respite.

Very slowly, the princess raised her head. The bright emissary was watching her, but the spark of pity was dimmed now, replaced once more by dispassionate implacability.

"Come, child," the being said quietly. "You must put your grief aside. It is time for you to go."

"Go . . . ?"

"Yes. There is no longer a place for you at Carn Caille. While we stand here, time is halted; but it must remain so no longer. All around us, those who have survived the demonic onslaught are trapped in a single, timeless moment. We must leave so that they may be free to begin the work of salvaging what is left of their lives."

Anghara's haunted gaze flicked quickly, furtively

about the so-familiar room. "I don't understand . . ." she whispered.

"To your own people, you are dead," the emissary told her. "They will mourn your family, and they will mourn you, for even though you still live and are their rightful queen, you can never claim your throne. Instead, you must take on a new identity and leave the Southern Isles."

"But this is my home." There was no color in Anghara's lips. "It has always been my home: I know no other—"

"You have no home now," the emissary told her emotionlessly. "The seven demons released by your hand are scattered across the world, and the world must be your hunting ground if you are to find and destroy them. But you cannot return to Carn Caille."

Anghara's face was gray as old parchment. "Never . . . ?"

The being smiled poignantly. "*Never* is an imprecise concept, child. But while your quest is uncompleted, Carn Caille is barred to you."

She wanted to protest, but couldn't articulate what she felt. Instead, mute, she hung her head and nodded.

"You are no longer Anghara Kaligsdaughter of the Southern Isles, save in the memories of those you are leaving behind," the emissary told her. "You must choose a new name for yourself, by which those you meet on your journeying will know you." It paused. "Perhaps it should reflect what you have now become."

The princess's gaze slowly scanned the room. Her mind silently and bitterly cried out against the emissary's imperative, although she knew she had no choice but to comply. She was Anghara no longer. From this moment she must shed her memories, her past, and become a new person.

Her gaze lit on the floor, where the broken shards of glass from the smashed timepiece still lay. One fragment, larger than the others, caught the morning light and winked back a rainbow flicker of purplish blue; it was the shade that to the people of Carn Caille had always been associated with death, the color with which they draped themselves and the walls of the old fortress when the kingdom was in mourning. It was also, by a terrible irony, the color of her own eyes.

She looked up from the shard of glass and met the emissary's gaze. Her eyes were haunted, and she said:

"I shall be called Indigo."

·CHAPTER·VII·

The bright emissary said: "Come, Indigo." And as her gaze followed the direction of its pointing hand, she saw the mirror on her wall, the mirror in which she had seen Fenran's tormented face, begin to glow with an inner light. The light intensified, blotting out the frame of the glass, spreading into the room like water encroaching, and the entity took her hand.

"Come," it said again, and the word was an imperative.

She wanted to cry out: *No! I won't leave—this is my home, my life, everything I have ever been!* But what she had been was dead. Anghara was dead. She was Indigo now.

Her feet moved with an impulse beyond her ability to control, and she walked toward the mirror, toward the shining light. About her the contours of the room began to waver, swelling and fading, as though she stood poised between dimensions, and in panic she tried to drink in the image of the familiar furnishings one last time, a final taste of the sights and sounds and scents of her home. Who had died? Who would live on? What would become of Carn Caille, with Kalig's line gone? She struggled to form the questions, but could only whimper. And the light was growing brighter, her beloved room receding now into a dim twilight as the cogs of time began to turn once more and she left her home and her world behind.

An intolerable brilliance flared suddenly from the heart of the mirror and she felt something press against her back, forcing her unwilling but helpless feet forward. For an instant her outspread hands touched cold glass—then the mirror dissolved, and she stumbled into it, through it, and with a silent concussion Carn Caille was gone.

Quiet enveloped her. She could feel the soft, cool breath of a wind on her face, stirring the shorn tendrils of her hair, but the wind made no sound. Beneath her feet, and beneath her rigid fingers as she crouched where she had stumbled, was the rough solidity of a stony track. And though the intense brilliance had faded, she could sense through her tight-closed eyelids that there was light.

Indigo, who had been Anghara, opened her eyes.

The Earth Mother's emissary stood before her, but its shining form was the only familiar anchor in a place of silence and emptiness. They were on a road that stretched empty and as straight as an arrow-shaft across a smooth, flat and featureless landscape. No grass, no trees, no hills, no hedgerows. No sun in the sky, no source for the shadowless light that bathed her. No clouds, no birds. Just the endless plain, brown and desolate, and the gray spear of the road.

She turned her head—even the gravel beneath her

hands made no sound as it moved—and looked behind her. The road. The empty plain. And, incongruously, the mirror through which the bright being had led her, hanging unsupported above the track. But the mirror was blank and reflected nothing.

She turned to face the bright emissary once more, and her mouth contorted with the effort of holding back further tears. "Please," she whispered, and barely recognized her own voice. "What is this place?"

"A world beyond your world. A place where the river of time flows on a different course."

"Carn Caille . . ." She felt panic rising within her. "What has become of Carn Caille?"

The being smiled sadly. "They mourn your family, child, as it is proper that they should. Look in the mirror again."

Indigo looked. And the glass was clearing. . . .

They formed an aisle through the throng that had flocked into the great hall, to let the young page lead Cushmagar to the high table. The old harper walked falteringly, gnarled hands clutching the boy's supporting arm, and those in the ranks nearest to where he passed saw the glitter of tears in his blind and empty eyes.

No man, woman or child in the hall spoke. Before the table four bodies lay wrapped in sheets of indigo linen, their shapes almost entirely hidden by wreaths made from the burnished autumn leaves of elder and ash and blackthorn. Only the lost, lonely sound of a single woman's weeping broke the silence: they had found old Imyssa a place by the hearth, and the other women stroked her hair and held her hands, knowing that they could not heal her pain but trying to give her what comfort they could.

Indigo stared numbly at the scene in the mirror, then

spun around to confront the emissary. "There are four bodies!" she cried, her voice anguished. "Four! *Who are they*?"

"King Kalig, Queen Imogen, Prince Kirra Kaligson and Princess Anghara Kaligsdaughter."

"But my mother—she was—" Indigo swallowed hard, unable to bring herself to form the words. "They couldn't have found her! And I still live!"

The bright being replied dispassionately, "*Indigo* lives. Anghara Kaligsdaughter is dead, and she will be mourned as is right and proper."

"But my *mother*—"

"Queen Imogen died of the same fever that struck down her lord and her children."

"Fever . . . ?" Indigo's face was ashen.

"A virulent fever that swept across the Southern Isles. It was short-lived, but it took a heavy toll, and among its victims was the royal family of Carn Caille. Kalig and Kirra died quickly, as did Anghara and the Northman Fenran. Imogen burned with fever for five days, then succumbed. There were many others who followed them to the Earth Mother's embrace." And, seeing her stunned bewilderment, the emissary smiled with faint pity. "Yes, there was a demon horde, and there was a battle.But the demons you released from the Tower of Regrets have no true physical existence in your world. They are the quintessence of evil, but their forms are allegories; they came through a rift between dimensions, and now that the rift has closed once more, those who survived their ravages have no memory of a battle. To them, the tragedy that befell Carn Caille took the form of disease: a brief but virulent plague. It is an ironic parallel, but apt enough, for in their way the monsters released by your hand are like a plague; no eye can see their true form, but their evil influence is wide-ranging, unpredictable and deadly."

Indigo stared at the dusty track. She understood—or believed she understood—what the emissary had said to her, but it left her with a numbness, a sickness of spirit that nothing could lift. Invisible horrors, an influence that was already spreading across the world like a disease . . . and she must find those demons, capture and destroy them, if the world was not to be doomed.

She said, her voice emptily bleak, "How many still live?"

The bright being touched her shoulder, making her shiver, and when it answered its voice was suddenly gentle. "Enough to ensure Carn Caille's survival. Look into the glass again."

Indigo blinked away tears, and the mirror swam into focus once more. At the high table in the hall of Carn Caille the cushioned chairs were empty, and before each place a gold dish, gold cup, knife and spoon had been set. Between the table and the draped corpses stood Cushmagar's harp. It hadn't spoken since the eerie moment when its voice had shocked the revelers at the hunting feast into silence: now, as the page helped him to his place and settled him, the bard ran his fingers over the strings, producing a shivering, melancholy ripple at which even Imyssa ceased her sobbing, and every face in the hall turned toward him. He looked pale and ill; fever had touched him, too, and he was but a day out of his bed. But no power in the world would have persuaded him to shirk the duty before him now.

"Mother of Dreams, Great Mother." Cushmagar's voice rose strong to the rafters as he intoned the ritual words. "Mother of our nights and our days, Mistress of our joys and our sorrows, to You I speak the litany of the Earth-sons. For our lord and our lady, who spoke with Your blessing and who ruled with Your hand, have passed through the portal whence none shall return, and we are bereft of them. They walk now as the deer in Your glade, and they swim now as the fish in Your sea, and they soar now as the birds in Your sky, and we are bereft of them. Their wisdom and their justice is gone from us, and we are bereft of them, and we sorrow. Mother of all the world, I sing the song of our lord and our lady, and I sing the song of the children of their union, that You may hear of our grieving and know that they were loved. I sing their song, that all may hear and bow their heads for our loss, and that their names and their deeds will be remembered while Carn Caille stands. Let all you sons and daughters of the Earth our Mother hear the song of our lord and our lady, and let all you sing, and while the sun stands in the sky let all you mourn with Cushmagar."

A soft, sad, breathless note shimmered from the harp strings as the old man's last word hung on the stillness; then the sound flowed into a lilting lament with the rhythm of the restless winter sea. Several of the men nearest the high table turned their heads away, not wanting their fellows to see the tears in their eyes, and Indigo's heart constricted as she recognized faces lined with sorrow and ravaged with the aftermath of sickness. Dreyfer the houndmaster. Angmer, her father's adviser and old friend. Lillyn, her mother's tirewoman. Little Middigane the seamstress. The head groom's three children with their mother, though their father was nowhere to be seen. Others, so many others. And yet more who were absent, who would always be absent. Then, like a surging wave, the massed voices of everyone in the hall rose and swelled in the ancient and beautiful Island Pibroch, the lament for the dead. Cushmagar, head bent, blind eyes closed, played as though possessed, and it was as though for a moment Indigo was within his mind, feeling the harmonies flooding through his bones as his harp led the choir.

Behind his closed lids he, too, wept: and she saw the images that he saw—of strong Kalig, of serene and lovely Imogen, of the young Kirra and Anghara cut down like sapling trees. He would speak the true oration to their memory at a later time, when the Earth Mother had touched him with her inspiration; today, Carn Caille mourned in the only way it knew, the old way, the proper way.

The sounds and images reflected within the glass faded and were gone. On the dusty road that ran eternally through the dead, featureless landscape, Indigo covered her face with her hands as a fresh wave of grief and remorse swamped her. How long she stayed still and bowed before the bright entity touched her again, she didn't know; but at last she felt its cool hand on her shoulder, and raised her head.

"It is time for us to leave," the emissary said quietly.

"No . . ." Her voice was a child's whimper and she reached out toward the blank, unreflecting glass before her.

"You cannot go back, Indigo. This road leads to your future, and you must follow it as the Earth Mother commands. Come with me."

Slowly, unsteadily, she rose. Then the pain and bewilderment got the better of her again and she turned to her companion, hands outstretched, pleading.

"I must have something to hope for! *Please*—I've lost my family, my home, my land; all I've ever known and loved. There must be something left for me—there must be *something*!"

The emissary looked into her eyes, and for a moment she saw again the pity that had shattered the barriers within her. Then it held out a hand, and though she didn't consciously will it, Indigo found her own hand rising to take hold of the outstretched fingers.

"We have a way to travel yet, child," the bright creature said. "Three encounters lie ahead of you, and two will take place on this road. The first is not long away, and you will fear that one, and you will have good reason. The second . . . the second may be your salvation or your doom, Indigo: an inspiration to your quest, and yet a threat to your resolve."

"And . . . the third?"

"The third lies farther in your future. It will bring you to a new and trustworthy friend, though appearances may at first suggest otherwise." The hand holding hers relaxed its grip, and the being pointed along the dead road to the hazy, unchanging horizon. "It is time to go."

Indigo looked over her shoulder just once as the entity began to move away. And even as she looked, the mirror, which had hung unsupported above the dusty track, began to fade. Its outlines quivered, dimmed; she thought that for a fleeting moment she saw Cushmagar's blind face again and heard the echoes of a harp and of singing, but the images were gone like a dream, and the mirror shimmered away into nothing.

For a little time Indigo continued to stare at the place where it had been. Then she bowed her head, and, turning once more, followed the bright emissary's footsteps along the featureless, endless road.

In Carn Caille the massed voices sang, and the sound of their lament flowed out from the hall to fill the ancient fortress with its melancholy beauty. Cushmagar wished that it might reach out across the farthest reaches of the Southern Isles, for the song was for all who had died: every forester or fisherman, every wife or serving-maid, every child. He didn't yet know how many beyond the walls of Carn Caille had succumbed to the virus, but guessed that there must be many, many bereaved families in the kingdom. In a few days, when his strength was restored, he would set out with other bards to travel the islands and visit the stricken homes and sing the elegies for those they had lost, as was his duty. And then when the grieving was over, there would be much more work to do. Shattered lives must be rebuilt, and a new king must be chosen to sit upon the throne of the Southern Isles. Cushmagar, as the royal harper, would preside over that sad task; he would sit at the head of what was left of the council, and the wise women would be summoned from the forest to add their voices and cast their divinations, and at last a choice would be made. But for now the bard led his people only in music, and the music flowed on until it reached every corner of Carn Caille. It filled the room which had been Kalig and Imogen's own: a room empty but for a stray shaft of sunlight and an easel on which stood the masterpiece of Breym the painter, whose dead body now lay, watched over by his sister, in another part of the fortress. The forms of Kalig and Imogen, Kirra and Anghara, were captured forever in the artist's pigment, and framed now, as they always would be, with draperies of indigo linen.

Indigo did not know how long they had walked. The bright entity was tireless, and so, it seemed, was she; for she felt no fatigue, only a numbness, an inner emptiness that reflected the emptiness of the road and the land around her. Her feet moved, her lungs drew breath, but beyond that all sensation was dead. And the road did not change.

Until, so far ahead that she couldn't convince herself it was anything more than illusion, she saw a figure waiting for them.

Her pulse began to quicken. The distant, solitary watcher was incongruous, sullying the plain's unending uniformity and looking somehow unnatural in this featureless world. Indigo remembered the emissary's last words to her and hastened her steps—the bright being was a few paces ahead of her—to catch up.

"Someone awaits us," she said.

"Yes."

"Is this—the first of the travelers we are to meet?"

"Yes." Her companion gave no further explanation but walked on, and she had no choice but to follow.

Slowly they drew nearer to the distant figure, until Indigo could see that the traveler was human, or at least had human form. A small person, she thought; perhaps even a child . . . Her heart lurched with a sudden, unbidden memory, but she thrust the thought away. Not here, surely not in this empty world . . . But her steps were slowing as a terrible foreboding began to take hold of her, and with it a reluctance to go on. It *wasn't* possible—yet intuition told her that it was, that her worst fears were about to be hideously confirmed—

"Child." The bright being looked at her, and she realized that she had halted.

"I . . . can't." Indigo's voice was ugly; she was staring fixedly at the waiting figure by the side of the road ahead.

"You must."

"No!" Her throat tightened painfully, and the ground seemed to lurch beneath her as panic boiled in her mind.

"You must." And her eyes met the emissary's, and she was stumbling forward, compelled to move despite her terror. She tried to protest but had no voice, she was moving on and now she could see what awaited her, what she had dreaded.

A child with silver hair and silver eyes stood on the sere earth beside the endless road. It was dressed only in a simple gray tabard, and haloed by an uneasy, phantasmic aura. It smiled, showing cat's teeth, and the smile was cruel, malevolent, monstrous.

Shock made her swear savagely, and she swung around, every muscle rigid. The bright emissary stopped and looked back, saw the dreadful echoes of memory in her eyes. Indigo didn't think, didn't pause to recall the being's earlier exhortation, but hissed through clenched teeth:

"What is that creature?"

Soft, malignant laughter breathed past her, but the silver-eyed child didn't move, didn't acknowledge her presence in any way. The emissary said: "Do you not know its nature, Indigo? You should—for you gave it life."

"I?"

"Yes. It is your own nemesis. A manifestation of that part of yourself which led you to enter the Tower of Regrets and release the demons incarcerated there." It looked at the still-smiling child, and an expression that combined compassion and revulsion showed on its beautiful face. "While you are on this road, it cannot harm you; it has no foothold here, and what you see now is only a reflection. But when you leave the road, your nemesis will be your deadliest enemy, for of all the demons you must face, it is the worst."

Indigo's face tightened and her mouth twisted. "I'll kill the filthy thing! I shall *destroy* it!" Violence in every movement, she started toward the silver-eyed creature, but the emissary held her back.

"You cannot kill it, Indigo. It is part of you, despite the fact that it has taken on an independent existence. And you cannot escape it, for wherever you go, it will dog your steps. Walk on, child, walk on with me, and do not attempt to stray from the road."

She stumbled forward, but her venomous gaze didn't leave the apparition's face.

"This creature has but one goal: to thwart you in your quest," the bright being told her gravely. "And it is a powerful demon. It will appear to you in many guises, but always, *always* it will be treacherous."

Indigo's heart was thundering beneath her ribs. Harshly, she said, "If I cannot kill it, or even recognize it, I can't hope to stand against it!"

"Ah, but you can. It has one weakness: it cannot manifest without showing some part of its form as silver. Silver eyes, silver hair, perhaps silver adornments—even a silver tooth. Beware of silver, Indigo; for silver is the color of your nemesis."

She looked quickly at her companion. "Why? Why silver?"

It shook its head. "No more questions now. We must continue on our way."

Indigo wanted to argue. She turned her head, looked again toward the demonic child—

There was nothing to be seen but the empty road.

How long they walked again after that first encounter she didn't know. The landscape flowed on unchanging, the flat light never altered, the road was endless. And then far ahead Indigo saw a shape moving slowly, as though racked by weariness or pain, toward them.

The second encounter. Her mouth was dry as she remembered the hated visage of the demon-child, and she wondered what would be in store for her now. *Your salvation or your doom*, the bright emissary had said: *an inspiration to your quest, and yet a threat to your resolve.* She shuddered, and forced herself to walk on.

The distant figure drew nearer, and she realized that, like her nemesis, it did not stray onto the road but walked on the barren earth beside the track. Again an instinct she couldn't name told her, long before the traveler was clearly visible, that when their paths crossed she would know him.

And the sense of recognition, when it came, was more terrifying than her nemesis could ever have been.

An awful sound broke from her throat and she put the back of one hand to her mouth, biting the skin as her mind tried to reject what her eyes told her. The emissary stopped and looked back at her.

"You cannot turn aside from it, Indigo. You must face your second encounter."

She couldn't answer, couldn't protest. He was walking toward her still, his gait loose, uneven, as though he stumbled through some mad, solitary dream. He was oblivious to Indigo's presence; though he seemed to gaze straight at her, his eyes looked into another world, and what they reflected made her recoil in horror. His hands pushed at something invisible that seemed to impede his way, as if he struggled like a swimmer through deep water. And he bled. The blood ran from wounds in his body, in his legs; it streamed from a gash on his bleached, stark face; it matted his black hair, constantly running, an inexhaustible crimson river that left no stains or traces on the earth behind him.

The hiatus of shock broke, and a cry ripped from Indigo's throat.

"Fenran!"

Before the emissary could stop her she rushed forward, arms outstretched and clawing, toward her dead lover. She broke from the road—and slammed into an intangible barrier, solid as a stone wall, that sent her reeling dizzily back. She recoiled screaming as, for an instant only, she glimpsed another world beyond the barrier—a world of shrieking skies and sulfurous fogs, where warped and disfigured trees twisted their rotting branches into a dense, foul thicket through which Fenran struggled like a fly in a spider's web. Then the hideous image was gone and there was only Fenran's broken form stumbling on like a crazed mummer by the side of the endless road.

Cool hands took her arms as Indigo tried again to go toward her love. She didn't have the strength to fight the emissary, and so could only watch as Fenran shambled on, ignoring them, fighting his way through the strangling, monstrous trees that only he could see.

"But he's dead," Indigo whispered. "I saw him *die*. . . ."

"He lives—but not as you would understand living." The bright creature watched the shambling, departing man with deep pity. "And therein lies your hope. The demons may have mutilated Fenran's body, but they could not destroy his soul. He is trapped in their realm, a dimension beyond this world. If you succeed in the task the Earth Mother has set you, then he can be freed from captivity and restored to you: but *only* if you succeed; for until the seven demons are destroyed, Fenran is and will remain their prisoner."

Indigo stared miserably after Fenran's retreating figure, then shut her eyes as thoughts of the torment he must be suffering overwhelmed her. Desperately, she said through clenched teeth, "How can the Earth Mother be so cruel?"

"She had no hand in inflicting Fenran's suffering, Indigo," the entity replied gravely and with a touch of severity. "The demons are man's creation, not Hers; She cannot control them, and She cannot release your beloved. Only you have the power to do that, if you will."

"If I will?" Bitterly, Indigo turned on the being. "Don't you think I would give my life, my *soul*, to save him? Do you think anything else matters to me?"

"I know your feelings perhaps better than you know

them yourself, child. And therein lies the greatest danger, for in your desire to save the man you love, you might all too easily forget the greater quest. That is what I meant when I said that the second traveler on this road would symbolize your salvation or your doom."

She began to understand. With great deliberation, and forcing herself, though with difficulty, not to look again in the direction the apparition of Fenran had taken, she said: "Will you answer one question?"

The emissary inclined its head. "I will."

"How can I find and destroy the seven demons?"

The entity sighed. "The Earth Mother wishes the answer were as simple as the question. All I can tell you is this: you will encounter the seven demons one by one, though the nature of each encounter may vary. Some you will find in the guise of human evil; others may lead you into astral realms. It is for you to confront and destroy these harbingers with the resources of your own mind and heart; but with each triumph your strength will grow." The being smiled with sympathy. "It will be a long road, Indigo. You will see the world change about you, whilst you yourself remain unchanging, unaging. But whilst you may not die a natural death, you must still beware, for you are vulnerable to other forces. But you will know your enemies when you meet them. And you *can* prevail, if you use what you have wisely and are not afraid. You have the power to redeem yourself and your love. That much the Earth Mother vouchsafes you, and gladly."

Indigo gazed down at the dusty ground beneath her feet. "You try to offer me hope," she said at last, her voice old. "I only wish that I could take comfort from it."

"In time, child, perhaps you will learn to do so."

The being held out a hand toward her. "We must go. The end of the road isn't far away."

She couldn't look over her shoulder, for she didn't know which she feared more: seeing Fenran's lurching, mutilated form again, or seeing nothing but the empty land. Together, they walked on.

And then ahead of them was a gateway. One moment there had been nothing but the unending road; the next, an arch of pale light shimmered into existence directly ahead of them. Whatever lay within the arch was obscured by a shifting, milky mist, and Indigo hung back uncertainly, but the emissary smiled.

"Don't hesitate, child. This is the end of our road together."

They approached the arch, and as they drew close to it the mist began to agitate, shredding apart to reveal a latticework pattern of branches and the vivid green of young leaves. Something about the emerging scene made Indigo feel a sharp pang of familiarity—and then they had passed through the arch and were standing on soft, lush grass, with sunlight dappling through the trees that formed a canopy over their heads.

"We have returned to your world," the entity told her. "These woods lie half a day's walk from Ranna Port. I will leave you now, to return to my own realm, and you must go to Ranna and take ship from the Southern Isles."

Indigo gazed at what would be one of her last sights of the great woods of her homelands—then stopped. Her knuckles whitened as she involuntarily clenched her fists.

"But—" Again she looked around, wildly this time as she thought she must be hallucinating. But her eyes didn't deceive her. The leaves on the trees surrounding her were new, young; too brilliant to be autumnal.

"It's spring . . ." Her voice was throaty with the shock of realization. "But when we left Carn Caille, it was—"

"I know, child. But I told you that the currents of time flow differently on the road we traveled. Seven months have passed on the Earth while we walked."

Indigo's face was gray. "Seven months . . . ?"

"Yes. The world has turned, and new life is burgeoning." The being smiled kindly. "It is a time of hope."

Hope? she thought bleakly. Somewhere a bird uttered a sharp, rising trill of exuberant song, and she felt her lips moving in an unlooked-for ironic smile, though she didn't truly know whether to laugh or cry.

The emissary said: "It is time to go, Indigo. Take up your belongings."

For the first time then she saw the two bags that lay on the grass a few paces away. One, made of fine hide, had a familiar shape, and she bent down to touch it with uncertain fingers.

Her harp. It was a poignant link with Carn Caille, Cushmagar and all she had been forced to leave behind. The emissary smiled gently.

"Music has its own powerful magic. Always remember that." It stepped forward and, to her surprise, laid both hands on her shoulders in a way that hinted at affection it would not or could not express. "We may encounter one another again; but in the meantime remember all I have told you. There is danger for you on the road ahead, yet there is also hope. You have skills that are yet undiscovered; use them well, if you can, and you will not find yourself unrewarded." The being paused, then smiled. "And you will not go on your quest entirely without friends. Your third encounter is not long away, and it will be one you can trust. The Earth Mother wishes you well, Indigo."

The air shimmered as though the sun had abruptly fluctuated and brightened. A second later Indigo saw the arch of light behind the emissary shiver, its colors whirling with new energy—then a sweet-scented breath of wind touched her face from nowhere, and the arch and the bright being were gone.

·CHAPTER·VIII·

Ranna was the busiest port in the Southern Isles; and all the more so at this time of year with the sea-lanes newly reopened after the winter storms. The road into Ranna was hectic with traffic now through most of the lengthening daylight hours, and the vast natural harbor crowded with ships of every size and kind, while on the docks activity was ceaseless. A big and ponderous merchant square-rigger of the Bear class was wallowing out of harbor on the afternoon tide in the wake of a lighter, faster barque bound for the eastern continent. Flanking the square-rigger, two pilot boats danced on the glittering water like dolphins around a whale, seeing her safe out of coastal waters.

Shortly after the square-rigger had cleared the harbor, the *Greymalkin*, a sleek Lynx clipper with a mixed cargo of ore and timber, hoisted her departure pennant and sailed on the last of the tide under the command of her master, Danog Uylason. And from the clipper's deck, a woman with shorn gray hair, dressed in a man's hunting-garb, looked back for the last time at the receding coastline of the Southern Isles.

Indigo felt as if she were trapped in some dull and lonely dream. She had left the wood to find herself on an unfamiliar road, and had walked throughout the cruelly brilliant day in an increasing miasma of misery and grief as the small spark of hope kindled by the emissary's last words to her faded with her memory of the bright being's face. She felt as though phantoms trod in her wake; her family, Fenran, the people of Carn Caille; all aware of what she had done, all accusing her. And she felt the burden and the responsibility that she had incurred lying like a leaden cloak upon her shoulders.

A wagoner, overtaking her on the road and seeing her harp in its bag on her shoulder, had offered to carry her into Ranna in exchange for a lively tune, but she had declined with a shake of her head, unable to bear the thought of company. And so the tricky shades of dusk were beginning to encroach on the landscape when at last the lights of the coastal town appeared as a hazy shimmer ahead.

Ranna was the hub of the kingdom's mercantile power. Indigo had never before visited the town, and though her first sight of its sprawling chaos unnerved her, she nonetheless felt thankful to be in an anonymous place where she might blend in with the itinerant throng and thus go unnoticed and unremarked. In Ranna she had no memories; she was nobody. Reaching the harbor with its forest of ship masts, its huge granite piers, its jumble of warehouses, she had sought a quieter alley away from the racket of ceaseless activity and had examined the contents of her two bags. The harp she touched, but only once; the sweet sound it gave as her fingers stroked the strings almost tore her heart apart, and she quickly moved on to the second bag. In this she found a water-skin, a small purse of coins, flint and tinder, her hunting knife, a few simple cooking utensils and a small scrying-glass which Imyssa had given her and which she had hardly ever tried to use. Strapped to the bag was her crossbow, together with a supply of bolts, and she smiled wanly. The Earth Mother's emissary knew her well enough to have granted her the weapon with which she had the greatest skill; whatever befell her from now on, she was at least unlikely to starve.

She sealed the bag again and, though her heart wasn't in it, took stock of her surroundings. She didn't want to take a room at one of the many taverns that fronted on the harbor; her few coins were precious, and she couldn't face the thought of having to speak to a stranger or lie in a strange bed. As darkness fell, torches were lit in brackets and the harbor was almost as bright as day; she would do well enough without sleep.

Indigo made herself as comfortable as she could in the shelter of the dock storehouses, watching as Ranna's endless activity, which was dictated entirely by the tides, continued through the night. She paid little heed to *Greymalkin* or to the man and woman who yelled orders to the men filling her holds; the clipper was simply one ship among many. But when the thin gray light of dawn began to rival the flames of the torches, she woke from an uneasy and dream-racked doze in time to see the woman pause in her work and glance in Indigo's direction with undisguised curiosity. For a moment their gazes met and held; then the woman smiled and, in an involuntary reflex, Indigo smiled back.

Why Laegoy, Danog Uylason's wife, took pity on the hapless stranger with her bewildered eyes and her few coins, neither she nor Indigo would ever know. But somehow, during a lull in her work, Laegoy found an excuse to pass by the stranger, stop and speak to her. And on hearing that the girl wanted to leave the Southern Isles, Laegoy was moved to offer her passage on the *Greymalkin* in exchange for a few coins and her harp music.

Laegoy stood now at *Greymalkin*'s rail. She was a big, rawboned woman approaching middle age, with filed and tobacco-stained teeth, and long black hair tied into four greasy braids. She wore seaman's clothes and a good deal of jewelry; copper and brass bracelets bit into the flesh of her brawny arms, while a heavy brass torque adorned her shoulders, and the wicked-bladed knife thrust carelessly into her belt had a hilt encrusted with moonstones and agates, her personal luck-stones. Her sharp, water-green gaze was divided between the dipping hulk of the square-rigger ahead of them, now turning into her northeasterly course, and the solitary figure near the stern. Why their passenger should want to sail to the Redoubt, a journey that would take her almost from pole to pole, Laegoy couldn't imagine; but there was something about this girl-turned-old-woman that evoked both compassion and discomfort in her. She'd learned nothing about the girl, save that she called herself Indigo: a bizarre choice and obviously not her birth-name; its association with death and mourning had made Danog suspect that she might be jinxed, though Laegoy had scorned the idea and ridden roughshod over her husband's doubts. But there *was* a strangeness about her, a privacy, an inner darkness and emptiness that she held back from her face yet which showed in her shadowed eyes. And Laegoy, for all her outward hardness and termagant sway over the ship's crew, was a warmhearted woman and easily moved to pity.

The departure pennant—a blue triangle with a single diagonal white stripe—came rattling down the mast as *Greymalkin* cleared the last of the buoys anchored in the harbor lanes. Laegoy paused to yell a stentorian order to a slacking seaman, then turned from the rail and made her way to the stern.

Indigo looked up as she approached. *Those eyes*, Laegoy thought: *so empty.* Aloud, she said, "We're clear of port now, lass. Nothing more to see but the water."

"Yes . . ." Indigo suppressed a shiver.

Curious, and wanting to draw the girl out of herself, Laegoy continued. "There'll be little else to look at until we're in sight of the Scorva coast. With the wind out of the south, that shouldn't be more than four, maybe five days. We'll put in at Linsk Port in the Horselands to take on fresh food and water, then cross the Serenity and go on up through the Snakemaw Straits to the Redoubt." She paused, but there was no reaction. "The western way makes for harder navigation, but with the currents as they are this time of year, we'll save a sennight or more on the voyage."

Still Indigo said nothing, and the seawoman frowned. "Whichever way we go, it'll be a long journey, lass. You must have a reason for wanting to travel such a way—no," as Indigo tensed and mistrust glittered in her empty eyes, "I'm not prying into your private concerns. But I hope you've friends to greet you when we finally get to Mull Barya. The Redoubt can be a lonely place without friends."

Laegoy's concern was kindly meant, but Indigo couldn't assuage it by telling her what lay behind her decision to travel to the great island in the far north. She had few illusions that she'd find friendship among Fenran's people, for Fenran had been estranged from his father long before he came to the Southern Isles.

But the entire world was open to her; though the Redoubt might hold little for her, she felt, however illogically, that to venture there would bring her closer to Fenran, and that lent her a little comfort.

She said to Laegoy: "I'll be well enough, thank you."

"As you please." Laegoy shrugged, then nodded toward the companion-hatch. "You should get you down to your cabin and rest awhile. There'll be nothing afoot until the crew starts clamoring to be fed, and you look as if you could do with the sleep."

Indigo said, "No," so quickly that Laegoy heard the edge of fear before she could disguise it. Her black eyebrows lifted.

"What is it, lass? Afraid of bad dreams?"

Confirmation showed in the girl's eyes, and the seawoman smiled grimly. "There's ways of keeping them at bay. I'll mix you a draught and bring it to you below—I promise, you'll sleep like a babe in arms and no need to fear shadow-demons." She put an arm around Indigo's shoulders and squeezed, not gently but with rough warmth. "Go on with you now."

Laegoy's brusque mothering reminded Indigo like a stab in the stomach of Imyssa. She looked away, blinking back the threat of tears and reminding herself that the time for crying was past, and nodded.

"I . . ." But there were no words of explanation; she had the taste of ashes in her mouth. "Thank you."

Careful not to let Laegoy glimpse her face, she walked, unsteady with the pitch of the ship, toward the companion ladder.

Thanks to the draught Laegoy prepared for her, Indigo slept through the night and most of the following day, and as the seawoman had promised, there were no dreams. When she woke, *Greymalkin* was running with a high sea under heavy cloud-wrack: Laegoy told her that, with the wind so strong from the south, they were ahead of schedule and should sight the coast of the Horselands within two days and reach Linsk another day after that.

As a windy dusk began to fall, the ship's crew gathered on deck to eat under the shelter of tarpaulins, and, remembering that music was to be part payment for her passage, Indigo brought out her harp. She played sea-songs, chanteys which they all knew and could sing, and, finally, the Amberland Wife's Lament, a poignant and beautiful piece created long ago by the widow of a fisherman who had watched her husband's boat go down off the notorious Amberland Point. When the piece was done, Laegoy, visibly moved, hugged her while the sailors thumped the deck planks in gruff approval, and for the first time since the hideous night that had shattered her life and her world, Indigo felt the seeds of comfort stir within her. The rhythm of sea and wind, the dip and rise of *Greymalkin* as she surged on, the music, the men's voices in harmony . . . it all had awoken an unlooked-for sense of warmth and companionship, a feeling that Indigo still had friends in the world and that her quest, however lonely and however hard, had a real and vital purpose.

But her peace of mind wasn't to last. When the food was eaten, Danog Uylason broke open a keg of cider and, with tongues loosened by a mug or two of drink, the crew began to talk. At sea with no sight of greenery to tell the season, it had been easy for Indigo to forget that months had passed while she walked the strange, otherworldly road with the Earth Mother's emissary, and now it came as a shock to hear of the changes that had taken place in the Southern Isles.

The worst of it was that she could glean only a small amount of the truth. She dared not ask questions:

Greymalkin's crew knew she was an Islander, and so assumed she would know as much about recent events in the kingdom as they did; if not more, for they'd been at sea through all but the worst of the winter. To avoid the risk of being questioned in turn, Indigo pretended to be asleep, whilst listening intently.

There was as yet no new king at Carn Caille. The fever that had swept the islands as summer waned had been short-lived but horrifyingly virulent: hundreds, so Indigo gathered from the seamen's conversation, had died or come close to death, and the stricken islands were only now beginning to recover. And in Carn Caille the remnants of the royal council, barefoot and with hair knotted as signs of mourning, consulted the bards and the forest witches, cast runes and watched the natural omens around them, in their efforts to find a worthy successor to Kalig.

There had been fears that one or more of the neighboring countries not closely allied to the Southern Isles might try to take advantage of the tragedy to wrest superiority on the seas from the Southerners' hands; Indigo learned that *Greymalkin* and many of her sister ships had spent much of the winter patrolling the sea-lanes lest hungry opportunists in the east or on the big island of Scorva should attempt to assert their own power. There had been skirmishes, but none serious enough to warrant widespread alarm; now all was quiet again, and the Islanders believed that the name of the new king would be known before many more days had passed.

Still feigning sleep, Indigo listened to the talk and forced herself to show no emotion, but inwardly the thought of a new monarch, a new reign, a new family at Carn Caille was like red-hot embers in her gut, for it brought home to her, perhaps as nothing else had yet been able to do, the cruel irony of her situation. She was, by right of birth, queen of the Southern Isles. But instead a newcomer, possibly even a stranger, would sit on the great chair in Carn Caille's hall, and her dynasty would soon be nothing more than a chapter in the islands' turbulent history.

Not, she told herself bitterly, that she would have wanted to be queen. She wanted her father alive again, with her brother as destined heir. She wanted her mother, sophisticated and gracious. She wanted Fenran . . .

At the thought of Fenran, tears squeezed themselves between her shut eyelids despite her efforts to hold them back. Her body shook with a spasm and she huddled further into her corner, hoping that no one on *Greymalkin*'s deck had noticed.

But someone had. Laegoy moved to sit beside her and nudged her ribs. When she opened her eyes Indigo saw the seawoman gazing down at her with open pity, but when Laegoy spoke she sounded careless enough.

"Sleeping, lass? I doubt if the men'll let you go below without another tune to send the watch to their posts and the rest of us to our hammocks."

Indigo blinked and struggled upright. She was grateful to Laegoy for helping her to maintain the deception, but wondered what, if anything, the woman had inferred from her momentary lapse. Laegoy smiled kindly.

"Music's good for the soul, girl," she added in an undertone. "Yours as well as ours. One piece more, and then get your sleep."

One or two of the crewmen grinned encouragement, and there were approving shouts as Indigo reached for her harp. She returned Laegoy's smile wanly and said, "Another chantey?"

"That's it, lass." Laegoy pinched her arm hard but affectionately. "Another chantey. And make it a rouser!"

* * *

Although the days were lengthening, the sun still had a low meridian in these latitudes. When Indigo woke the next morning it was barely above the horizon: she had slept this time without the need for Laegoy's dream-banishing potions, and through the two days that followed she worked alongside the ship's crew, turning her hand to whatever labor she could. The taxing physical activity gave her, to her own surprise, a sense of being cleansed, so that as time passed she felt that she was very slowly beginning to recover from a wound that she had thought might fester without hope of healing. Then as the grayness of twilight started to touch the sea and turn it to pewter on the fifth evening out of Ranna, the lookout's stentorian yell alerted them all to the smudge of a coastline and the distant, winking beacon of Linsk harbor.

Indigo stood with Laegoy at *Greymalkin*'s rail to see, for the first time in her life, the great western continent take form out of the gathering dusk. Linsk was the foremost trading port in the staunchly independent little principality known as the Horselands, and much of what she saw as pilot boats guided the clipper to shore reminded her of the busy sea-towns of the Southern Isles. Behind the rocky harbor a jumble of warehouses and dwellings scrambled up shallow cliffs, rain shining on slate rooftops, while the harbor itself was a forest of tall masts. Lights glimmered about the quays, reflecting in dancing patterns from the water; in the distance, where the evening mist was coming down, she saw the gray-green smudge of moorland stretching away inland.

Greymalkin was brought to a berth at the southern end of the docks, and a port official—a small man with broad, flat features, dressed in a motley of fur, leather and bright-hued woven wool—came aboard. Danog

Uylason took him down to the captain's quarters for a cup of mead, and the crew at last began to relax. Laegoy told Indigo that they'd sleep on board that night and have the next day free before leaving on the evening tide, and suggested that she might benefit from a few hours' exercise before the next leg of the voyage began.

"They don't call this province the Horselands without reason," she said. "They probably breed the best riding animals you can find anywhere in the world, and there are always plenty for hire in Linsk. Danog will arrange it for you." She grinned and nudged Indigo's ribs. "And if you could put that crossbow of yours to good use on the moors, some fresh meat wouldn't go amiss!"

The idea of a long ride to clear her head appealed to Indigo, as did the chance to repay Laegoy's kindness in however small a way. So, after a fitful night's sleep—she'd become accustomed to the clipper's rhythmic motion on the open sea—she collected a hired mare the next morning and set off inland. On her back she carried her harp, which was too precious to risk leaving behind, her travel bag, belt-pouch and crossbow: if game was as plentiful as the landscape implied, she should have little difficulty in carrying out her errand.

Laegoy had been right about the horses of this district: the hired mare—a tall chestnut—was as lively as she could have wished, and reminded her, with a pang, of her own lost Sleeth. On the rough track beyond the harbor town Indigo gave her her head, and the moor opened up like a great landlocked sea before them, the wind rushing in her face with an exhilarating chill. Far ahead she could see dense woods edged by the glittering ribbon of a river, and away to the west a small herd of the wild horses from which the region took its name grazed the springy turf.

She rode until the mare began to tire, then at last slowed her to a walk and halted. The woods were much closer now, maybe half a mile away at most; she'd ridden farther than she had intended, but was glad, for the gallop had done more than refresh her mind and body; it had eased something in her soul. Maybe the feeling wouldn't last; maybe within a few minutes or a few hours or even a few days the torment would come back to haunt her. But while the respite lasted, she was deeply grateful for it.

The mare tugged at the bit, wanting to stray off the track and crop at the young grass, but Indigo pulled her back. Apart from the wild horses, she had seen no animal or bird life, and if she was to hunt, then the woods held far better promise than the moorland. She kicked the reluctant mare forward and trotted on more sedately until she reached the riverbank beyond which the forest began.

The river was wide, but the early spring spate had abated, and though the water still flowed fast, it was no more than a few inches deep. Her mount splashed across the stony bed, pausing midway to drink, and within minutes they were among the trees.

It wasn't like the forests of the Southern Isles. There, deciduous trees had to struggle for survival among their coniferous cousins, which were better adapted to a cold climate; but here oak and ash and birch and hornbeam ran riot in a brilliant patchwork of young green. The undergrowth was dense and varied, and from the canopy overhead came intermittent snatches of birdsong.

There were paths through the forest, encroached on by the vegetation but clear enough to follow without risk of becoming lost. And in the soft leaf mold underfoot were the slotted prints of cloven hoofs.

Indigo smiled and unslung her crossbow. She lashed the reins around the saddle pommel and guided the mare forward with knees and heels, her eyes alert for any sign of movement.

Something away to her right . . . She hissed softly through her teeth, edging the mare off the path in the direction of the telltale disturbance. Just ahead of her was a small natural clearing where, with more light to encourage it, grass grew unusually lush. It was a likely haunt for grazing animals, and as she eased cautiously among the branches toward it she was gratified to see another flicker of motion through the leaves, a glimpse of something dappled by the filtered shadows. A deer, its size and the hoofprints told her; enough to provide a venison feast for *Greymalkin*'s entire crew. She began to skirt the clearing, wanting to move downwind of the animal without leaving the trees' shelter, and as quietly as she could she fitted a bolt into her crossbow, drew the string back, set it—

The undergrowth on the far side of the clearing rustled. Indigo readied herself to shoot, expecting the deer to emerge at any moment from the forest canopy; but instead there was a new disturbance among the leaves, as though something had caught hold of a branch and pulled it violently. The mare laid her ears back and her nostrils flared; Indigo could feel sudden tension in her muscles and realized that she had sensed something untoward, and beyond the reach of human perceptions.

"Hush." She dropped her voice to the peculiar, inflectionless whisper used by skilled Southern Isles hunters. "It's only a deer."

The mare's ears flicked forward but only briefly; she was still uneasy. Indigo started to unloop the reins to gain better control, then froze as the undergrowth rustled again to the tread of a foot, and she glimpsed her quarry.

It wasn't a deer. Though it looked as large as a fallow doe, its body was the wrong shape: too low, too sleek; the neck too short and the muzzle too long. The deceptive shadows made it impossible for her to discern any detail, but she felt with an instinctive tightening of her stomach muscles that this animal was as much of a predator as she was.

The indistinct shape moved, and she knew that it had seen her. The head, its outline distorted by the bushes and tree trunks among which the creature lurked, swung around—and brilliant eyes, not a gentle, bovine brown but shimmering amber, focused on her face.

Without any warning her mount's nerve snapped and she danced sideways, snorting. Indigo felt herself slipping in the saddle and snatched at the reins, trying to bring the mare and her own body under control. But before she could regain her balance the leaves and the branches on the far side of the clearing agitated furiously, and an alien shape erupted from cover and shot like a living arrow straight at her. She had a chaotic impression of brindled fur, a massive, powerful body, as the snarling creature hurtled by an inch from the mare's flank. She reared, panicking, and swerved wildly: Indigo lost a stirrup, was jerked back in the saddle, saw a bough come flailing toward her as the horse bolted. She tried to scream, but a mad confusion of leaves and branches exploded in her face; the bough struck her full on the forehead and she was unconscious before she hit the ground.

The sailor whom Laegoy sent out to the edge of the town to look for any sign of *Greymalkin*'s passenger returning came back to report failure. Danog Uylason, who had been pacing the clipper's deck for the better part of two hours, torn between arguing with his wife and anxiously watching the ebbing tide, finally put his foot down. They could wait no longer. Dusk was falling; if they didn't sail now they'd not have the draught to clear harbor, and another night's delay would be a setback to their schedule, especially if they ran into one of the periodic calms in the Serenity, which were a constant hazard.

Laegoy gave way. She disliked the idea of leaving without Indigo—aside from the fact that she'd taken a liking to the girl, there was the moral question to consider—but acknowledged that her first duty lay with *Greymalkin*, her crew and her cargo. Nonetheless as the lines were cast off she watched the higher reaches of the town, hoping that at the last minute she'd see a solitary rider coming off the moor. But there was nothing. And at last *Greymalkin* eased from her berth in the wake of the pilot boats, and her sails filled and bellied as she headed toward open water.

Laegoy was uncharacteristically quiet for the next few days. She thought a good deal about Indigo; wondered why the girl hadn't returned to the ship, what her fate would be. But there were other demands on her time and on her concentration. Guilt faded, worry faded, memory faded.

Only once in a while did she wonder if she'd ever see Indigo again.

·CHAPTER·IX·

The angle of the light had changed. All day the sun had been breaking through the cloud cover in fitful moments, and now it seemed that the overcast must have cleared, for amber rays were slanting into the forest, etching tree trunks and pooling in bright patterns on the littered floor. But the vivid shafts were coming in low, and she realized as she sat up that hours must have passed since her fall.

That realization was followed by a sick moment of panic. *Greymalkin.* She had few illusions that the clipper would miss the tide for her; chances were that she was already preparing to leave. Indigo started to her feet in alarm—then fell back with a sharp cry as her left leg refused to take her weight, and pain shot through her ankle as though she'd stepped in a steel trap. She lay still, breathing hard and sweating; then, when the pain receded enough for her to regain her breath, she tried cautiously to twist her foot from side to side. It hurt, but not unbearably, suggesting—though her knowledge was very limited—that the ankle was twisted rather than sprained. Not that it made much difference: either way, she couldn't stand. And the hired mare was nowhere to be seen.

Putting her weight on her arms, she dragged herself backward until she could rest against the bole of the oak whose overhanging branch had knocked her out of the saddle. Her head was throbbing, though her vision seemed unaffected; the blow she'd taken had, it seemed, done no real damage. The crossbow, which she hadn't had the wit to fire, lay almost buried in a bramble bush a few feet away, and her harp had come to rest beside the tree; if she stretched, she could just reach it without disturbing her injured leg. It seemed to be unscathed, and though the feeling was irrational, she was more relieved by that than by anything else.

Then she remembered what had caused her to fall, and her skin crawled.

Quarry turned predator, erupting from the undergrowth in a flash of deadly savagery to vanish into the shadows as swiftly as it had manifested. What manner of animal had it been? She'd had only the briefest glimpse of it, but it was far larger than anything she had ever seen in the forests of her homeland. And it was at large in the vicinity still; had prowled among the trees while she lay unconscious; might even now be watching her, unseen, awaiting its moment to strike.

Suddenly, Indigo was frightened of being alone.

She struggled into a more upright position, wincing as a lance of fire pierced her ankle, and wondered how far the mare had bolted. Depending on the nature of her training, she might have found her way out of the forest and run for home, or she might still be in the vicinity. It was possible—though the chance was remote, Indigo knew—that the mare might respond to the whistle that Southern Isles horsemen used to summon recalcitrant mounts.

Indigo pursed her lips and blew, but her mouth was too dry for the chirruping call to form. She worked her jaw, trying to induce saliva; at last she tried again and this time, though wavering, the whistle shrilled in the wood.

A bird answered her querulously, but nothing else. She tried again . . . and moments later heard something approaching, skirting the clearing and coming through the undergrowth. Something big, her ears told her; certainly a horse, or—

Her skin crawled again as the thought came, unbidden: *or what*? Memories of what she had seen before she fell ate at her, and involuntarily she tensed, pressing her back hard against the tree trunk and fumbling for the crossbow, heart pounding—

A chestnut muzzle appeared from a tangle of leaves, and the mare whickered a greeting. Indigo shut her eyes and started to shake with laughter that was also a desperate release of tension. Tears trickled between her tight-closed eyelids and she bit them back, knowing how easy it would be to succumb to hysteria. The mare ambled to her and nudged at her shoulder; she reached out and hugged the soft nose as gradually the fit subsided.

She was no longer alone. All she needed to do was climb into the saddle and she could ride out of the forest, back over the moors to Linsk. If *Greymalkin* had left port without her, there would be another ship soon enough. But when, with the aid of a stirrup-leather, she heaved herself painfully up on her good leg, she realized that she wouldn't be able to mount without help: her ankle simply couldn't cope with the strain. The mare shifted restlessly, not understanding the delay, and after several minutes of fruitless effort followed by equally fruitless thought, Indigo gave up the attempt. She'd need to find some high point from which she could drop down onto the saddle, but there was nothing of any use in sight, and she couldn't travel far to find a more suitable spot. Besides, the slanting sunlight was now fading from amber to blood-red, and she realized that the day was dying. It would soon be dark, and to attempt to find her way out of this great tract of woodland in darkness would be foolhardy. She had no idea how far the forest extended; by morning, if she missed her way, she could be hopelessly lost in its depths. Better to stay put until the daylight returned, by which time her ankle might be strong enough to enable her to climb into the saddle.

She sank back against the tree. This was a good enough place for a makeshift camp; certainly she didn't want to risk another fall by trying to struggle to some better location. Looping the trailing reins around a knobby, protruding oak root, she began to take stock of what she had about her to see her through the night ahead. Water—early training had taught her never to go riding or hunting without a full waterskin. No food: but there might be edible shoots or roots within reach if she searched for them, and if not, the pangs of hunger were nothing to worry about. Her greatest problem was shelter. Despite the heavy leaf canopy, the open forest offered little protection against rain or bitter cold, and her coat, though warm, might not be enough to save her from cold-sickness if the night temperature here dropped as severely as it did in her homeland. There were no convenient caves or even bushes dense enough to give her a lodging, but she could at least have a fire: flint and tinder, together with her knife, were stowed safely in her belt-pouch, and there was enough debris on the forest floor to make a fair blaze.

While the mare cropped the grass at the edge of the

clearing, Indigo set to work. She had never had to make a fire for herself before, but she remembered watching servants build pyres in the hearths of Carn Caille or in the woods on two-day hunts, and soon had a good-sized heap of brushwood, bark and leaves ready. Persuading the pile to ignite proved less easy; the material was damp, and by the time the first spark reluctantly caught and she blew it into life, shielding it with a cupped hand, she was tired and dispirited.

As the fire finally blazed up, however, she had an unexpected and unlooked-for piece of luck. Whether the light or the scent of the burning wood had aroused its curiosity or whether it was simply blundering aimlessly through the forest, she didn't know; but a rustling alerted her, and in the fast-fading light of sunset she saw a small wild pig emerge beside a birch tree. It was very young, probably no more than two months old, and she tensed immediately, aware that its mother could well be nearby and that an adult sow could be dangerous. But there was no sight or sound of any larger animal: the piglet simply stood staring at her as though hypnotized by the firelight. Even when she reached slowly and cautiously for her crossbow, it didn't move, and only at the sound of the bowstring being drawn did it turn and scramble away.

Indigo fired, and the piglet leaped into the air with an agonized squeal as the bolt slammed into its side. It rolled over, kicking and shrieking, then after a few seconds became still but for an occasional twitch.

Clenching her teeth against pain, Indigo crawled the few feet to where the wounded piglet lay, and dispatched it with her knife, silently thanking the Earth Mother for her hunting skills and for the fact that Imyssa had insisted that, princess or no, she should know how to prepare and cook the game she caught. Gutting the pig was messy and unpleasant, but she managed it, then hacked off a haunch and speared it on a peeled twig which she propped at an angle beside the fire, so that the meat was suspended over the flames. The haunch sizzled, giving off an aroma that set her stomach juices churning. The mare continued to graze. And, tired after her efforts, and perhaps still suffering the effects of her fall, Indigo dozed against the bole of the tree.

When she woke, it was pitch-dark. The fire was still burning, but only just; neglect and a heavy dew had reduced it to sluggish embers. Hastily she scrabbled for more kindling, and sighed with relief as the flames rose again and the encroaching shadows slid back from the renewed circle of light.

The forest was very quiet. The mare was no longer cropping but stood with her head down, sleeping in the peculiar way of horses. The birds were mute now; there was not enough wind to disturb the leaves and set them rustling, and Indigo felt her spine prickle with the uneasy loneliness of being isolated in a vast, dark silence. This was no place for a solitary human; the firelight cast bizarre shadows, turning the undergrowth into a dim, silhouetted threat without form or symmetry, the trees into eerie, sentient watchers, creatures from the realm of old stories and superstitions. Though she fought against the impulse, Indigo couldn't help recalling Imyssa's tales, deliciously but safely thrilling in the comforting warmth of her firelit bedroom at Carn Caille, but now conjured horribly into the realm of possibility. The Brown Walker, tall as an oak but thin as the youngest sapling, with his one eye and the mouth in the center of his chest, from which came the ceaseless hooting that was the last sound his victims ever heard. The Scatterers: squat, brindle-furred, with five hundred teeth apiece, whose name came from their habit of scattering the bones of those who fell foul of them, when the last of the marrow had been drained. Ginnimokki, who, it was said, had once been female but was now a living skeleton who crawled, and glowed, and howled.

A great shudder ran the length of her spine like a shock wave and left her breathless. She didn't want to think of those old, ghoulish stories, but they crowded into her brain unbidden, drawn by the forest's depth and blackness and silence. At any moment any one of those horrors or a dozen more like them might step out of the shadows, out of the realm of dreams, to confront her. And she had no defense, no stone walls to shield her, no nurse to croon her to sleep.

Indigo felt a sick fear that she hadn't experienced since childhood rise within her. Fear of the unknown, of solitude, of the formless monsters that haunted lonely nights; a deep-rooted terror that was far worse than the more natural fear of lurking predators. She reached out and snatched at the bag that contained her harp, pulling the instrument out with cold, fumbling fingers. The hunger that had assailed her earlier was swamped by the nauseous dread; the piglet's haunch continued to cook, but the idea of food turned her stomach. Her need was one of the spirit, not of the body. Only music could keep the horrors of the night—and of her own mind—at bay.

The harp was badly out of tune and moaned like a banshee when she plucked the strings. Shivering, Indigo tuned it, then settled herself and took several breaths before beginning, softly at first but with growing confidence, to play a gentle sea-song. The sound of the harp against the forest's backdrop was breathtakingly beautiful; with no walls to confine them, the liquid notes shimmered and shivered in the dark, and she felt herself responding, her pulse slowing, mind relaxing as the music soothed her. After the sea-song she played a Hawthorn-Month dance, a celebration of the coming of summer; then a harvesters' song that rose and fell with the rhythm of rippling corn and sweeping scythes.

She was halfway through the harvesters' melody when she saw lambent eyes gazing at her out of the dark.

The music stopped on an ugly discord, and the harp fell over with a protesting *twang* as Indigo's hands lost all control. Rigid with shock, she stared at the patch of undergrowth, at the twin golden orbs that caught the firelight and reflected it back with feral brilliance.

Reason struggled to assert itself. This was no supernatural manifestation; it was simply a forest animal. The glow of the flames, the smell of the roasting meat . . . of course they would attract predators. A cat? She had seen wild cats in the Southern Isles, and it was possible that they inhabited the Horsclands, too. But those weren't a cat's eyes. *What, then?*

Something moved, a shadow darker than shadows. With a hunter's reflex Indigo tried to start to her feet, forgetting her injured ankle; it gave and she fell back, yelping. When she recovered and looked again, the eyes were closer.

A few feet away the mare nickered, a low, uneasy sound. The horse's instinct confirmed her own, and Indigo reached toward the fire and plucked out a piece of blazing wood. Sparks showered over her arm and the unburned end was blisteringly hot, but she ignored the pain and hefted the brand threateningly.

"Haah!" She snarled deep in her throat, a challenge and a warning. The eyes didn't move.

"Back!" Again she brandished the burning branch. *"Go!"*

Something dark, bulky, shifted just beyond the periphery of the firelight, as if whatever lurked there were deciding whether to flee or pounce. Indigo's heart crashed against her ribs and she groped for the crossbow but couldn't find it; silently she cursed herself for forgetting the most vital rule of the hunter's code, that a weapon should be to hand at all times.

And then she heard something so incredible that her thundering heart almost stopped beating in disbelief.

A voice spoke to her out of the dark, from the deep shadow where the feral eyes shone. It wasn't a human voice—it was far too guttural, too harsh, with a chillingly stilted inflection, as though the creation of such sounds gave their maker terrible pain. But it spoke a language she knew.

"Mu . . . sic." There was agony in the voice, and desperation. *"Li-ike. I . . . li-like. Muuu . . . sic . . ."*

Indigo swore in shock, and her self-control snapped.

"Get out!" Her voice rose to a shrill scream, and she flung the firebrand with all her strength at the source of the hideous voice. "Get out of here, go, *go*!!"

The eyes winked out. Her stunned mind registered an immense dark shape that flowed like water, huge, muscular shoulders, a head whose outline was somehow familiar, sharp-pricked ears. Then it was gone, leaping fluidly into the night and vanishing. She heard a crash and rustle of underbrush, diminishing—and then something that dried the saliva in her mouth. Distant, but shudderingly real, a mournful *yip-yip* that rose to a long-drawn, desolate howl before falling away into a silence so acute that she felt as though she could have reached out and touched it.

A wolf. Indigo slumped back beside the fire, trying to control the hammers that pummeled blood through every vein in her body. In that last split second as the intruder sprang away she had recognized its shape, and the dismal cry in the distance confirmed it beyond any doubt.

She had never been afraid of wolves. In the Southern Isles they presented no threat; their skill and cunning were respected, and human and lupine hunters left each other alone. But she had never seen a wolf of such gigantic size. *And wolves couldn't speak in human tongues . . .*

Indigo checked, and sternly told herself to be rational. The dark played tricks with the eye; it would have been easy enough to mistake the size of the creature as it fled. And little was beyond the capacity of an overwrought imagination; her frightened mind might easily have turned such an animal's stertorous breathing into words. Her childhood nightmares hadn't come back to torment her: the unwelcome visitor had been a wolf, nothing more. And even if Horselands wolves were far bigger than their cousins in the Southern Isles, there was nothing supernatural about them. This one had been drawn to her camp by curiosity and the scent of food; it had been frightened away by fire and a show of aggression. She didn't think it would come back.

The brand she had thrown had guttered away to nothing in the damp undergrowth; the mare had settled, and the forest was quiet once more but for the crackle of her fire and the intermittent sputtering of the roasting pig haunch. The wolf's visit had brought Indigo back to earth, replacing the terrors of nightmare with solid reality and thus banishing her superstitions. She set the crossbow down, smiled, a little wryly, and rescued her meal before it burned to cinders, scorching her fingers when, her appetite restored, she tried to pull pieces from the cooked haunch before it had cooled.

She ate and, sated, slaked her thirst from the waterskin. She had no way of knowing how much time had passed, but an inbuilt instinct told her that dawn was not long away, and the thought was comforting. The forest held no more terrors for her. She thought of playing one last tune on her harp, a lullaby to soothe her subconscious mind until morning, but when she lifted the instrument her fingers were slow with weariness, and she set it aside unplayed. Her ankle ached with a dull, throbbing pain which she could, with a little effort, ignore; the bole of the oak tree was comfortable now that the muscles of her back had grown used to it. The fire sputtered, the mare hung her head peaceably once more. Pain and satiation and the flickering flamelight melded into a soft, numbing blanket, and Indigo slept.

When she woke, dawn had broken; gray light filled the woods and the birds were singing. The fire was nothing more than a circular smudge of dark gray ashes. And something had come while she slept, and carried away the carcass of the piglet she had killed, leaving nothing but a faint bloodstain in the dewy grass.

She tried not to think about it as she drank from her waterskin and gathered her scant possessions around her, but it was there in her mind nonetheless. The wolf had returned, had padded into the circle of firelight and taken the remains of the piglet without disturbing her or the mare. It could have killed her. Such a thing was unknown in the Southern Isles, but here—and especially when she considered the wolf's size—it might be another matter. But instead it had come and gone like a ghost, and her only loss was a few days' meat.

For some reason that thought made her feel sad, and the sadness triggered memory of the dreams that had haunted her while she slept the rest of the night away. Not nightmares this time, but melancholy images of things loved and lost. She had heard her mother's voice, seen Kirra's laughing face, felt Fenran's touch. And there had been something else, running like a woven thread through her sleep: a sense of pity that moved her to forget her own torments and reach out to a stranger who had loved her music and begged her to play more. . . .

She shook her head, and the images shattered and fell away. She was being fanciful; it was morning, the forest was no longer an unknown quantity and she must be away back to Linsk. Her ankle seemed better, though the swollen joint still pressed painfully against her boot, and with a little patience and a good deal of care she was able to pack her belongings and scramble onto the mare's saddle.

The chestnut was eager to be away. Indigo squinted up through the forest canopy, trying to get a bearing on the climbing sun. But the dense leaves and a return of the heavy overcast made it impossible, and so she guessed at the right direction and turned her mount's head, she hoped, southeastward.

She realized that she'd judged wrongly when the forest thinned and finally petered out and they emerged at the top of a long, gentle hill with the vast moorland plain stretching below and before them. The river that skirted the forest bisected the plain, spreading into a slow, meandering network of small tributaries like a giant spider's web across the landscape; though the sun was invisible, the morning light was bright enough to give the scene a hazy, shimmering quality. It was beautiful—but it wasn't Linsk. Turning in the saddle, Indigo saw that she had emerged on the forest's northeasterly boundary; behind her, the tree line followed a natural curve of the landscape, and she could see across the moors to the distant glitter of the sea.

The mare pawed the ground. She could smell the grass of the plain and wanted to enjoy it. Indigo clicked her tongue, holding the reluctant animal back as she tried to judge which would be her quickest route back to Linsk. There was a chance, though a slender one, that Danog and Laegoy would have delayed their departure, and *Greymalkin* might even now be waiting for the turn of the tide before setting out on the next leg of her northward journey. If she rode fast she would reach the port well before noon, and might be in time to rejoin the ship. There was flat land along the delta which would make for safer riding, but she might save time by cutting across the rougher, higher ground close to the forest. And time was all-important.

The mare didn't want to turn away from the prospect of the lush delta, but Indigo won the brief battle of wills, and they set off at a ground-eating canter along the sloping flank of the forest boundary.

She knew something was wrong when the easy pace at which she'd been riding slowed suddenly and unexpectedly to a lurching, uneven trot that made her teeth ache. A few minutes earlier the mare had stumbled, catching a hoof in one of the countless burrow-holes that were a constant hazard, but she had seemed to recover and Indigo had thought no more of the incident. Now, though, she realized that the chestnut had gone lame. They slowed, stopped, and Indigo slid out of the saddle. She still couldn't put any weight on her left ankle, but managed to hobble around to the mare's head to examine her. She stood with her right foreleg cocked; when Indigo ran her hand down to the hock, the mare tossed her head and twitched nervously, and Indigo cursed herself. Anyone with a grain of sense would have taken the lower country by the river rather than try to ride fast across this pitted ground. But she'd ignored the risks for the sake of haste, and now—ironically, in the wake of her own injury—the stumble had resulted in a strained tendon. She could only be thankful that the mare's leg wasn't broken.

She stepped back and looked at the landscape around her. What she saw wasn't encouraging; the coast was still a long way off, and closer to, all she could see was the uninhabited plain stretching endlessly away, the only signs of life one of the wild horse herds grazing by the river below her.

Indigo slumped down onto the grass. The mare couldn't carry any weight now, that was certain; and though she might be able to walk at a gentle pace, Indigo herself could make no progress without a crutch and had nothing from which to make one. There was no question of continuing on to Linsk; they were, effectively, stranded, either until someone came to rescue them—which seemed unlikely—or until their injuries healed sufficiently to allow them to travel on.

Or until night fell, and the wolves came out again. . . .

Alarmed, she looked quickly about her, as though expecting to see a gray muzzle, a long, sleek shape, stealing up on her across the turf. In broad daylight such a fear was irrational, but night would be another matter, and with difficulty Indigo stood up again to scan the landscape more carefully in the remote hope of seeing some form of shelter not too far away.

The horse herd drew her attention, and for the first time she noticed several animals among the milling throng that appeared to be carrying riders. Herders—of course; the horses weren't entirely wild, but would be husbanded by local tribesmen. Which meant that there must be a village not too far away.

She studied the milling animals, squinting against the flat light of the river delta. At this distance the herdsmen were unlikely to see her, much less hear her if she hailed them, but a fire would be sure to attract their attention. Indigo pulled hastily at the grass, gathering together a reasonable pile which she hoped would be dry enough to burn—but as she made ready to strike her tinder, she wondered suddenly if she was wise to draw attention to herself. The herdsmen might well be hostile to an interloper in their territory; though she had no possessions worth stealing, she could be robbed, raped, even killed—

Or she could stay out here on the plain. And her second night in the open might bring far worse terrors than wolves. . . .

Cupping her hands around the heap of grass, she set spark to it. Whatever the herders might or might not be capable of, there was no alternative open to her. At least this way, she thought grimly, she would have a fair chance of survival.

A small tongue of flame licked at the grass, flickered and grew. Indigo fanned it with her coat, trying to create more smoke, and after a few minutes she was gratified to see two of the distant riders wheel their horses away from the main herd, gesticulating and shouting to each other. They held a brief conference, then spurred their mounts into a canter and splashed across the river, heading toward her.

Indigo got to her feet again as the two riders approached. One of the herder ponies whinnied; the chestnut mare returned the greeting, and Indigo surreptitiously let her hand fall to the knife at her belt.

The herders pulled their ponies to a halt. They were small, stockily built men, with broad faces the color and texture of old leather, and almond-shaped eyes. Their clothes echoed those of the harbor-master at Linsk but were more colorful: short leather boots, loose felt trousers, jerkins and coats trimmed with a bizarre collection of felt patches, fur scraps and silver and copper disks. They both wore embroidered felt caps with long earflaps over their oily black hair—and they both carried lances, the vicious tips of which hovered a few inches from Indigo.

She tried not to let her nervousness show in her face, and bowed, putting the palms of both hands flat together in what she hoped was a universal gesture of friendship.

"Greetings to you, goodmen." She spoke slowly; there was a chance that they would have some knowledge of a neighboring country's tongue.

They stared at her, then one jerked his lance in a gesture she couldn't interpret, and replied in a language she didn't comprehend. It was a peculiar mixture of the guttural and the singsong, and she shook her head.

"I'm sorry. I don't understand you." To emphasize her words, she spread her arms out helplessly.

They conferred rapidly; then the one who had addressed her edged his shaggy pony closer, and pointed at the mare with an interrogative sound.

"My horse is lame." Indigo pantomimed, as best she could, an animal limping, and reached down to touch the chestnut's foreleg. "And I, too, have hurt my leg."

They must have understood the gist of what she said, for the herder jabbed the lance at her, making her move aside while his companion dismounted and went to examine the mare. His touch was expert; the animal hardly flinched, and when she did he chirruped three soft notes that seemed to calm her. The examination done, he turned his attention to Indigo, pointing at her belt-pouch and saying something that she interpreted as an order to set it down.

Uneasily, she unbuckled the pouch and laid it on the grass beside her harp and crossbow. While the first herder kept his lance pointed at her stomach, the other carried out a brisk, silent inventory, and Indigo watched in trepidation as her possessions were loaded into a pannier on the back of one of the ponies. When all was complete, her guard stamped out the remains of her fire, then reversed his lance and prodded her with the haft, gesturing toward the unladen pony. She nodded to show that she understood. If they meant her to ride, it was a favorable sign; at least they didn't intend to kill her immediately.

When she proved incapable of climbing into the saddle unaided, the herder swore—she assumed, anyway, that he was cursing her—and legged her roughly up onto the pony's back, taking hold of the reins. The lance tip still hovered uncomfortably close to Indigo's unprotected body, but she seemed to be in no immediate danger, and made no protest as, with the second man leading her mare, they moved off and away from the delta.

·CHAPTER·X·

The herders' village was tucked between two folds of land, a collection of dun-colored buildings against the greening slopes of the hills that protected it. As they approached the gated palisade a gaggle of children gathered to stare mutely at the stranger; dressed in bright clothes but with small, solemn faces, they were their elders in miniature. A woman's shrill voice called them away, and they reluctantly dispersed as Indigo's hosts—or captors—led her through the gate.

She had little time for first impressions of the village, gathering only an image of thatched, single-story houses set in a rough circle around a patch of dusty and hard-trodden earth with a well at its center. Small fields straggled up the slopes beyond the buildings; near the top of the rise she saw an irrigation pump worked by two dogs harnessed to a whim. More dogs, distant kin to the hunting hounds of the Southern Isles, came fawning or snarling, each to its nature, around the horses' feet; the chestnut mare sidestepped nervously and rolled her eyes until a curt order from one of the herdsmen sent the dogs slinking away.

As the mare settled again, an old woman shouldered through the crowd toward them, and the villagers made way for her with a deference that suggested she was an important personage. She was grotesquely fat, and in contrast to the bright colors around her, her many layers of clothing were plain black. Her only adornment was a headband of beaten copper disks; beneath it her eyes were black and sharp in a face seamed like rock strata. She stopped, and looked Indigo up and down as though assessing a carcass at a market. Then she turned, gestured imperiously to two women standing nearby and uttered a shrill, staccato volley of orders.

The women hastened forward, and the herdsman's lance jabbed toward Indigo's thigh, indicating that she should dismount and give herself into their care. She could barely put her left foot to the ground; seeing her disability, the women chattered like agitated birds and half walked, half carried her to a long, thatched house, larger than the others, which seemed to be some kind of communal hall. They lowered her onto a heather-stuffed pallet near the sluggish peat fire that burned in the center of the hall, and with a good deal of gesticulating began to ease the boot from her left foot. She sat mute while they clucked over her swollen ankle, and submitted to the application of a poultice. Though she couldn't understand a word of their voluble conversation, she was reassured by their attitude, which seemed to imply that she was a guest rather than a prisoner.

They had almost finished their work when the door opened, spilling light into the hall, and the old woman in black entered, accompanied by an equally elderly man with a bald pate and a thin fringe of beard under his chin. He, too, wore disks of copper at his brow, and from the haste with which her two ministrators sprang respectfully to their feet, Indigo guessed that these two must be the senior village elders.

She made an apologetic gesture to show that she couldn't rise to greet them, and the old man held up a hand, his seamed face breaking into a politely reserved smile.

"Not to stand," he said in Indigo's own tongue.

She blinked, surprised. "I . . . thank you."

"I be Shen-Liv," the old man told her. "You be . . . ?" He lifted his eyebrows interrogatively.

"Indigo." She made a bow as best she could from a sitting position. "From the Southern Isles."

"*South*-ern Isles." He pronounced it with an odd emphasis. "Ah, yes. We know well."

"You speak our language excellently, sir."

Shen-Liv's smile became self-effacing. "We trade Scorva, *South*-ern Isles, other places. Horse for . . ." He sought the right word. "For metal."

The old woman, who had been watching Indigo with a disquieting lack of expression, abruptly uttered a string of unintelligible questions. Shen-Liv answered them rapidly, then looked at Indigo again.

"The Grandmother want to know: how come you to here, you with sick leg, your horse with sick leg?"

Indigo smiled a little ruefully. "I hurt myself in a fall and had to spend the night in the forest. This morning I was on my way back to Linsk when my mare caught her foot in a burrow-hole and went lame. Two of your herdsmen found me and brought me here."

"Ah." Shen-Liv nodded, then looked her up and down. "You fall. From horse?"

"Yes."

"Good horseman do not fall without proper reason,

and your mare seem not ill trained.'' The implication that she was probably incompetent was obvious.

''No,'' Indigo said with a slight edge to her voice. ''My mare was frightened by an animal we encountered in the forest.'' She paused, remembering the huge shape, the glowing eyes, the panic.

Shen-Liv interjected quickly: ''Animal? What animal was this?''

Tiredly, she shook her head. ''I don't know. It happened so quickly, I couldn't be certain.'' She licked dry lips. ''Maybe . . . a wolf.''

The Grandmother said, ''Ha!'' as though it were a word she knew, and Shen-Liv's face took on a sharp, closed look.

''Wolf?''

''Yes. I . . . think so. And later, in the night, something came to my campfire. I didn't see it clearly, but I—heard it.''

The old man narrowed his eyes and studied her carefully, as though he suspected that she might at any moment turn into a wolf herself. ''You *think* it was wolf,'' he said, emphasizing the verb suspiciously. ''What mean you by that? Wolf is wolf: either you see one or not.''

''I can't be sure.'' She didn't meet his eyes, and the Grandmother shuffled forward until she was only a pace from where Indigo sat. She stared at the girl, her expression still unreadable, then backed off and rapped out something to Shen-Liv. Indigo had the impression that the old woman either disliked or distrusted what she had seen.

''The Grandmother say you do not tell all the truth,'' Shen-Liv informed her. ''She say there is something else, something you keep secret.''

So the old woman was a seer. She should have known; should have realized that, like the witches of the Southern Isles, she would sense evasion as a dog scented a hare. She'd already done her own cause enough harm; to dissemble further would only make matters worse. Let them have the truth, however incredible it might seem.

Shen-Liv said curtly, "We wait."

Indigo sighed. "Very well. There *is* something else. I didn't tell you, because I didn't think you would believe me." She looked up at last, candidly. "I don't know if I believe it myself. But the creature that came to my camp—whatever it was—I thought it . . . *spoke* to me." She swallowed, wishing she had a cup of water. "Do you know of any wolf that can do that?"

There was silence. The elder stared at her—then the Grandmother nudged him, hard, and demanded imperiously, "Ha?"

He turned to her and spoke in a rapid undertone, and the old woman made a hex-sign and hissed a reply. Shen-Liv listened carefully to what she said, nodded and bowed to her, upon which she turned abruptly and moved toward the door. The two women who had tended Indigo hastened after her, and moments later the rickety door closed behind them, leaving Indigo and Shen-Liv alone.

Shen-Liv eased himself down onto a pallet on the opposite side of the fire and folded his hands in his lap. In the flickering flamelight his face looked as though it had been carved out of granite, and red pinpoints reflected in his eyes.

"Now," he said, quietly but in a way that wasn't to be trifled with. "You tell me all your story, I think."

And so Indigo related all that had happened to her since her arrival in the Horselands on board *Greymalkin.* The story was brief enough; but when it came to describing the creature that had prowled around her fire, and the guttural sounds which, to her, had seemed shockingly like human speech, Shen-Liv demanded to know every detail: what she had seen, how she had reacted, what she thought the unwelcome visitor had said to her. Indigo found that her memory was painfully acute; the tortured words, *Music, I like music,* echoed in her mind as she repeated them to the elder, and when she finally finished he sat back on his heels, his face grave.

"It is as the Grandmother tell me," he said. "You was very fortunate you did not die in forest. It was music, I think, that save your life from demon."

The color drained from Indigo's face. "Demon?"

"Yes. Wolf was not wolf. It was *shafan*."

And, seeing that she was both baffled and unnerved, Shen-Liv went on to explain. The shafan was a Horselands demon, neither man nor animal but with elements of both; a devourer of flesh, a marauder, a slayer. According to legend it could assume the shape of any creature but usually chose the form of a predator—wolf or white leopard or wolverine. In living memory, Shen-Liv said, there had been no incidence of a shafan on the plains or in the forest; magic rites and sacrifices performed by the old women kept such devils at bay. But on the first full winter moon, two herders had reported seeing an unnaturally large wolf near the river. Hunters went in search of it, fearing for their mares in foal, but found nothing. Then from a village a day's ride away came news of depredations among the pony herds. One predator, or two at most; not a wolf-pack, the message said: but no wild beasts of the region were large enough to tackle a fully grown horse in anything other than large numbers. Then further sightings, each adding fuel to the fire: a huge wolf glimpsed in the woods, a creature roaming the plains that called with the voice of a man and in a human tongue but when challenged ran snarling, a dark, sleek apparition with fiery eyes seen lurking just beyond a village palisade. Suspicion and rumor flowered at last into certainty: the plains were being haunted by a shafan. And now Indigo's own experience had confirmed it beyond all doubt.

"You was very lucky," Shen-Liv told Indigo with emphatic gravity. "Is rare for human and shafan to come face-to-face, and for human to live." He frowned. "Is not a pleasant death, I think."

Indigo repressed a shiver. "You said that my music saved my life. I don't understand that."

"Ah, yes. Music is a magic thing, so the women say. It can . . ." He hesitated as the unfamiliar language failed him momentarily. "Can *lure* shafan, make it not to attack, if music is right. You understand?"

Cushmagar had instructed her well in the peculiar magic of music. Indigo nodded. "I understand."

"So it is that you be favored of the Earth Mother. That, I think, is omen." Stiffly, Shen-Liv got to his feet. His gaze was intent as he looked down at her. "I must tell of this to other *het* of the village. Women will come back to finish tending your sick leg; later here we will eat, then we will talk more." He nodded, a curt but courteous acknowledgment of his satisfaction. "There will be very much to say."

And with that, Shen-Liv left the house.

The two women returned, completed their ministrations and departed once more, and Indigo saw no one else for the rest of the day. Her attendants had left her a pitcher of water but no food; and although she was comfortable enough, and grateful for their help, she still felt uneasy about the villagers' attitude toward her. The women's attentions and Shen-Liv's reserved politeness implied no hostility, yet she had been left alone and effectively helpless, bereft of her possessions, until such time as they wished to question her again. Her only grain of comfort was in Shen-Liv's assertion that she must be "favored of the Earth Mother": an unwittingly ironic statement but one that, she felt, must surely ensure her safety whilst he continued to believe it.

Beyond the long-house the sun moved around and cast shafts of dusty, dun-colored light through the narrow window at Indigo's back. The fire made the room stifling; tired still after her broken night, she dozed most of the afternoon away, and woke to find the day fading, the fire burned to embers and the house filled with deep shadow. Outside she could hear sounds of activity, hooves clattering and men's voices mingling with women's shrill chatter and children's shrieks: a dog barked furiously, then howled as it was kicked into submission. The herders, it would seem, had returned from the plains; and a few minutes later the door of the long-house opened and several women and young girls came in and began to build up the fire and move the pallets into a circle around the hearth. Rushlights were lit, giving off little illumination but a good deal of smoke that reeked of sour tallow; then the serving-women brought in trays laden with bowls of what looked like assorted pieces of meat and vegetables. Lastly they set a heavy trivet over the fire, and on this was placed a large iron cauldron in which some heavily spiced liquid began to bubble.

As the women withdrew, a young man entered the house. He was tall for a Horselander, and dressed less elaborately than most of the men she had seen. From his manner and posture, Indigo guessed him to be, or at least fancy himself, a warrior. His expression was supercilious and unfriendly; he made a brief survey of the preparations, then turned and stared down at her.

"So; you be woman of foreign place," he said with

undisguised contempt. The words were clipped and unnatural; the young man's command of her language was poorer than Shen-Liv's. His gaze raked her, focusing on her hair, her face, finally dwelling shamelessly on her breasts. "Is not of my approve."

Indigo, who had felt instant and violent antipathy at first sight of him, returned his look with a withering glare and retorted, "Then I will not trouble you for the pleasure of your company."

He clearly didn't fully understand, and frowned angrily. "You will talk as proper at me, like woman should!"

"And you will keep a civil tongue in your head!" Indigo fired back, furious. "If—" And she broke off at the sound of voices outside.

The young man turned quickly, and his frown deepened. Resentment flickered across his face, then abruptly he backed off.

"Het of village come now to eat," he said, and shook a finger at her. "You will be respecting, and answer when spoke at!"

He turned on his heel and walked stiff-backed to the door. Every muscle radiated frustration at the thwarting of his attempt to assert his dominance, but he tried to hide it and stood to attention as the village elders—the het—filed in. The Grandmother, Indigo noticed, was not among their number: this was a gathering only of men, and she realized suddenly why the young warrior was so resentful. To the Horselanders, women—except wise women like the Grandmother—were little better than chattels, and the idea that she should be privileged to sit among the elders at their evening meal had offended the young man's sense of propriety. She smiled with faint irony as, the gathering complete, the warrior stalked out and shut the door with a force that nearly shook it from its hinges.

The het ignored the display and took their places on the pallets, forming a semicircle that radiated out from Shen-Liv. Stilted bows were exchanged, then the meal began.

There was, Indigo quickly discovered, a good deal of rigid protocol to be observed in the simple business of dining. Before anyone was permitted to eat, Shen-Liv intoned ritual words over the simmering cauldron, ending with a flourishing gesture to which his fellow hetmen grunted approval and slapped the earth floor with the palms of their hands. Following this, all present drank, in strict order of precedence, from a communal pitcher. Indigo's turn came last; as the men had done, she lifted the pitcher with both hands and put the lip to her mouth, drinking as deeply as she dared. The brew was a tepid herbal tea, bland and innocuous; with this rite completed, the company began to eat. Pieces of meat or vegetable were carefully dipped—again, a strict order was observed—into the simmering cauldron and eaten without the aid of plates or knives; Indigo watched her hosts and followed their every example, noting, too, that the feast was conducted in stony silence. The food was probably wholesome enough, but to her palate it was unappetizing. The vegetables were tasteless, and she suspected that the meat might be horse or even dog, its flavor disguised by the liberal addition of spices to the cauldron. From politeness she did not demur as the bowls were repeatedly passed around the fire, but she was thankful when at last the meal was over.

With great formality the hetmen brought out short-stemmed pipes, which they filled with cured leaves and began to smoke. To her relief Indigo was not expected to join in this ritual; and as the smoke of the pipes mingled with the smoke of the fire to form a scented pall among the rafters, Shen-Liv broke the silence which had persisted now for more than an hour.

"I have spoken with het," he said to Indigo, "and the Grandmother have read the signs. We are agreed that there be much good omen in the events that brought you to here."

The other old men were now watching Indigo intently, and one or two who, like Shen-Liv, obviously understood the Southern Isles tongue translated to their fellows in whispered asides.

"The Grandmother say," Shen-Liv continued, "that one who has come face-to-face with shafan and taken no hurt must have strength against such demons."

"Shen-Liv, I am no spell-caster!" Indigo protested hastily. "If the Grandmother thinks—"

"Not to interrupt." Shen-Liv held up a hand, and his fellow elders frowned their disapproval. "I say, *strength.* Not magic. Is gift, like horse-skill, like singing. Grandmother say is gift of Earth Mother, and gift must be used to drive shafan from here. Now." He leaned toward her, one finger uplifted as though lecturing a child. "You have instrument for making music which is not known to us."

"My harp . . ." Indigo's voice was thin.

"Harp." He repeated the word as though to imprint it in his memory. "Good. You will use harp. And also you have a weapon, like bow but not the same. It will shoot a long way, I think, and with much force."

She nodded. "It's a crossbow. The principle is the same as the longbow, but it is, as you say, more powerful."

"And you can use this? You have skill?"

"Yes. I was taught by my father, the—" Indigo stopped, aware that she had been about to speak Kalig's name and aware that she must not, *could* not. She swallowed and felt a hard knot in her throat. "My father was a skilled hunter."

This was duly translated, and some of the hetmen shook their heads, clearly finding the idea of a woman learning a man's skills hard to comprehend. Some further rapid discussion followed, in which Indigo heard the word *shafan* spoken several times. Then Shen-Liv looked at her again.

"Very well. The het have agree, and I shall now tell to you what is to be done. When you heal, and your horse heal, you shall go back to forest where shafan come upon you, and you shall play music to bring shafan to where you are. When shafan come, you shall be ready. You will kill shafan, and send it back to the dark place where it came."

The ensuing silence was acute. Indigo stared at Shen-Liv, who had a small, satisfied smile on his face, while she struggled to bring her furious tide of reaction under control. *As simple as that. You will go out, and with nothing more than a harp and a crossbow you will kill the demon that has been plaguing the Horselands. . . .*

"Shen-Liv." She took a deep breath and bit on her tongue to stop the anger from overflowing and making her hurl the nearest empty bowl at the old man's head. "I think I must have mistaken your meaning. You're surely not saying that I should return to the forest, and kill this—this thing, this demon—single-handed?"

Shen-Liv's smile broadened a fraction. "Yes. As I have told to you."

"And as I have told *you*, I am not a spell-caster!" Indigo knew the pitch of her voice was rising, but didn't care. "Nor am I superhuman—if your own hunters can't kill the shafan, why by all the seas do you think *I* will succeed?"

He was unmoved. "I have explain this. All is clear and simple—"

"Simple?"

"Not to shout," Shen-Liv said severely. "The Grandmother say that you have the strength against shafan; therefore is no danger for you in this."

"Shen-Liv." She had to try once more, make him understand that the Grandmother's pronouncement was not enough, that she had no innate power against whatever creature it was that lurked in the forest and threatened the village. "Please, listen to me. As I said before, I am not a spell-caster. I have no power against demons, and I know nothing of your shafan. If I go alone to the forest to banish this creature, I will fail, or it will kill me. Or both."

"You will not go alone," Shen-Liv assured her blandly. "Hunting men of here will accompany, and will be close by in case of trouble." His eyes narrowed suddenly, and there was an overtone of threat in his next words. "Het have decided. This thing must be done."

Indigo realized what lay behind his implication. They were offering her no option.

She carefully interlocked her fingers and looked at them. "And if I . . . find myself unable to attempt what you ask of me?"

Shen-Liv pursed his lips. "That will be unfortunate," he said. "Het will find the need to keep harp, and keep weapon, that the men of here may succeed where you have fail." He met her eyes, his gaze coolly intimidating. "And doubtless keep horse, too, as payment for kindness shown to you in your trouble."

"I see." He had, indeed, made the position quite clear. Bow to their wishes, or find herself turned out of the village without a mount of any of her belongings, to survive as best she could. Effectively, Indigo thought, she had no choice but to concede.

The hetmen were waiting for her to reply. She wished

she could say something that would wipe the small, complacent smile from Shen-Liv's face, but she knew what her answer must be.

"Very well, Shen-Liv. Since you have seen fit to offer me this opportunity, I shall not be so churlish as to refuse."

Her irony was lost on the old man. The smile became a beam, and he nodded, setting the copper disks at his forehead rattling. "Is good. And now that all is as should be, there is much arrangement to make." He drew his knees up and, with some effort, began to get to his feet. The other elders followed his example. "Women will see to your need. When all is ready, you will be inform."

They bowed politely to her, one after another, and moved toward the door. Shen-Liv was the last to leave, and on the threshold he paused and looked back.

"We wish you good night," he said, and smiled with the satisfaction of a man well content before following his fellow hetmen out into the darkness.

•CHAPTER•XI•

Indigo spent the next three days in the herders' village. Her ankle healed quickly, but she soon discovered that she was effectively a prisoner, for she was forbidden to leave the small hut, part storehouse and part jail, to which she had been removed after her encounter with the hetmen. Nor did she see any more of Shen-Liv: her only visitors were the women who came morning and evening to bring her food and water, and who either didn't understand her questions or had been instructed not to respond to anything she might say.

The elders, it seemed, had no further interest in her well-being; she had agreed to do what they wanted, and until the time came to carry out their plans, they considered her unworthy of notice. Those plans, meanwhile, were being completed, but Indigo was not privy to the earnest discussions that took place in the nearby long-house. She was but a pawn, and a woman at that;

her role, in the eyes of the het, was to carry out the orders given to her without demur or question.

The arrogance of the old men's attitude maddened Indigo, but two furious explosions which were met by indifference from the women who tended her, and the discovery of an armed guard outside her door, cooled her temper as she realized that she was powerless to change matters. She had no allies, no weapons, couldn't even communicate with her guardians; and if she refused to cooperate, the best she could hope for was to be allowed to walk out of the palisade gate in the clothes she stood up in. All she could do was wait, and try to be patient.

With nothing else to occupy her, she slept away as many of the tedious hours as possible. But sleeping brought only an ugly mental and physical miasma; her muscles craved exercise and her thoughts slipped all too often into a feverish confusion between dreaming and wakefulness. And she suffered nightmares; sometimes images of the past, but more often dark and fearful premonitions of the ordeal that lay ahead of her.

Shen-Liv's bland assurance that she would be in no danger when she faced the shafan brought Indigo little comfort. It was all well and good for the smiling old man and his complacent fellows: they would not be called upon to risk their own lives confronting a demon, and theirs were not the hands which would be raised to kill it. They had brushed aside her doubts, ignored her fears and refused even to grant her the privilege of knowing, before the time came, exactly what they expected her to do. Often when anger and misery got the better of the patience she struggled to engender in herself, Indigo resolved to tell the het, when they finally condescended to see her again, that their plan was sheer madness and she would have no part in it. But always the impulse faded as she reminded herself, as Shen-Liv had none too subtly pointed out, that she had no other choice.

So the hours and the days passed, until, as the murky sunlight leaking in beneath her door began to alter its pattern (she had formed a crude system for judging the time from the changing of the light, and guessed that it was midafternoon), the door was shoved carelessly open and the young man whom she had encountered briefly on her first evening in the village appeared on the threshold.

For a few moments he stood staring down at her, and this time the contempt she'd seen before in his face was mixed with a deeper-rooted and more personal dislike. Then he jerked a finger toward the daylight and said curtly. "You. Come."

Indigo's mental hackles rose at his offensive manner, and she replied icily, "I *beg* your pardon?"

"You hear me. Do as telled." A short-thonged riding whip hung at his side; he fingered it. "You go to forest at set of sun."

"*What?* With no warning, no—"

He interrupted, regarding her as he might have regarded an ordure-pit. "All is ready. Not for you to say more."

"Oh, but I think it is!" Indigo got to her feet, feeling fury well up uncontrollably inside her. "Who in the name of the Great Mother do you think you are, to march in here and order me about as though I were your trained dog? If your benighted het want anything from me, they will have the common courtesy to come here themselves and *ask*, not issue demands through their strutting minions—and you may tell them that with my compliments! Now get out of my sight!"

Whether the young man understood all she said, she couldn't tell; he merely continued to stare at her. Then, so unexpectedly that she was caught completely off guard, he lunged forward and snatched a handful of her hair, jerking her toward him and grabbing her arm with his other hand. He twisted her around, making her gasp with shock and pain, and his voice grated in her ear.

"I say to come, you come! You will learn proper place!"

Indigo's fury bubbled over. She wrenched her arm free, spun on her heel, and her fingernails raked across his face with all the strength and violence she could muster. He yelled, and as he staggered back she kicked out. Her foot connected with his thigh and he lost his balance, crashing against the hut door. As he sprawled, Indigo whirled back to her pallet bed and snatched up her coat. She'd have this out with Shen-Liv and his crew—and she'd teach them that neither they nor their pet cur could treat her like a serf and get away with it!

She turned back to the door—and saw that the young warrior was on his feet, and barring her passage.

Her jaw muscles tightened. "Get out of my way."

She heard a faint serpentine sound as he unhooked the short whip from his belt and drew the lash through his hands.

"You . . ." His face was twisted, and the four parallel scratches on his cheek stood out livid and bleeding. "You get teached now, I think. You learn that woman not to disobey with me!"

She forced herself not to step back. "Touch me, and I'll kill you."

He laughed, a snort of contempt. "*You* kill? You to be nothing!" Suddenly he flicked the whip against the wood of the door, and the savage *crack* made her jump involuntarily. "Woman must learn, like dog, like horse, to do what she be telled by master. You learn that quick, I think. Or you be very, very sorry."

Indigo's heart was thumping painfully. He was barely

taller than she was, but his build was far heavier, his strength greater—and she had nothing but her bare hands with which to defend herself. Rage and loathing were a suffocating presence in her throat and chest; she longed for her crossbow, her knife—

"I'll say it once more." It was pure bravado, she knew, but it was the only weapon she had, and she had to take the risk. And she suspected that, like so many arrogant bullies, the young warrior was at heart a coward. "Move aside, or I'll make you regret the day your mother birthed you!" Mustering her nerve, she took a step toward the door.

The whip sang through the air: she saw it coming, instinctively flung up one hand to protect her face and felt the lash's stinging, agonizing impact as it cut across her thinly protected forearm. She cried out, and the cry was cut off in a grunt of forcibly expelled breath as the warrior's full weight came down on her, throwing her to the floor with jarring force. He pinned her arms behind her back, dragging her into a kneeling position and cursing volubly in his own language, and again she felt the whiplash, on her back this time, cutting like fire into her skin.

Tears of pain blurred Indigo's vision—and then the blur turned scarlet as her control snapped. She heard her own voice screaming, but this time it was a shriek of fury. With the strength of blind rage she twisted in the warrior's grip, and her knee pistoned up, driving into his stomach. As he fell back with a furious roar, she leaped to her feet and ran for the door. It vibrated back on its rickety hinges; the warrior made a grab for her but missed, and Indigo stumbled out into the thin sunlight.

Wildly, she looked about her. The village square was almost empty: a gaggle of women by another hut were staring openmouthed at her, and farther away a tethered dog started to bark furiously, but there was no one else in sight. Indigo dragged breath into her lungs and shouted to the women:

"Your het! Where are they?"

They only continued to stare blankly—and suddenly there was a rattle and the thud of stumbling footsteps, and Indigo's attacker appeared in the hut doorway. He saw her, and launched himself at her with a furious yell. Indigo tried to jump out of his path, but the uneven ground betrayed her and she tripped, sprawling in the dust as he bore down. Her hair was snatched, she felt herself dragged backward, felt a booted foot slam into her side and tried to twist free, her scrabbling efforts to get purchase kicking up a cloud of choking dust. The dog was barking hysterically now, others joining in, the women were adding their shrill voices to the clamor—

"Tarn-Shen!"

The stentorian bellow stopped the young warrior in his tracks, and Indigo fell back as he released his hold on her hair. Coughing and spitting, she struggled into a sitting position and blinked dust particles from her eyes to see Shen-Liv striding across the square toward them.

The hetman stared down at Indigo, then glared at the warrior and snapped out a question. Tarn-Shen mumbled a reply, and the old man turned to Indigo.

"What is happen?" he demanded.

Indigo got to her feet. "Shen-Liv." Her voice shook with fury. "This mongrel's whelp has insulted me, assaulted me and attempted to use a horsewhip on me! He seems to be under the impression that I am some kind of chattel to be kicked into submission at his whim. I suggest—" She flashed Tarn-Shen a look of pure hatred. "I suggest that you teach him the error of his ways, and a sharp lesson in courtesy!"

Tarn-Shen started to object indignantly, but a curt command from Shen-Liv silenced him. The old man followed the order with another, and, red-faced and with fists clenched at his sides, Tarn-Shen turned abruptly and stalked away.

Silence fell. A number of onlookers had gathered by now, drawn by curiosity from various huts about the square. Someone had kicked the barking dogs to quiet them, and for a long moment Shen-Liv stared at Indigo. His face was a stiff, unreadable mask, but she could see hostility flickering in his eyes.

"You will please to return inside," he said at last, indicating the hut. "This matter is not to be settle before all of village."

She nodded brusquely and preceded him back inside. Shen-Liv shut the door and adopted a pained expression.

"It displease me that you quarrel with my grandson," he said severely. "We wish to spill only the blood of shafan, not of each other."

So Tarn-Shen was his grandson. It made an ironic kind of sense. "I had no intention of quarreling with him," Indigo retorted. "But neither had—or have—I any intention of tolerating such treatment! You seem to forget, Shen-Liv, that I'm not one of your village women, to be ordered about like a slave." Her eyes narrowed. "And that you have an interest in securing my cooperation."

"Very well." He made no attempt to hide his resentment. "Tarn-Shen shall be deal with most severely. Such a thing will not to happen again. I myself shall see for it."

Indigo inclined her head. "Thank you," she said with heavy irony. "I appreciate your concern. And now there is one more matter to be settled. Before our altercation, Tarn-Shen informed me that you have completed your plans."

"This be true." Shen-Liv nodded with a degree of self-satisfaction. "All is ready for shafan to be trap tonight."

"I see. Then you will kindly tell me what you intend. In detail."

He looked surprised. "Is not to be necessary. Hunting men will tell you what is needed when time come."

"*No*, Shen-Liv." Indigo paced across the hut, then turned to face him again. "That is just what I'm trying to explain to you. After the treatment I've received at your grandson's hands, I see no reason on the good Earth why I should lift one finger to help you in any way. However, you have, effectively, blackmailed me into agreeing to your scheme, and so I have no other choice. But I will *not* play my part unless you explain to me, in every detail, exactly what your plan involves and what I am expected to do. Do I make myself clear?" She paused, saw his scowl and added emphatically, "I must know *everything* before I leave. Otherwise, you may look elsewhere for you demon-hunter."

She could see the struggle taking place within Shen-Liv. Chagrin, indignation, anger . . . but caution, too; and finally caution triumphed. Though it went against the grain, prudence dictated that, for once, he should give way.

"Very well," he said curtly. "It shall be as you wish. You will come with me, and all will be telled to you." With great dignity he turned to lead her out of the hut, then on the threshold stopped and looked back. Dislike showed clearly in his eyes. "You have much to learn, I think."

Four hours later, Indigo and her escort rose out of the village. The sun was a crimson ball on the horizon of a sky brassy with evening haze; behind them the village was steeped in the hills' shadows, while before them in the distance the river gleamed blood-red, like an open artery.

There were six men in the group flanking the girl on her chestnut mare; all were heavily armed with knives, spears and their own short bows—far simpler than Indigo's crossbow but doubtless highly effective in their own way—while one of their number carried Indigo's harp and bow over his saddle. At their head, pacing them, rode Tarn-Shen.

Indigo's temper had exploded when Shen-Liv informed her that his grandson was to lead the party, but this time the old man had been adamant. She had to admit, however grudgingly, that his reasoning was plausible: Tarn-Shen alone of the village huntsmen could speak her language tolerably well, and without him she would be unable to communicate with her escort. Tarn-Shen's presence, though in one sense regrettable, was a necessity, and very stiffly Shen-Liv added his assurance that Indigo need not fear a repetition of earlier events. His grandson had his orders, and knew his duty to the het.

With great reluctance, Indigo had finally capitulated, but as they prepared to leave she had ignored the young warrior's resentful glares and kept as far from him as possible. Now, though, with the village falling behind them, she wondered if her agreement had been wise. At the palisade gate she had heard a sharp, whispered exchange between Tarn-Shen and his grandfather, and it made her uneasy. The other hetmen had not been pleased to learn of her ultimatum, and she had the impression that Shen-Liv had lost considerable face with his fellows by giving way to her. If all went well tonight, she might be better off not to return to the village, but to take leave of her escort in the forest and ride through the night back to Linsk.

Assuming that she would be allowed to do so. . . .

Indigo glanced quickly, covertly at Tarn-Shen. She had made two enemies in the village today, and one of them, at least, was nurturing a smoldering desire for revenge. Aware that a sense of place and protocol ran very deep in the herder people, she also suspected that Shen-Liv's assurances were worthless, and that the old man would consider it no more than the merest justice if his grandson chose to exact that revenge once her usefulness was expended.

She tried to concentrate her energies on controlling the mare, who was fully recovered from her strain and skittish after three days' inactivity; but the ugly conviction was growing stronger. Her life was in danger from more than the shafan. One mistake, one momentary lapse of caution, and she had little doubt of what would happen. She glanced covertly at Tarn-Shen, and shivered inwardly. Until she had a weapon in her hands and the freedom to use it if necessary, she would be well advised to take great care.

The party strung out into single file as the track they were following narrowed between tracts of long grass riddled with hillocks and burrows. In the distance Indigo could make out the gray-green swathe of the forest encroaching on the landscape, and she judged that they would reach its borders just as the sun dipped completely below the horizon. This, according to the grudging explanation she had finally received from Shen-Liv, meant that the hunters could set their trap under cover of the post-sunset hour, yet be ready to spring it by the time the absolute blackness of night fell. The shafan, he had said, was primarily a denizen of the dark, and with care and good fortune it would suspect nothing untoward until too late.

It seemed to Indigo that Shen-Liv and his fellow elders had relied a little too heavily on such tenuous factors as care and good fortune in forming their plan to trap the shafan. When the details were at last revealed to her, she had been astonished and chagrined: the scheme was simplistic, naive, and allowed no contingency for any of the dozen or more things that might go wrong. She had tried to express her misgivings to the old man, but each argument she put forward was dismissed as worthless. Nothing would go wrong, Shen-Liv assured her. The het had pronounced their approval of the plan; and did she not remember the Grandmother's assertion that she was strong against demons, that she was blessed of the Earth Mother? What more assurance could she possibly need? Success was certain: Indigo need do no more than follow her instructions.

And her instructions were starkly clear. She was to be the bait in the trap, the lonely bait set to lure the shafan. With her harp she was to first draw and then lull it, and with a bolt from her crossbow, over which the Grandmother had muttered the appropriate magic, she was to kill it.

When the hetmen proved impervious to reason, she had shouted at them. It was a pointless protest, but the frustration invoked by their blind complacency had been beyond her control, and she had sworn, raged, cursed them until she had no more breath. They merely waited impassively until her fury abated; then Shen-Liv repeated his instructions as though she hadn't uttered a word of dissent. There was, however, a subtle but unmistakable hint of menace in his voice—reinforced by the sudden quiet emergence, as he was speaking, of two herders armed with spears from the shadows at the far side of the room. At that Indigo's anger had crumbled before cold reality. She couldn't fight them. If she tried, they would kill her; she had pressed them as far as they were prepared to go.

So now she rode toward the forest in the company of six guards, led by a man she loathed and distrusted, to fight a demon. And she must fight that demon alone, with nothing more to her hand than a harp and a crossbow over which an old woman had mumbled incantations. It was madness. *Madness.*

Tarn-Shen turned his head at that moment and caught her eye briefly as he looked back at the convoy. He smiled, not pleasantly, and Indigo had an ugly, superstitious feeling that somehow he had read her thoughts and agreed with her sentiments. And if he, too, believed that she rather than the shafan was likely to die tonight, he made no pretense of regret.

Her fingers tightened on the reins and, trying to quell the queasiness in her stomach, she looked quickly away.

The only sound on the periphery of the forest was the insidious rustle of leaves as the wind stirred them. Indigo stood at her horse's head, staring into the deeper gloom while she waited for three of the herder huntsmen to light the lanterns they carried. With a last glimmer of daylight still in the sky, the absence of birdsong was eerie, giving the impression that the forest was devoid of all life, a gateway into a petrified, dead world. The chestnut mare was nervous, and even when the lanterns were finally alight and etching shadows on the tree trunks with their stark, bluish radiance, she refused to settle, as though her animal instinct told her that something was wrong.

Tarn-Shen swaggered across to where Indigo waited, and stared at her. In the uncertain light of the lamps his face had the sickly pallor of a corpse.

"You go us," he ordered her peremptorily. "Leave

horse here.'' And he took hold of her arm, twisting it to pull her away.

''Take your hand off me!'' Indigo snarled at him, teeth clenched with a blend of anger and pain. He released her, making a pacific gesture that wasn't confirmed by his eyes, and sardonically bowed toward the trees.

Her spine tingled as she walked, with the two men flanking her and Tarn-Shen just behind, into the wood. She heard the muffled thump of hooves as the remaining huntsmen led the horses in their wake, keeping their distance. Bizarre shadows loomed in the lanternlight, stark outlines of branches, shapeless masses of dark that contorted with brief menace, then fell behind. The undergrowth rustled damply underfoot; wet leaves caressed her face with a touch that made her shiver. They pressed deeper into the forest: no one spoke. Once, a horse whickered uneasily, but a soft, cajoling sound from one of the men soothed it.

At last they came to a clearing. Not the one in which Indigo had camped, but smaller, the trees encroaching in a tight circle about a patch of lush grass overgrown with bramble. Tarn-Shen shouldered ahead of the others and walked into the middle of the clearing. After a quick appraisal of the site he said something in his own tongue, and one of the men brought forward Indigo's bow and harp, setting them down on the damp ground. Another handed her knife, travel bag, belt-pouch and a small bundle of crossbow bolts to Tarn-Shen; the leader examined the items briefly, then held them out to Indigo.

''Here you sit, and you make fire.'' He grinned, showing crooked teeth, and her jaw tightened at his implication that to help with the fire-building would be beneath him or his men. ''Then you take harp and bow, and you wait. When shafan come, you know what to do."

"Yes." Indigo didn't disguise the contempt she felt, both for Tarn-Shen and for the hetmen's plan. "I know well enough. And if I were a gambler, I'd take no wager on its chances of success!"

Tarn-Shen grinned again and shrugged. "That problem is for you."

"Thank you. I appreciate your concern." Indigo turned her back on him as he strutted away.

As she settled herself at last before her newly made fire, she wasn't relishing the vigil ahead of her. The only kindling she could find had been damp, and the flames refused to burn brightly but were blue-tinged and sluggish, casting very little light. She didn't even have the mare for company; Tarn-Shen and his fellow hunters had taken her with them when they left the clearing and scattered to their hiding places. Knowing that they were still in the vicinity was cold comfort; if anything, she would have felt safer had she been truly alone.

She glanced at her crossbow, which lay in the long grass beside her. It was loaded, the string drawn, and one of the five bolts her captors had given her gleamed a wicked slate blue in the firelight. One shot. There would be no time to reload. One shot, and if the shafan failed to die she would be its next victim, whatever Shen-Liv had promised to the contrary. Indigo tasted something sulfurous in her throat and swallowed saliva, forcing herself to turn her attention from the bow to the harp on her other side. No one had tampered with it; a little warming of the cold wood, a little retuning, and it would be ready.

There was no point in delaying longer than she must. She settled the harp on her lap and experimentally drew her fingers across the strings. The answering ripple of sound was like water falling, with only a few sour notes. Indigo spent a few minutes—more time, she was aware, than was really necessary—perfecting the tuning, then damped the last vibrations with her palm and took several deep, even breaths.

Not the Hawthorn-Month dance or the harvesters' song tonight. They were too light, too redolent of brightness and celebration. She played an experimental chord which, from a subconscious blend of memory and instinct, flowed into the first notes of the Amberland Wife's Lament. This was right. The liquid, lilting, ineffably sad refrain was perfect against the green-black sea of the forest. Haunting, yearning, lonely . . . Indigo closed her eyes and an image of a dark, endless sea filled her inner vision as the lament rippled from the harp strings. She could almost feel the slow and inexorable flow of its currents in her veins, hear the hushing roar of the waves in rhythm with her fingers, feel the icy touch of cold, deep waters. The forest was lost to her, Tarn-Shen and the huntsmen might never have existed. There was only the night and the music.

A part of her mind tried to warn her that she was slipping away from reality toward a dreaming, entranced doze, but the warning voice was too small and too distant to be heeded. Indigo played on, hearing the melody change but no longer knowing what she played or why. All sense of time and place was gone, and consciousness was fading, so it seemed that one moment she was sitting cross-legged on the damp grass before the fire's sluggish embers, and the next she was afloat on a vast cushion of darkness, rising and falling, rising and falling . . .

The harp stopped on an awful discord that shocked her awake. She felt sudden heat on her face and, blinking rapidly as the world swam back into focus, realized that she had fallen asleep, slumping toward the fire, and her wrist had caught the harp strings as the instrument slipped from her lap. She stilled the last unpleasant echoes and shifted her cramped body, rubbing her eyes and shaking her head in an effort to clear her mind.

No movement in the trees around her. How long had she been in that half-waking, half-sleeping trance? Her head felt heavy, eyes tired, and her thoughts wouldn't marshal properly; the only clear concept that came to her mind was that she was still alone at her fire. The shafan had not come.

I am not a demon.

But it *was* a demon, at least according to the men of—

A mental bolt shocked Indigo to the core. Still half asleep, she had silently replied to a thought—but the thought had emanated from outside her own mind.

Her bones seemed to crawl beneath her flesh and she took a ferocious grip on herself, denying the fearful idea even as it rose within her. The voice which had seemed to speak with such peculiar intimacy in her head had been no more than a momentary slip back into a dream state. She'd experienced the phenomenon often enough on the verge of sleep; it was nothing to be afraid of. A brief hallucination . . .

She reached out for her harp.

Yes; please play again. There is nothing to fear. I mean only kindness.

The harp thudded back into the grass and Indigo swore aloud, whirling around to grope for her crossbow as stark terror wiped out the last traces of torpor.

The smooth wood of the bow, the feel of the taut string, the cold metal of the bolt—she concentrated on every nuance of the weapon in her hands, striving by it to push away the dark and the horror that crawled over her skin like phantom spiders. She couldn't speak—her throat muscles were locked—and her eyes stared into the darkness beyond the firelight's small circle, straining for any untoward movement among the shadows.

The darkness was utterly still. She stopped breathing, holding the air in her lungs as she listened, disconcertingly aware that the night was *too* quiet, *too* empty. Then a piece of the black vortex beneath the trees detached itself, flowed into form and outline, and she saw what had crept out of the forest's depths to her camp.

It was far too big to be any normal wolf. Massive, densely furred shoulders hunched behind a broad, brindled head that tapered to a near-white muzzle; the tufted ears were laid back, whether in aggression or defensiveness Indigo could not and dared not ask herself. And eyes like dimmed amber lamps, alien and unhuman yet filled with a stark and sad intelligence. It took three paces out of the dark to where the flamelight could just touch it, and stopped, staring at the girl as though it stared into her soul.

Indigo felt her hands tighten on the crossbow, felt the weight as she slowly raised it. She took aim at the creature, the impossible denizen, the shafan she had come to kill. But as her white-knuckled fingers curled on the bow's trigger, an unnameable instinct made her pause. The lambent eyes of the shafan gazed back at her, and mingling with the sad intelligence was a hope, a pleading . . .

She didn't want to kill it. Something beyond her volition was making her trigger hand relax, and that same urge also told her that to harm the creature would be wrong, unjust—

Time seemed to slither to a halt as she and the shafan continued to stare at each other. Indigo felt like a fly caught in amber; though she struggled against the compulsion, she felt her hands moving, setting the crossbow down, withdrawing. She was unarmed now, helpless. Only the fire stood between her and the demon. . . .

Muscles worked spasmodically in the wolf's throat and it panted, tongue lolling. Then every nerve in Indigo's body came alive with shock as a harsh, smoky voice emanated with painful effort from the beast's mouth.

"Not . . . demon. F—Fr—*Friend* . . ." It couldn't properly enunciate; the stuttering *Fr—* came out as a hard, dry cough.

Indigo's jaw worked and saliva filled her mouth. She couldn't swallow it back, felt it dribble down her chin as she gaped at the wolf, unable to believe what she had heard.

The great shaggy head swayed from side to side; then the throat vibrated again.

"Pl—ease. Fr—Friend . . . Mu-sic . . ." And an awful sensation of sorrow and pity flooded through Indigo, drowning the fear and releasing her from its thrall. Her hands clenched into fists, an involuntary protest against something so impossible, and at last she swallowed convulsively, able to force her tongue to form words.

"What are you?" She whispered the question, awe and uncertainty in her voice.

It panted, breath rasping. "*Wolllf* . . . N-not harm. Not kill . . . mean . . . kindness." It swung its head in distress.

A new and trustworthy friend, though appearances may at first suggest otherwise. . . . The words came up from her memory with no forewarning. But it wasn't possible; not this, surely not such a friend as this—

Indigo remembered her mission, and the unspoken threat of what would happen to her if she should fail.

But she couldn't kill this creature. Animal or something beyond, she didn't know; yet instinct made her certain that it was anything but a demon.

And somewhere in the forest at her back, Tarn-Shen and his hunters were waiting. . . .

The wolf stiffened abruptly and its hackles rose. Indigo started, made to turn and look over her shoulder, then realized that the animal was still staring directly at her. The amber eyes were intense, as though it was looking into her mind and reading her thoughts, and it said in a harsh exhalation, *"Dan-ger!"*

"What—" Indigo began, but was silenced by a snarl. For a few seconds that seemed to last a lifetime they were both motionless, listening intently; but she could hear nothing beyond the faint stir of a breeze among the leaves. Then, mingling with the breeze, the sound of the wolf's quickening, panting breath.

"Away!" The guttural voice was urgent, and the creature's hindquarters braced as though to spring. "Quick-ly. *Quick-ly*!"

She tried to answer, started to get to her feet, but her reaction came too late. In a blur of movement she saw the wolf leap, twisting in midair, heard the *twang* of a bowstring and lurched off-balance as a silver dart flashed past her head.

"No!" Indigo shouted a furious protest, whirling toward the enemy at her back. Something dark and massive loomed out of the night, and she connected with a stunning blow that had been meant for her skull but instead caught her on the temple. Scarlet lights erupted in her head and she fell, yelling as the dark shape toppled out of the sky toward her. Then something took hold of her shorn hair, dragging at the roots, swinging her up and about so that she sprawled in the wet undergrowth, groveling and fighting to control a spasm of nausea.

There were soft-booted feet in the grass before her unfocused eyes. And she felt the heat, the bulk, the nearness of someone looming over her and looking down as an angry master might look down on a crawling, penitent servant. Slowly, and with an effort that tore apart the last shreds of her dignity, Indigo dragged her arms back until she was able to raise herself first on her elbows and then to her knees. Her head swam; dizzily she looked up. And met the narrow eyes, red-lit by the fire and filled with hatred and vengefulness, of Tarn-Shen.

·CHAPTER·XII·

Tarn-Shen was breathing hard and his face was stone, contempt carved in every muscle. Indigo thought of reaching for her crossbow, but her head was swimming still from the blow he had struck her; she couldn't find the weapon, didn't even know where it was.

"So." Tarn-Shen smiled, cruelly. "Is what I have think. You be bad betrayer."

Under other circumstances she might have found his crude use of her language comical; as it was, with the unpleasant revelation spreading like poison in her mind, she made no move and no answer.

"You let shafan to go." Tarn-Shen shifted forward, the toe of his right boot now mere inches from her kneecap. "Is doing of betrayer, of—" He used a word in his own tongue which she didn't understand but could guess was a contemptuous insult. "Het will not be please. Het will maybe learn now to listen at me." He paused, then suddenly and savagely kicked out, catching Indigo off guard and sending her sprawling on her back. His foot came to rest on her stomach, lightly but firmly enough to quell her instinctive urge to retaliate. "And *you* will learn what is to be against Tarn-Shen!"

He was enjoying this moment, Indigo realized with sick disgust. It mattered nothing to him that his avowed quarry had escaped; his underlying resentment, both of her and of the hetmen who gave him orders, was a stronger motive than the desire to see the shafan dead.

She said, her voice low and dangerous: "Don't dare to touch me, Tarn-Shen. Or I swear, I'll make you regret it!"

He laughed, but continued to watch her carefully. "I be not afraid of you. You be black thing, worm thing. You be *nothing*." His foot pushed a little harder against her midriff and she drew her breath in against the pressure.

Indigo's head was clearing at last, reflexes sharpening, but she had seen the short bow that Tarn-Shen held negligently in one hand, an arrow already nocked. Her own bow was out of reach, her knife trapped between her body and the grass; she dared not so much as turn her head, for she didn't doubt that he could draw the string and shoot fast enough to impale her if she made any incautious move.

But at the same time she couldn't dislodge the uneasy feeling that he didn't intend for her to die quite yet.

"You will learn good lesson, I think." Tarn-Shen spoke softly and his tone was redolent suddenly of his grandsire: complacent, righteous, satisfied. "First I hurt you, but not much." Slowly he began to raise the bow; she heard the creak of wood flexing as the string was gradually, lovingly drawn back. "Like to hurt animal; not to kill but to stop from running. Then men of me will hurt you, but in different way. Like man to hurt woman which displeases." He grinned, feral in the dark. "So by, you learn how to obey what you be told, as woman should."

His meaning was clear, and he believed he was adding to the insult by implying that he would take no part in however his huntsmen chose to use her. Indigo willed her face to remain a still mask; to show emotion now, whether fear or anger, would give Tarn-Shen even greater satisfaction.

"Then when men be done, you be took back to village and het will know that you betray them." A slither and faint touch of iron on wood as the arrow poised to fire. "You not to live much after that, I think. Maybe you not *want* to live, I think."

He raised the bow and took leisurely aim at her left thigh. Helplessly, irrationally, one thought burned in Indigo's mind: *a friend; a trustworthy friend—*

Then a snarl sent a shattering shock wave through her, and she was knocked aside by a streaking shimmering form that exploded from the cover of the brambles and hurled itself at Tarn-Shen. Powerful muscles pistoned the wolf into an incredible leap, and its massive weight bowled the herdsman off his feet in a flailing cartwheel of limbs as they crashed together to the forest floor. Tarn-Shen was bellowing, the wolf snarling, rabid; they rolled like a single macabre, eight-limbed monster—

Sounds of racing feet erupted in the undergrowth, and as the hunters came running, Tarn-Shen's hand appeared momentarily among the battling, ravening shadows. Silver flashed; Indigo saw the blade of a murderous knife—

She didn't stop to think; *couldn't* stop. She shrieked a piercing, ululating cry of the Southern Isles hunters, a warning, the desperate alert to danger.

"Aware! Aware! Knife!"

The blade sheared and the wolf leaped aside, evading the deadly strike by inches. Tarn-Shen rolled like an acrobat, was on his feet, bow drawn even as the slavering animal turned and crouched. He couldn't miss at such close range, and Indigo flung herself frantically toward the dying fire where she knew her own bow must be. Her clawing hands closed on wood and metal, and she rolled in a rapid, economical movement, no time to sight, no time to aim, and fired.

The crossbow sang with heavy, deadly authority, and the bolt flashed vicious blood-crimson in the flamelight for an instant before it slammed into Tarn-Shen's side. He howled like a wounded dog and staggered sideways, his own bow flying from his grasp, and Indigo yelled at the top of her voice, "Run! *Run*!"

Brindle gray rushed past her, a streaking projectile, displaced air buffeting her as she scrambled to her feet. *Her harp*—She snatched it up by a handful of strings, not caring for any damage, not waiting to see the fate of the howling, thrashing Tarn-Shen.

Men's voices echoed among the trees, shouts of chagrin, anger, protest, shrill imprecations. Something whined close by her ear and an arrow thudded into the bole of a nearby oak. Indigo leaped over the fire, feeling heat scorch her ankles, and plunged into the gaping darkness that opened like a huge maw ahead of her. She cannoned into a tree, rebounded, ran on, hampered by the crossbow in one hand and the harp in the other. Two more arrows almost found their mark and she could hear the undergrowth being trampled behind her; breath sawing like vinegar in her throat, she stumbled on a zigzag course deeper and deeper into the dark.

Desperation gave her the edge she needed to outrun them. But even when the sounds of pursuit had faded and there was only her own staggering, chaotic progress to shatter the quiet, she kept going, neither knowing nor caring where she was, until at last an impenetrable bramble thicket forced her to halt. She dropped to hands and knees, panting like an animal, shoulders heaving as she dragged the dank night air down into her lungs. Her harp had tangled in the briars and she hardly had the strength to pull it free, but finally the thorns released it with a discordant protest and she curled over the instrument, her forehead pressed against the curve of the wood.

She had to rest. No matter who pursued her, no matter how close they might be, she was too drained to go on. After a few minutes she raised her head, blinking against the forest's intense darkness. Though she could barely see her own hand, she sensed that she was in a dense thicket; she could feel the proximity of the trees, the low-hanging branches, the encroaching briars. She would be as safe here as anywhere, at least until dawn.

Indigo crawled as far as she could into the shelter of the thorn tangle. By hunching and twisting her body, she made herself tolerably comfortable in the undergrowth; drawing up her knees to protect her harp and her bow, she pillowed her head on her hands and fell into a dark pit of sleep.

Indigo?

She felt as she had done once in childhood, swimming back toward the real world after the passing of a severe fever. She seemed to be bobbing in the wake of something vast and dark, released from its hold yet lost, bereft, not knowing where she was.

Indigo . . .

There was hard ground beneath her, but she couldn't coordinate her thoughts; had to drag herself out of a lingering dream—

No; don't try to wake. When you are awake, I can't speak to you like this. You can't hear me. Please . . . answer me in your mind, not with your tongue.

She knew the voice. It had spoken to her in the forest and she had thought it was illusory. . . .

She formed a thought, but tentatively, not wanting to break the fragile thread that held her between sleep and waking.

"Who are you?"

I am called Grimya. And with the silent reply came wordless concepts: wolf; female; friend.

This was insane, Indigo told herself. There were no such things as telepathic wolves. And yet she couldn't argue with bald facts. The creature that had spoken at her campfire, that had saved her from Tarn-Shen, had been no illusion: and that same creature was speaking to her now.

She marshaled her thoughts and projected: "How do you know my name?"

I looked in your mind as you slept, and I saw many things about you. A pause. *I didn't mean to pry. Please forgive me.*

Indigo felt her face muscles move as she smiled in her half dream. Why would she be angry? What had she to fear from sharing her secrets with a wolf?

"Then you know much more of me than I know of you," she replied.

Yes. Suddenly, though the voice in her mind had no tone beyond a sibilant whisper, Indigo sensed reluctance and uncertainty. Grimya was afraid of something.

"What is it, Grimya? What do you fear?"

No answer.

"Grimya?" She made the question as gentle as she could. "Why are you afraid to tell me of yourself?"

Because . . . Again a hesitation, and Indigo sensed

the internal struggle taking place within the creature. Grimya longed to communicate, but something held her back. Then at last there came a sigh, a breath in her psyche, ineffably sad.

I saw in your mind that you are lonely, and that you are sad. I, too, am lonely and sad, and I thought that perhaps you might be my friend. But if I tell you what makes me lonely, you may turn your face from me.

Indigo realized that what lay behind the deep and apparently sourceless sense of pity that had touched her during previous moments in the forest. Grimya had been trying to reach out to her then, trying to share her thoughts. But though she had sensed the wolf's presence, Indigo had been unable to hear her: any telepathic skill she might possess was too embryonic, too untrained, to manifest except in sleep.

She said: "Why should I turn from you?"

Because I am different. That is my shame.

Indigo smiled again, sadly. "I know all about shame, Grimya. I have more than enough of my own. Besides, I owe you a debt. You saved my life."

A gruff sound, as though, bizarrely, the wolf was clearing her throat. *As you saved mine.*

"Well, then. Doesn't that make us equals?"

Once more there was a long pause.

"Grimya?"

I can't tell you my story. I don't know all the right words. I could show you the pictures in my memory, but I don't think you will see them clearly, not now you are so nearly awake. Perhaps when you sleep again.

"Try for me, Grimya. Please."

No. The response was emphatic. *It is day. You should rouse now, before the men of the village come to avenge their dead leader.*

A shock went through Indigo, almost jolting her out of her trancelike state. "Tarn-Shen is dead?"

The one who attacked you. I smelled death on him before I fled to find you. He went to darkness before morning—I can always tell. His men will come back to find us, and kill us. You should rouse.

"I—" And Indigo gasped, physically gasped, as the threads of the dream snapped and the nerves in her body came suddenly alive to the feel of hard, uneven ground, damp grass, the sense of something closing over her. For a moment a gray-green film clouded her inner vision; then she opened crusted eyelids, blinking at the dull forest daylight, and turned over to see Grimya sitting in the shelter of the brambles not two paces away.

For the first time she looked fully and clearly at the creature she had previously seen only in shadow-shot darkness. Grimya was indeed far bigger than any normal wolf, but under the luxuriant pelt of gray, brindled fur she was starkly thin, bones angular and staring through the long hair. And her face, especially around her muzzle, was a mass of old scars that had never properly healed. Weals, gashes, bite-marks; the skin of her lower jaw had clearly once been badly torn and now no hair grew there, and the flesh was puckered over her right eye, slightly distorting its shape. How she had come by such injuries Indigo couldn't begin to guess, but it was clear that life hadn't treated Grimya kindly. Yet something in the wolf's amber eyes made her beautiful despite her blemishes; they held warm intelligence and a depth of genuine kindness that Indigo had rarely encountered in any living creature, animal or human.

They looked at each other for what seemed a very long time, neither liking to make the first move. Indigo didn't know how to greet her new found friend; she couldn't clasp hands with a wolf, but to stroke or pat Grimya, as she would have done a dog, would be crude and insulting. Finally, though, it was Grimya who broke the awkward stillness by rising to her feet, padding two paces toward Indigo and, with an artlessness that touched the girl's emotions, licking her face. It was, Indigo realized, the only form of greeting the wolf knew, and she responded impulsively by putting her arms about the shaggy neck and hugging tightly.

Grimya made a pleased, puppyish sound at the back of her throat, and formed words with a panting effort. "Wel-come. Wel-come!"

"Grimya . . ." Indigo sat back on her heels, then shook her head as her mind tried to assimilate too many things at once. "Forgive me, I—I've never before met a wolf who could speak."

"There are—no others," Grimya said. "Only me."

So she was a mutant. But a natural freak or bred for some purpose? Indigo wondered about the scars on her face. Animals, she knew, tended to be intolerant of any of their own kind who were in any way different from the norm. Little wonder that Grimya was lonely. . . .

The guttural, faltering voice broke in on her thoughts. "We must—not stay here. Men will come."

Indigo shook off her speculations. There were dogs in the herders' village, and doubtless some were trained as trackers. If, as Grimya believed, Tarn-Shen had died of the wound she'd inflicted on him, the het wouldn't rest until they had her blood in return.

Indigo and Grimya crept out of the brambles and into a small clearing. In this part of the forest the trees grew so densely that it was impossible even to judge the angle of the sun. Grimya realized what Indigo was thinking, and said, "I—lead us to safety. But we must be quick. Go now."

"Where are we to go?" Indigo asked.

"F-*far* away." Grimya had great difficulty with the

first word, and she was already pacing restlessly, her tail twitching, anxious to be on the move. "Away from the men. Now."

"But *where*?" Indigo started to say. "If they're truly determined to find us, they'll—" And she stopped as Grimya interrupted her with a snarl.

"Hush!" The she-wolf's head was raised, ears pricked forward, and the coarse hair of her ruff and along her spine was bristling.

Though she concentrated with all her will, Indigo could hear nothing but the chatter of birds. "What is it?"

"Hun-ters." The reply was a thin, dangerous growl, barely discernible as speech. "Men; dogs. Hear them. Smell them."

"I can't."

Grimya dropped to a crouch and her haunches quivered. "Upwind," she snarled, "but near." Her eyes, glittering like bronze now and feral, focused on Indigo's face. "No more time. Follow. *Run.*" And before Indigo could react she sprang away, swerving past the tangle of black brambles and into the dense wood.

Then Indigo's spine chilled as for the first time she heard what the wolf had sensed long before. A distant baying: the eager, frantic and mindless voices of hunting dogs scenting a kill. The crowding wood distorted her sense of direction, but she judged that they could be no more than a quarter of a mile away.

She swung around, biting her tongue to stop herself from calling after Grimya, and among the trees glimpsed a flicker of something gray and more corporeal than the shadows. Then a chilling howl rose demonically from the dark of the forest as Grimya gave voice to a defiant challenge.

Indecision crumbled. With one rapid movement Indigo snatched up her harp and bow from the thicket, then without pausing to look back she plunged in the direction Grimya had taken. Branches whipped her face, snagging in her hair; she slashed them viciously aside with the hand that held the bow, saw a protruding root just in time to jump over it, ran on. Grimya was waiting, and as the girl came up to her she took off again at what must have been for her a slow lope, but which soon had Indigo panting like a wolf herself in her efforts to keep pace. As she ran she swore, silently and ferociously, cursing her human clumsiness that smashed down undergrowth and set bushes shaking and rustling, so that the noise of her passage seemed to fill the forest. Sometimes she lost sight of Grimya ahead of her; then the she-wolf would appear again, a silent ghost, waiting to urge her on with lolling scarlet tongue and hot eyes. How close their pursuers were, whether they were gaining or falling back, Indigo didn't know, but Grimya's agitation grew as they forged deeper into the woods, and she began to feel close to despair. The hounds must have picked up their scent by now, and she knew the breed. They were tireless; even if they couldn't catch their quarry, they would run it down until it dropped from exhaustion. Grimya might escape them, but she could not.

"In-di-go!"

The cry was so like a rasping, panting breath that for a moment she didn't realize that Grimya was calling her name. Only when the wolf loomed out of the crowding trees ahead did she slither to a halt, one arm flailing to keep her balance on the treacherously uneven forest floor.

"Water!" Grimya's jaws hung wide, fangs yellow and deadly. "Follow!"

She didn't comprehend. This was no time to stop and drink—but she didn't have the breath to protest, and Grimya had already turned again and was loping away at a sharp angle to the path they'd been following. Indigo stumbled in her wake, and when the trees thinned unexpectedly to reveal a steep, moss-grown bank with a stream running below a drop of some ten feet, she understood what her companion had meant.

It was an old, simple trick, but effective. Their scent would be obliterated the moment they entered the water; the dogs could comb the banks, but while they ran along the streambed they would be untraceable.

Grimya stopped at the top of the bank, where ancient oak roots had twisted around a weathered boulder to form a petrified and strangely shaped overhang. She looked back briefly, then vanished over the edge in a slithering scramble, splashing into the water at the bottom. Indigo followed, slipping and sliding, hampered by the cradling of her precious harp and crossbow but managing to stay upright. The stream was shallow, chuckling over stones which thankfully were free of treacherous weed growths. Grimya had already turned downstream, and Indigo glanced back at the bank. Even the most inexperienced tracker would have no trouble finding the telltale signs of their descent, the flattened grass and crushed moss, the place where the miniature soil cliff at the stream's edge had crumbled under the pressure of a careless foot; but it didn't matter. There the trail would end.

She paused for a moment to listen for any untoward noise, but could hear nothing other than the sounds of the stream and the ever-present birds. Grimya was waiting, less frantic now but still impatient. Indigo adjusted the thong that secured her harp over her shoulder and set off down the watercourse.

They had been following the stream for more than an hour when Grimya finally indicated that it was safe to rest. The ploy, it seemed, had worked; there had been no signs of their pursuers and the forest was quiet and undisturbed. Nonetheless, as she scrambled up the bank the she-wolf was cautious, ears pricked alertly, pausing at the top to watch and listen before allowing Indigo to follow her.

By this time Indigo was hopelessly lost. The trees extended seemingly without end in every direction, and from the greenish quality of the light and the profound quiet, she guessed that they must be deep in the heart of the vast woodland. Alone, she might wander ceaselessly without finding a way out; if any doubts still remained about the wisdom of trusting Grimya, she had no choice but to abandon them.

The wolf had already set off into the trees, and she followed. After perhaps ten minutes—time was hard to judge in this still, quiet place—they came to a shallow ravine formed long ago by a landslip. Huge oaks overhung the drop, and their roots, partly exposed to the air, formed a natural shelter on the moss-grown slope.

"Here we rest," Grimya said. "Safe."

There was a ledge under the oak roots, large enough to accommodate them both comfortably. Indigo sank down with her back against the ravine wall, thankful to rest her aching legs. Grimya peered out, sniffed the air carefully, then said:

"All is good. Men too far away to smell. Safe." She turned to regard Indigo, her eyes seeming to ask assurance that the girl had confidence in her.

Indigo reached out and, though still a little tentative, laid a hand on the wolf's shoulder. "I don't know how to thank you, Grimya. I owe you a great debt."

Grimya's tongue lolled, jaws gaping in a show of pleasure, and her tail thumping against a gnarled root. Then she turned, looking out again at the forest.

"You st-ay here," she said throatily. "Wait."

"Where are you going?"

The wolf's hindquarters twitched. "Hunt," she said. It was almost a bark. And before Indigo could say any more, she had wriggled between the arching tree roots and was scrambling up the ravine side. For a moment she stood poised at the top, a sleek silhouette; then she was gone, bounding away without a sound.

Indigo sat back and closed her eyes. She was grateful for this respite from running, from the fear of capture and what it would have meant. And for the first time she had the chance to consider the bizarre events of the past few hours.

The fact that her life had been saved—twice—by a wolf would in itself have been strange enough to contemplate, but even that was eclipsed by the extraordinary nature of the wolf herself. She had yet to learn Grimya's story, but was certain of one thing: the she-wolf was one of a kind. An outcast, perhaps a pariah; a solitary survivor with only her own resourcefulness to rely on. The parallels between them were painfully clear.

Not for the first time, the parting words of the Earth Mother's emissary came back to Indigo's mind. A new friend, who could be trusted. In the days that followed that strange encounter she had had no cause to consider the idea, but suddenly it seemed sharply pertinent.

A wolf whose mind had touched hers with a sense of sympathy and comradeship. A creature who had saved her, guided her, helped her . . . Indigo smiled a private smile. She had believed that true friendship, when she found it, would be in human guise.

It seemed she had been wrong.

·CHAPTER·XIII·

Grimya returned an hour later, with the corpse of a hare dangling from her jaws. Indigo's own hunger was tempered by reluctance to light a fire; woodsmoke could be detected from a great distance, and though her stomach was gnawing, the risk was too great. When she explained this to Grimya, adding that she would prefer not to eat raw meat, the she-wolf's dismay was acute, but she finally agreed to take the kill for herself while Indigo made a nutritious if unappetizing meal from shoots and a few young wild carrots.

Once convinced that her friend would make good enough shrift without meat, Grimya was naively and innocently uninhibited about devouring her meal. Trying not to watch her, or to listen to the sounds she made, Indigo sat staring out at the forest canopy and took silent stock of her situation.

Her chances of being able to return to Linsk now were very remote indeed. If, as Shen-Liv had implied, the herders traded in the port, she dared not take the risk of showing her face there. She could do without the possessions she had left behind; she had her harp, knife and bow, tinderbox and a warm coat—enough, in other words, to fulfill her basic survival needs—and replacements for her lost bolts could be found or fashioned in good time. But without a horse she was badly hampered.

There could be, of course, no question of trying to retrieve the chestnut mare from the herders' village, nor of attempting to steal a mount from among the herds on the plains. Either would be far too dangerous. But as a lone and inadequately armed foot-traveler, she would be vulnerable; all the more so while Tarn-Shen's hunters continued to search for her. Until she could leave the Horselands altogether, she was and would remain a fugitive.

She sighed, and Grimya looked up. The wolf's jaws were crimson. "You are . . . trr-oubled?"

"No; no." Indigo shook her head. "Just thinking, Grimya."

"We have . . . much to say. But to talk this way is h . . . *hard* for me. When you—" Grimya's sides heaved with effort and she growled as though protesting against her own inadequacy. "When you sleep, then we can . . . speak."

Indigo glanced at what little she could see of the sky through the thick tangle of branches high above them. She doubted if the day was more than half done; the idea of sleeping at this hour seemed bizarre, but Grimya was right; they had much to say to each other, and while she was awake anything beyond a very one-sided communication was impossible. Time, too, was not on their side; the hunters might have abandoned the chase for now, but they would not give up the search for her.

Grimya had turned back to her kill. Bones crunched,

and Indigo turned away, shifting her body until she could lie down in reasonable comfort. Despite her doubts she found herself suddenly sleepy; the spring day was mild and she felt warm inside her coat and, at least for the moment, safe. She closed her eyes and a quiet greenness seemed to envelop her, punctuated by the small, almost subliminal sounds of the forest. Leaves whispering, birds calling with bright, distantly echoing voices, the faint hum of a bee searching for early flowers somewhere nearby . . . the sounds melded, softened and finally faded away into the quiet of sleep.

Can you hear me, Indigo?

Grimya's soft, toneless mental voice penetrated her dreams and she felt her mind rise through the deeper layers of consciousness until she hovered, as she had done before, midway between sleeping and waking.

"I hear you, Grimya."

You have slept for a long time. The light in the sky is fading.

"Are we still safe?"

Yes. I have been to the forest's edge. The hunters have given up the chase for now.

Relief was like cool water flowing through her veins. "Then—" she began.

No. The response cut across her thoughts, as though the she-wolf had read them almost before they could be clearly formulated. And again Indigo sensed fear and doubt in Grimya's mind.

She waited for the space of five heartbeats, then felt herself draw breath. "Grimya, you mustn't be afraid. There's so much I want to know about you, and nothing you tell me can ever erase the debt I owe you."

Words alone, she knew, couldn't convince Grimya,

and she tried to project a feeling of kindness, warmth, comradeship. There was a pause. Then Grimya said:

I can see a word in your head, The word is "mutant." I don't know what it means.

"It's just a word, Grimya. It isn't important. And you're no more of a mutant than I am."

I still don't understand.

Indigo felt bitter pain welling up in her. "Don't you?" she asked gently. "You've seen into my mind, Grimya. You know what I am."

A sense of negation: *No. I know only that you have come from far away, and that you are sad and lonely. When I tried to look further there was a dark place in your head, and I knew it was wrong for me to go there unless you should ask me to, so I did not.*

The simple honesty of that statement touched the girl to the quick. A dark place . . . was that how Grimya saw the appalling chasm that separated her from her own past? And if the wolf knew the real truth, would she be able to comprehend it, let alone understand?

Indigo saw suddenly and with awful clarity the nature of Grimya's self-doubt, for she shared it. What rational creature would not turn its face away in loathing, on learning the story of the threat brought upon the entire world by Anghara Kaligsdaughter's foolhardy arrogance?

A shock, chill as a hoar-month frost, ran through her as she realized that for the first time since leaving Carn Caille, she had formed the syllables of her own former name in her mind. And following on the heels of the shock came chagrin, when she saw that Grimya had picked it up.

Anghara . . . There was wondering curiosity in the thought the wolf projected back to her. *How can you be Indigo and yet Anghara, too?*

There were red flames before Indigo's inner vision, and she couldn't force them away. "I was Anghara," she said softly. "But I have forfeited the right to my true name."

I don't understand. Is this what makes you so sad?

"Ah, Grimya . . ." She hadn't cried since her second night aboard *Greymalkin*, but now the tears were coming, welling up; she couldn't stem them. "I can't explain to you, not in words. Look into my mind, if you can. Look into the dark place. And maybe then you won't fear that I might turn my face from you."

She could sense Grimya's hesitation as curiosity warred with a taboo against prying into another's innermost secrets. A little bleakly, Indigo projected the thought that she welcomed such an intrusion, that if Grimya was willing to learn, she was willing to open herself: and moments later she felt the first tentative probing as the she-wolf's mind and hers began to merge.

There were faces in her inner vision, faces she'd striven to blot from her memory but which had lurked in dark recesses, only waiting for their chance to rise into her consciousness again. Fenran, Kirra, her father, mother, Imyssa, Cushmagar. And other beings: things which had never been human, abominations, monstrosities, twisted parodies of life shambling and lurching across the burning landscapes of her inner eye. She felt her lungs and heart contract agonizingly as her mind was plunged deeper into her own past. There stood the Earth Mother's emissary, the serene face merciful yet without pity for her. There was the dusty road that lay beyond time and space, and on it she saw again the visions—if visions they were—of the maleficent, silver-eyed child, and of Fenran, torn and bleeding, struggling through the invisible thicket that had no end.

In her sleep Indigo's body shook as dry sobs, tearless now, racked her. But there was another presence in her mind: warm, animal, openly and simply comforting, with an undertone of distress.

I am beginning to understand now, Grimya said. *But why did you do such a thing, when it has brought you only sadness?*

It was such an innocent question, uttered without any hint of censure, and the unwavering trust it implied made Indigo wish that the earth might open and allow her to crawl away down to its uttermost depths.

She said: "I did it because I was a fool." Much worse than a fool, but could Grimya understand the concept of a crime against the Earth herself? "I was greedy and I was arrogant. I thought I knew better than all the world's bards and sages, and I tried to prove that belief without thought for the consequences."

Grimya considered this for a long time. Then: *I don't think I understand humans very well. Why do they desire to know so many things? What does it gain them?* She paused. *I know things, too. I know the day and the night, the forest, the plains, the river. I know how to hunt, and how to call to the moon, and what is sweet water and what is bad. I know that when I am tired I must sleep, and when I am thirsty I must drink. I know all these things, and I need nothing more.*

"But you know more than that, Grimya. The way we're speaking now is proof of it. You know far more than any ordinary wolf."

A soft, melancholy sound came from Grimya's throat. *Yes. But I did not seek for those things, and they have made me very unhappy. Yet when men seek, and are made unhappy by what they find, still they seek more. I don't understand that. I don't think I ever shall.*

"You shouldn't try," Indigo told the wolf softly. "Your philosophy is far saner then ours, it seems."

Phil-os-o-phy . . . Grimya tried out the syllables with grave caution. *That is a new word. But a word for humans, perhaps; not for me.*

Silence fell for a little while. Then Indigo said:

"Grimya, now you know the full truth about me. Are you still willing to be my friend?"

Why should I not be?

"Because of what I've done. Because of the curse that's laid on me."

Your curse is not mine. Mine is different.

"But among my own kind I'm an outcast, a pariah."

I don't know "par-iah." But I am outcast, too, and that makes us alike. I want to be your friend.

To feel relief at gaining the trust and the loyalty of a wolf was a strange concept, but the sensation was there, and with it came a warm feeling of gratitude.

"Then will you tell me your story?" Indigo asked. "Please, Grimya. You have done a great deal to help me. I want to try to help you in my turn."

There was hesitancy still, but it had faded to nothing more than an old reluctance to speak of something that gave the she-wolf pain. Grimya said: *I will show you the pictures from my memory, Indigo, if I can. Watch now, and listen. . . .*

Green darkness, the rich green of woodland moss, flowed across Indigo's inner eye. She felt the touch of something warm and fur-clad, and though the contact should have been alien to her, somehow it was not. A bird, somewhere overhead, trilled a flying cascade of notes that might have been a mating call or simply an expression of joy at being alive. And suddenly she was no longer Indigo, and no longer human. . . .

The den was a place of dark security, and her eyes, which had opened for the first time only a day or so ago, couldn't yet focus properly on the furry and—to the tiny cubs—vast flank of the mother-wolf who suckled her and her three brothers. Her world consisted of the bed of dry, crackling leaves, the squeals of her siblings, the warm body and rough, rasping tongue that cleaned her own downy fur, and a seemingly endless supply of milk. But her newly formed mind was aware of another world beyond the den, a world which, in her infantile dreams, sometimes seemed as real as waking, and which she seemed to see and hear in a way that was unlike normal seeing and hearing.

The warm presence and tiny cries faded then, and suddenly that other world was translated into reality before her eyes—eyes now sharp and alert and avid for new information. Small, sturdy legs carried her on explorations that grew more adventurous with each day that passed; though at the end of them there was always the return to the den and the warm presence. Sometimes she would sit at the mouth of the den, watching as her siblings played in the undergrowth a few paces away. Head cocked on one side, she listened to their yappings and growlings and longed to join in; but when she began, tentatively, to beat her tail on the dusty ground, or approached them with a hopeful whine, they drove her away.

Other experiences followed: scenes of the forest, becoming more familiar and less awesome; of her own growth mirrored in the growth of her brothers; of tasting meat for the first time; of her mother's increasing restlessness as the cubs approached maturity. And with the tapestry of those experiences, which seemed to be unfolding faster and faster, came a growing awareness that something was not quite right. A sense of not belonging, of *difference*. But what manner of difference? She couldn't understand. All she knew was that the mock assaults her brothers made on her were suddenly becoming more frequent and more serious. She was no longer welcome in the den; tolerated, but not welcome.

And more and more often she could only find refuge from their constant torment in solitude.

Until the day when they finally and irrevocably turned on her, and for the first time Grimya learned the real meaning of her *difference*.

She had always known that she could "hear" the thoughts of other creatures, but had believed it nothing untoward; nor had it occurred to her to wonder why neither her mother nor her brothers seemed able to reply when she tried to speak to them in that *other* way. And so she was unprepared for the events of that morning in late autumn.

The cubs, almost fully grown now, were in the clearing just outside the den. Their mother had not come out to join them, and Grimya had been thinking about ways to assuage her hunger when the attack came. Her brothers were on her so fast that she had no time to react, let alone defend herself; one moment the clearing had been quiet, the next Grimya was bowled over by three snapping, snarling bodies. This was no game: they were going for her throat, her face, teeth snatching at her fur, tearing at her skin—and in their crude, half-formed imaginations Grimya saw her own imminent death.

She fought them, instinct coming to her aid when, in her panic, she couldn't consciously remember the self-defense lessons she had learned. Yelping, biting, scrabbling, she stood her ground, and was only dimly aware of relief when her mother, disturbed by the noise, appeared at the den mouth.

But her mother didn't come to her aid; didn't call her brothers off. Instead—and the knowledge was like a hammerblow to Grimya's unquestioning faith—the she-wolf sprang into the fray, her snarls deeper and more deadly than those of the cubs, attacking the pariah, the strange one, the *different* one. Her mother's fangs sank into the soft flesh above Grimya's eye, and Grimya howled, protesting at the pain and the betrayal. She was lost—no one would help her; and her assailants, her own family, would not be content until she was driven from their midst, or dead.

She had one hope of survival—to run. Twisting about, she squirmed between two of her brothers and, breaking into a momentarily clear space, fled with her tail between her legs. They pursued her, but desperation gave her an edge and the chase was halfhearted; once certain that she was out of their territory, the four wolves let her go.

Alone, bewildered and far from the only home she had ever known, Grimya huddled miserable and wounded in the forest's dank undergrowth. And Indigo, her mind inextricably bound with the mind of the young she-wolf, felt her own lungs heaving, her own tongue lolling, the slow trickle of blood from her own torn face and flank. She was betrayed, she was bereft. She had no family and no friends; her only companions had rejected her, driven her away because she was *different.* In her loneliness she raised her head toward the impassive leaf-canopy and uttered a long, dismal howl that set birds chattering with alarm; a cry of wretched despair.

New sensations and images came then. The harsh reality of solitude, with no pack to give her security and comfort. Learning, step by painful step, to hunt alone, catching only small game that barely satisfied her needs. Bitter winters—two, the part of the wolf-mind that was Indigo counted—during which starvation was an ever-present threat. Often in those icy days she saw men who came from the surrounding villages to hunt in the forests, and sometimes she followed them when they returned to the plains and the horse-herds. The *difference* that had turned her own kind against her also enabled her to understand, and awkwardly mimic, human speech; language, it seemed, had no barriers for Grimya. But to men, as to her fellow wolves, she was an object of hatred . . . until the night when, hungry and lonely, she had been irresistibly lured to a stranger's camp by the smells of woodsmoke and meat, and the faint strains of harp music. . . .

Release from the thrall of merged minds came abruptly, like falling into a twisting, turning vortex, and the shock jolted Indigo awake. She sat up in a confused flurry, almost cracking her head on a protruding root, and suffered the secondary shock of disorientation as she realized that suddenly she had hands and feet instead of four paws, that her body wasn't covered by a thick pelt of fur, that she no longer knew how to howl. Gasping, she turned her head. And there beside her—a separate entity now—was Grimya.

The she-wolf's flanks heaved and she spoke in her halting, pained way. "Now you . . . know . . . all of me."

Indigo swallowed, but couldn't dislodge the blockage in her throat. "Yes . . . I'm sorry, Grimya. So sorry for your suffering."

"I . . . cannot change it. But you . . ." There was something odd in Grimya's manner, an underlying excitement that put Indigo abruptly and inexplicably on edge.

"Me?"

The shaggy, brindled head swung from side to side and Grimya's jaws opened wide, tongue lolling. It was a sign of frustration, of distress at her own inability to communicate more clearly. "You have . . . I do not know a word! When I sh-showed you . . . pictures, you—*became*." Her eyes were amber lamps in the shadows. "Became *me*."

"In my mind, I—"

"No. Not mind. Not *just* mind. I *saw* you."

Indigo's pulse missed a sharply painful beat as she realized what Grimya was trying to express. "You mean . . . I *changed*? I became—a wolf?"

"Yes, yes!" Grimya was almost wriggling with excitement. "Face, coat, body—like me!"

Shape-shifting . . . It was one of the oldest and rarest of the ancient witch-powers. Indigo had never met anyone who possessed that eerie ability, but she knew such people existed. As a child she had listened enthralled to bards' tales of encounters with the few elusive and secretive sorcerers who could alter their bodies at will into the forms of birds, or cats, or bears; the stories were well documented, as was the fact that such a talent could not be learned but was something inborn, a gift from the Earth Mother to a chosen few.

Was it possible that she could be one of those few? The thought made her skin prickle, and a rivulet of ice-cold sweat ran down her spine. Imyssa, who was herself a witch, albeit with little power beyond the skills of herbalism, scrying and weather-lore, believed that some measure of power lay dormant in her young charge; but even Imyssa had not foreseen *this*.

Yet the evidence of Grimya's eyes couldn't be denied. In her own mind Indigo had known, briefly, what it was to be a wolf, and with that experience had come the awesome manifestation of the shape-changer.

Suddenly Indigo began to shiver, and couldn't make the spasms stop. If she truly possessed such a power, then she was both blessed and cursed. Blessed because it was, in potential, a weapon beyond price to aid her in the grim quest ahead. But cursed because she had no knowledge of how to harness and use it. And without that knowledge, without the skill and the training needed to control and wield such a force, her innate talent was useless. Worse than useless; for its random and unchecked manifestation could endanger her life. And Imyssa, the one person who could and would have helped her to understand and use what was awakening within her soul, was lost to her forever.

Grimya whimpered softly, and she realized that the she-wolf had been watching her, sensing her distress and anxious.

"Indigo? What is wr-wrong?"

Indigo wiped both hands across her face, attempting to clear her mind. "I don't think I can explain it, Grimya."

"You have magic, yet that makes you more sad then before. Wh-why?"

"Ohh . . ." Indigo shook her head. "Because even if—*if*—I have that magic, I don't know how to use it!" She blinked rapidly, aware that she was beginning to feel very sorry for herself. "I didn't *know*, Grimya. And because I didn't know, I refused to listen to those who did, and I refused to learn from them. Now it's too late; there's no one to help me, and I've only myself to blame!"

Grimya was silent for a few moments. Then she said: "*I* can help you."

Indigo felt a stifling sensation in her throat, and tried to smile. "You're kind, Grimya, and a good friend. But—"

"No," Grimya interrupted. "I meant more than by—by being your friend." She paused, panting. Human speech was taxing her, but she was determined to say what was in her mind. "Something *else*. I know of a place in the forest, where men . . . will not go, because . . ." Again her tongue lolled with frustration. "I have not the *words*!"

A dim memory stirred in the depths of Indigo's consciousness and she felt tension creep through her muscles. "What kind of place?"

"A place of . . . water and dark. Deep among the trees. The hunters . . . fear it, but . . . there is magic there. Humans' magic. It is very strong." The she-wolf's nostrils flared. "I have smelled it, but not been too near. It may be that s-such a place can help you."

A faint, unfocused mental impression accompanied the words, and Indigo's spine crawled as the nagging memory slipped abruptly into place. In the depths of the Southern Isles forests were sacred groves, always at the site of a spring or natural well. They were used only by the most powerful and devoted of witches, those who had dedicated their lives exclusively to the Earth Mother's service, and no outsider ever dared enter one uninvited, for the groves were guarded by spirits which would not tolerate the presence of the uninitiated. Sacred sites, repositories of power, strong foci for the old magics . . . was it possible that such groves also existed here in the Horselands? She knew nothing of the occult practices of this wild country, but the people of the villages worshipped the Earth Mother, as her own people did. . . .

Her mouth dry, she said: "Grimya, is this place—the place of water and dark—still used by humans?"

"I . . . do not think so. Not for many, many moon risings. There is no man-scent there. But the magic is still strong."

As it surely would be. . . . Indigo sucked at the insides of her cheeks in an attempt to induce saliva, but when she spoke again her voice was husky with dehydration. "And you think that such a place might help me?"

A long, long pause. Then:

"I believe it is so. I have—*seen* things. In dreams. In sleep. I cannot speak of them. But they are there."

What have you to lose? Indigo's mind asked her silently. She knew the answer: *nothing*.

"Grimya, will you take me to the place of water and dark?"

The she-wolf's head swayed uncertainly. "Is it what you . . . truly wish?"

"Yes."

"Then . . . I will take you." Grimya blinked, and a long shudder ran the length of her back as she looked beyond their shelter into the green-lit forest, seeming to see something that was beyond Indigo's ability to perceive. "But I think," she added in a soft, throaty whisper, "I think I am afraid of what we might find there. . . ."

·CHAPTER·XIV·

Grimya did not want to begin their journey that day. The place of water and dark, she said, was a long way from their shelter, and night would soon fall. To set out now would mean arriving with only the moon to light them, and that prospect made her nervous. Indigo, however, was impatient, and her stubborn determination—coupled with the difficulty that verbal argument held for Grimya—finally prevailed.

They set out northwestward, with the sunset flaring through the forest ahead of them. Indigo was unwilling to trust the likelihood that the herders would have abandoned their hunt at least until morning, and kept her senses cautiously attuned for any untoward sights or sounds; but the woods were peaceful, and the small, natural noises of birds and animals slowly tapered off as the light faded, until they walked in darkness and silence.

Neither of them had spoken since they left their

makeshift camp. Once Grimya stopped to investigate a spring that bubbled sluggishly from beneath the ground by their track, but a growl was enough to warn Indigo that the water was not safe to drink, and they continued on their way. With the moon's passage invisible beyond the trees Indigo had no way of telling how long they had walked before the wolf, who was a few paces ahead of her, suddenly slowed and stopped. She too halted, and immediately felt something in the atmosphere that made her spine tingle. The night was very still, but it seemed as though the stillness itself were alive, a sentient presence, aware and anticipating.

She peered into the dark. Very little of the moon's radiance penetrated the dense canopy, but ahead of them—impossible to say how far; the night played tricks, and distances, she knew, were deceptive—a faint greenish glow shone among the trees, a pale column of light like a will-o'-the-wisp. Very slowly Indigo moved up to where Grimya stood, and laid a hand lightly on the wolf's shoulder. Her voice was a breathless whisper.

"Is that the place, Grimya? The place of water and dark?"

"Yesss . . ." Grimya's fur rippled beneath her touch and she sensed her friend's unease.

There was power here; she could feel it, a formless yet tangible presence in the air about her, and it conjured memories of places in her homeland's forests where she had been strictly forbidden to go. But unlike those sacred shrines, this grove seemed to beckon to her, calling her to approach . . .

Nothing moved; there was not the smallest breeze to stir a single leaf. Indigo took three paces forward, and heard Grimya whimper.

"Grimya?" She turned, saw that the wolf's hackles

were raised. "We *must* go on. We can't turn back now."

"I am . . . afraid."

"But there's nothing to fear." She looked ahead again. Was the strange radiance glowing a little more brightly, or did she imagine it? She took another two steps forward, aware that the trees and bushes were beginning to close in around her.

Grimya said: "This is not . . . a good place. I don't want to go in."

Abruptly, Indigo's conscience assailed her. This was her quest, not Grimya's; in bringing her to this place, the she-wolf had conquered her fear only with great difficulty. That sacrifice was enough; to ask more of her would be cruel.

She stroked Grimya's neck, hoping to soothe her and show her gratitude at the same time. "You need go no farther, Grimya. But I must. Do you understand that?"

"Yesss . . ."

"And will you wait for me?"

The shaggy head swung. "Of c-course. I will wait . . . here. I am not afraid here. But . . ."

"What is it?"

Grimya looked up at her, then impulsively licked her hand. "Promise me you will take care!"

She smiled, touched. "I promise."

Indigo carefully laid down her harp, unslung her crossbow and unsheathed her knife. To take weapons into a place sacred to the Earth Mother was the act of a desecrater; she laid them on the grass beside Grimya, then walked slowly in the direction of the faint radiance. The she-wolf settled to the ground; when Indigo looked back she saw her only as an alert silhouette, her eyes glowing pinpoints in the gloom. She raised one hand in salute, then set her face once more toward the dim, shining aura that called her on through the trees.

The woodland here was so dense that Indigo soon began to wonder if it was entirely natural. In places the trees crowded so closely together that she could barely move between them, and at every step she was forced to push aside resistant branches, like a swimmer forging against a heavy current. Several times she was obliged to veer aside when the undergrowth became impenetrable, and would have lost her way but for the distant glow of the strange column of light to guide her. But as she drew nearer to her goal the light seemed subtly to alter; it faded, brightened, faded again, appearing to dissipate until she feared that she might lose sight of it altogether. Indigo grew uneasy, and had to hold back a panic-borne impulse to hack and tear at the network of branches before her, trying to force a way through lest her only point of reference should vanish and leave her helplessly lost in the thicket.

The tangle of undergrowth ended so unexpectedly that she almost stumbled and lost her footing as she burst into the clearing. Shocked by the suddenness of the change, Indigo stood on an emerald carpet of moss-grown turf and gazed wide-eyed at the sheer wall of rock, not ten paces before her, that rose from the far bank of a still pool.

She breathed in slowly, and as though in answer the trees and bushes at her back whispered to the stirring of a faint breeze. Every inch of her skin was tingling with tiny, electric sensations; she could *feel* the focus of power here, could have reached out and cupped it in her hands, tasted it, drunk of its essence . . . She swayed, gripping a branch of a young sapling to steady herself as her mind spun headily. This was, indeed, a sacred place, and for a moment her courage almost failed her as she remembered old tales of what befell those who invaded the sanctity of these magical groves.

But she was not an invader. She had come in a spirit of reverence, to ask help of the ancient forces focused here. She carried no weapon; she intended no evil. All she brought with her was hope, and a silent prayer that the guardians of the grove, if they still kept vigil, would look kindly on her.

The moss beneath her feet felt soft and springy; the rough bark of the sapling held her to earth and reality. She took another breath and, conscious that what she did was an irrevocable commitment, stepped into the grove.

There was no sudden change, no howling gale, no shock of blinding light, no monstrous voice to boom a challenge or a condemnation. The quiet peace of the night still enfolded her, and as her racing pulse began to slow a little, she summoned the courage to cross the green carpet and stand at last before the pool.

It was perhaps two arms' length in width, a sheer-sided basin at the bottom of the rock face. How deep it might be Indigo couldn't tell; the water was like a black mirror, and when she dropped to her knees at its edge and looked in, she could see only a ghostly, distorted reflection of her own face. Nor was the pool's surface entirely still; faint ripples moved across it, and she realized that it was fed by a tiny rivulet of water that trickled from the rock above. Looking up to find the rivulet's origin, she saw that it ran down through a deep cleft in the rock face—and here was the source of the unearthly light, for the cleft exposed a dense vein of greenish, quartzlike ore that glowed with a peculiar phosphorescence. Reflecting and refracting from the crystalline surface, this phosphorescence formed the pale, shimmering column which had guided her through the trees.

Indigo knelt at the pool's edge, allowing her racing pulse a little time to slow and settle. Her senses were very alert and she was acutely conscious of the silence pervading the grove. Was she being watched? Her mind sought for a telltale sign, the smallest psychic hint of another presence, but found nothing. The guardians, if they still dwelt here, were not yet ready to make themselves known.

She focused her thoughts on the revelation which had brought her to the grove, and on the help she hoped to find, then closed her eyes and composed herself. Communion with the powers that inhabited other planes of existence had always been a silent and private matter among the witches of the Southern Isles. Panoply and ceremonial had its place in the mass celebrations of harvest, midwinter and spring, but for less public purposes it was held that the Earth Mother saw the hearts and souls of those who asked Her blessing without need of such trappings. Indigo's lips moved in a silent prayer of invocation and she opened herself to the grove and the power within it. She felt the greenness enclosing her, and the chill of the night seemed tempered by a warm, flowing sensation deep in her mind, as though she moved through dark, calm waters. A plea, a hope, an implicit trust: the images coalesced in her thoughts and took wing . . .

And something reached out from the darkness to touch her with the indefinable delicacy of a shadow.

Indigo's flesh tingled with ice and fire together as excitement and dread warred within her. Uncertainly, haltingly, her mind formed a question, a wordless hope—

"I hear you, Indigo. Open your eyes, and you will see."

Her eyelids fluttered and she shivered convulsively. Then the grove swam into focus and she saw that the eerie phosphorescence in the rock fault above her was glowing more brightly, the column of light taking on a hint of form. Even as she watched, the column wavered, flickered—and in its place, balancing on a narrow ledge inside the crevice, stood a slender figure.

It was almost, but not quite, human. Vivid emerald eyes gazed down at Indigo from a small, delicate face. Hair that was not truly hair but had the look of a cascade of young green willow leaves showered over the sprite's shoulders, falling almost to its waist. It was naked, sexless rather than androgynous, and its skin gleamed the color of pale, burnished maple. Prehensile toes clung to the ledge as a bird might cling to a branch; its fingers were tipped with long, translucent nails.

"What do you want, that brings you to this holy place?" it asked.

The voice had an oddly distant timbre, and Indigo found that her eyes wouldn't quite focus on the sprite. It was as though, she thought, it was not fully manifest in this world, but hovered between the dimension of Earth and its own otherworldly plane.

She dropped her gaze and said: "I seek the aid of the powers the Earth Mother has invested here. I come in peace, and in reverence."

There was silence for a few moments while the sprite weighed and judged her words. Then it inclined its head.

"I see that you speak without deviousness. What is the nature of the aid you hope to find?"

Haltingly, Indigo told of her experience and of the revelation that had followed. The being listened without movement or change of expression, and, occasionally daring to glance up at it, she wondered what thoughts ran through its alien mind.

When the tale was done, another and longer silence

followed, and Indigo felt her heartbeat quickening with trepidation. At last, the sprite spoke again.

"You are not an initiate in the craft of the wise, yet you seek the skills that the guardians of the grove grant only to that craft. What makes you think that you have a right to ask such a boon of us?"

"I have no right," Indigo answered. "But I believe that the power within me was invested by the Earth Mother, and I fear that I might offend Her by using it recklessly or unknowingly."

The sprite considered this. "It is true that all such powers are the Earth Mother's gift, and She does not bestow Her gifts without good cause." Its outline shimmered. "If the words of your lips are the words of your heart, then it may be that what you ask will be granted. But your sincerity must be tested, and if you fail that test, your deceit will be known to us and you will suffer accordingly. Are you willing to open your innermost secrets to us?"

Indigo looked up and saw that the strange being was smiling, faintly but, she thought, kindly. "Yes," she said without hesitation. "I am willing."

"Very well. It is quite simple. Merely put your hands in the water of the pool."

Indigo leaned forward. The pool's surface was a black mirror still, but as she bent toward it she could see, behind her own reflection, the faint shimmer of the sprite's ethereal form. Her fingers broke the surface, went through; she felt the profound, icy coldness of the water envelop her hands—

Without warning the scene about her tilted violently, and suddenly the pool wasn't a pool but was changing into a tunnel, a yawning vortex of a mouth opening up before her. She felt herself toppling forward, cried out—and in that split second, as she lurched between dimensions, she had a last glimpse of the sprite reflected in the black water before the pool winked out of existence. It was leaning from the crevice, its face twisted with demonic glee—and from its open mouth flickered a snakelike silver tongue.

Silver—

"Grimya!" Indigo heard her own despairing scream as though across a vast chasm, and she heard the answering howl, the crash of something heavy and powerful charging through the trees. She felt moss beneath her fingers and scrabbled frantically to grasp it as the forest turned in on itself and the ground beneath her heaved. Something vast and hollow came rushing toward her, she was snatched, buffeted—she heard a throaty snarling, shockingly close, tried to scream again—and lost her hold on the world to pitch helplessly into a void of chaotic light and impossible color, with the echoes of her own shriek dinning in her ears.

She had been aware of something whimpering close by for some time, but her mind and body seemed paralyzed and she was unable to respond. Only when the intense darkness began at last to give way to a gray, pearly gloom was she able to raise her head and look for the source of the sound.

She was lying on what felt like bare rock. Her surroundings were invisible; the darkness had lessened only enough to allow her to see a few feet in any direction. But the gray shape sprawled forlorn and frightened at her feet was unmistakable.

"Grimya . . ." Indigo struggled upright, reaching out toward the she-wolf as astonished relief swept through her.

Indigo! Grimya's head jerked up and her eyes glowed like twin pieces of amber. *You are not hurt!*

She could hear the wolf's thought-speech perfectly, Indigo realized with a shock. Did this mean that she was asleep, and dreaming? Or did it portend something far less pleasant?

She had no chance to dwell on that, for Grimya was on her feet, tail wagging with renewed hope. She licked Indigo's face. *I could not wake you! I thought you were not going to come back to me!*

"No, I—I've taken no hurt." She stared into the darkness, but still could see nothing beyond the bare surface on which she sat. "Grimya, do you know where we are?"

No. But I don't like it. I can see nothing, smell nothing. That isn't right.

Indigo struggled with recalcitrant memory. The last thing she recalled was falling, and a snarling at her back, and the pool changing into a great black mouth—

And silver. Ice clutched at her gut as an image of her last glimpse of the grove-sprite slipped into place. That warped face, suddenly taking on a look she recognized, and the silver tongue that darted from its laughing mouth, told her the truth. The creature in the grove had been no sprite, no guardian; it was Nemesis. The demon of her own dark self, architect of the evil she had wrought; her most deadly enemy.

The Earth Mother's emissary had warned her of Nemesis's treachery and urged her to take great care. But if the telltale signs had been visible, she had failed to see them in time. She had fallen prey to her demon's deception and had embroiled the innocent Grimya in the trap.

But what manner of trap? Of one thing Indigo was certain: they were no longer in the physical realm of Earth. And this was no dream: she knew the difference between reality and nightmare. They were, it seemed, on some astral plane; perhaps a part of—or at least a parallel to—the dreadful otherworld she had glimpsed when she walked the timeless road under the emissary's guidance. Her abruptly enhanced ability to communicate with Grimya was a further sign, but as to the form this world took, or its extent, she had no clues.

If only there were more light! It was impossible to tell if they were in the open or if the walls of some cell lay just beyond the borders of visibility. She thought she sensed openness, but knew how easily the mind could be deceived. And even if they weren't physically confined, this world itself, however large it might prove to be, was effectively a prison.

Grimya suddenly raised her ears. Her tail had stopped wagging and she stood stiffly alert, nose twitching as she sniffed the air uncertainly.

"What is it?" Indigo asked.

I don't know. There is something, but—And the reply broke off in a squealing yelp as, with no forewarning, the world lit up.

Indigo cried out in incoherent protest when light seared her unadjusted eyes, and jerked her head aside, covering her face with her hands as Grimya, with a howl of fear, bolted to take shelter behind her. It was some moments before she dared look again, through latticed fingers; when she did, she had to bite back the physical sickness of renewed shock.

As though an unseen hand had touched flame to a titanic lamp, the landscape around them was bathed in saffron-hued radiance that revealed a huge and bizarre vista of barren rock: peaks, crags, massive escarpments, sere and soilless and empty. They stood at the head of a bleak valley shot with shadows the color of long-dried blood—and overhead, hanging alone in a brooding crimson sky, was a black sun.

Indigo's hands fell to her sides and she stared, transfixed, at the valley, the crags, the insane sky, while her brain struggled to assimilate and make sense of what her eyes told her. The black sun had manifested in the sky from nowhere; it glared down, a celestial monstrosity surrounded by a ghostly, pulsing corona, and with each pulse the eerie daylight fluctuated as if the entire world were a vast room lit only by a single, failing candle.

At Indigo's back, Grimya howled again. Amid such desolation the sound was chilling, and Indigo dropped to a crouch beside the she-wolf, hugging her and trying to soothe her.

"Grimya, don't be afraid! It won't harm you—be calm now; try to be calm."

This is not my home! Grimya's anguished confusion battered her mind in a psychic shock wave. *I fear this place!*

Indigo, too, was afraid, but determined not to show it. She believed she was beginning to understand what had happened to them, and tried to convey it to the wolf. "It isn't *real*, Grimya! Can you understand that?" She clenched her teeth, gazing around and wondering how she could explain. "This is a demon world. It lies alongside our own world, but isn't a part of it."

Then we are far away from the forest?

"Yes . . . and no. The forest is close by, but we can't reach it, for it lies in another dimension."

Di-men-sion?

"Try to think of it as an invisible gateway between two worlds. We fell through that gateway, and now we've entered a world that didn't exist for us before."

Like dreaming? Grimya asked.

Indigo nodded. "Yes, very much like dreaming. But we're not asleep, and we won't awaken in the forest. If we're to escape, we must find the gateway again."

Grimya considered this for a few moments. Then: *The place of water and dark—was that the "gateway" you speak of?*

"Yes." She shivered, remembering the sprite, the

trickery, the revelation that had come too late. "The creature in the grove deceived me. I thought it was—"

A throaty growl interrupted her. *I know what it was! When you called me and I ran to find you, I recognized it as the demon I saw in your mind, and I knew it meant you harm.* Grimya looked up, her eyes feral crimson in the bloody light. *I tried to stop it, but I was too late. And then, when I tried to pull you back from the water, there were lights and noise, and . . . I found myself here. Now you have explained more, I think I understand what the demon has done.* She hesitated. *Do you think it means to kill us?*

Did it? Indigo wondered. If Nemesis was, as the Earth Mother's emissary had said, a part of her own self, then surely her death would result in its destruction. But if it had truly taken on an independent existence, matters might be very different. . . .

She shook her head, unable to reconcile her doubts. "I don't know, Grimya. I wish I could answer you, but I don't know."

Perhaps it doesn't matter, Grimya replied unhappily. *There's nothing to eat in this place, and nothing to drink. If we stay, we will die soon enough anyway.*

She was right—but the thought gave rise to another question. Had they been physically transported to this world, whatever and wherever it was, or did the crags and the bleak rock and the black sun exist only in their minds, whilst their unconscious bodies still lay in the grove? Experimentally, Indigo ran her hands over her torso, wincing as her fingers touched bruises on her rib cage. Pain was real enough, as was the growing thirst she felt. She turned her head to view the entire landscape, and shivered.

"We'll achieve nothing by staying where we are," she told Grimya. "Whatever form the gateway might take, there's no trace of it here." Her gaze was drawn toward the valley, a dark scar stretching ahead of them between forbidding cliffs. At their backs was the solid wall of an unscalable peak, to either side steep and treacherous shale slopes. The valley, it seemed, was the only route open to them.

Grimya, catching her thoughts, said: *Perhaps that is where the demon wants us to go.*

Perhaps it was. And Nemesis would have a reason, of that Indigo was certain. A trap, a confrontation . . . She took a firmer hold on her wavering confidence, aware that she had a simple choice to make. She could face the valley and whatever dangers it might hold, or give way to cowardice and admit defeat here and now.

She looked at the wolf. "Demon or no, I can see no option. I'm going into the valley. Will you come with me, Grimya?"

Grimya showed her fangs. *Of course. I am your friend.* Tentatively, her tail wagged once. *We won't know what lies ahead unless we look, will we?*

Her irrefutable logic brought a grim smile to Indigo's lips. "Indeed we won't," she said. "Very well, then; there's no point in delaying." Her eyes narrowed thoughtfully as she gazed into the lifeless valley. "And if we're fools, I suspect we'll discover the nature of our folly soon enough."

If the vale between the crags did indeed conceal the danger that Indigo feared, it seemed that the trap was not yet ready to spring. She couldn't estimate how long they had been walking through the narrow, shadowy defile; time, it seemed, had no relevance under the unchanging black sun, and minutes, hours, even days might have passed as they trudged along the valley floor.

There was still not the smallest sign of life. No grass grew anywhere among the barren rock, and not a single drop of water relieved the arid desolation. Once Indigo thought she heard the distant chuckle of a stream, and they quickened their pace eagerly to find its source. But the sound faded abruptly, and she realized that it had been an illusion.

After that, there were more deceptions. Odd echoes whispered between the crags, raising the hairs at the nape of Indigo's neck and making Grimya tense and crouch. Soft footsteps sounded in their wake, only to cease when they turned and saw the vale stretching empty and lifeless behind them. Petrified faces appeared and faded on the stratified rock walls to either side. And once, they saw a huge black boulder that blocked the way ahead. It seemed impassable, but as they approached it, it shimmered and took on, for a fleeting moment, the appearance of a vast, crouching beast before vanishing altogether.

As the hallucinations continued to haunt them, Grimya grew ever more uneasy and defensive, snarling at each new manifestation. Indigo's nerve, too, was badly shaken; so that they were both ill prepared for what lay ahead as they rounded a sharp curve in the vale.

Indigo, who was walking a few paces ahead, stopped and uttered a shocked oath, stretching out a warning hand to halt the wolf as she came alongside. A mere few feet in front of them, only now revealed as the path turned between two soaring crags, a huge crevasse cut across the vale. Massive rock buttresses leaned out to either side, and the far wall dropped sheer into utter darkness.

Grimya bared her teeth and the ruff of fur at her neck bristled. *Another illusion!*

"It may be; but I wouldn't care to wager on it." Experimentally, Indigo took a pace forward, feeling her foot slide suddenly on loose shale. The crevasse did not flicker and vanish as the giant boulder had done, and, mindful of her balance so close to the edge, she peered around the left-hand buttress. The black chasm stretched away into the cliff's deep shadows as far as she could see, and when she reached out a hand to the lip of the drop, she felt solid stone under her fingers.

"It's real." She straightened, backing away to put a safer distance between herself and the edge of the crevasse.

Too wide to jump, Grimya said. *What can we do now?*

"I don't know . . ." On the far side of the fault she could see the valley path continuing through the peaks. But there seemed to be a second path, diverging at the edge and running along a narrow ledge that overhung the sheer wall. Wondering, she leaned out, looking to the right—

Take care! Grimya warned.

"I will . . . but . . . *ah*!" Indigo's eyes gleamed as her suspicion that the path must surely lead somewhere was vindicated. "Grimya, look! There's a bridge!"

A bridge? Grimya edged cautiously forward until she too could look. And there, spanning out from wall to wall a short distance away, was a stone arch. Also on this side of the crevasse, a distinct track led to the bridge, following the curve of the cliff—which, they could now see, was far less steep than the opposite face. They way was easily negotiable, the bridge looked solid and uneroded; to traverse even the path on the far side, Indigo judged, would take no more than a strong nerve.

She turned to the she-wolf. "It's the only way across, Grimya. We *must* take it."

Grimya licked her nose, a little uncertain. *It will be easy for me. But you—*

"I used to go climbing on the cliffs of my homeland." Indigo smiled sadly at the memory of her flagrant childhood recklessness. "I'll be safe enough." And before Grimya could argue, she turned and moved toward the cliff edge.

The path was even easier than it looked. The slope of the crevasse was quite gentle, at least at this height; a few feet down, Indigo imagined, it must drop away as sheer as the far wall. But the gloomy light and the intense shadow in the cleft made it impossible to tell how deep the canyon below them was; she could maintain an illusion of safety that kept the dangers of vertigo at bay.

Cautiously she stepped onto the path, hearing the pad of Grimya's paws behind her. Negotiating the track proved a simple matter, providing she kept one palm flat against the rock wall for balance; in less than a minute she reached the wider ledge from which the bridge soared away across the canyon, and waited for Grimya to catch up.

"Well, the path was real enough," she said, stroking the wolf's head in an effort to reassure her. "Now it only remains to test the bridge."

I don't like it, Grimya insisted unhappily. *I will not feel safe until we are on the other side.*

"No; in truth, neither will I. And I'd suggest that we cross as quickly as we're able." She smiled, but the smile was uneasy. "I trust nothing in this place." Speculatively, she looked at the arch spanning out ahead of them. Though it had no parapet, its surface was broad and fairly even, and the distance to the far side seemed—

Indigo stopped in mid-thought as her mind and body froze.

Indigo? Grimya's anxious query seemed to come from a thousand miles away; she couldn't relate to it, couldn't answer. An inarticulate croak sounded deep in her throat and she stared, horrified, disbelieving, stunned, at the hunched and pain-racked figure amid the shadows on the far side of the stone bridge. Dark hair, tangled and lank with sweat; body twisted, eyes half blind and feverish in their sunken sockets. And he bled. Still he bled . . .

Illusion, her mind screamed; *illusion*! But logic was crumbling under the onslaught of a wild, longing hope, and she felt her control slipping.

"F—Fen . . ."

Indigo! Grimya's mental cry was frantic as the she-wolf realized the danger, but her warning went unheeded. Indigo gasped harshly, her voice barely recognizable:

"Fenran . . ."

The man across the bridge raised his head, and even that small movement seemed to cause him great pain. His eyes, dimmed by cataracts, tried to focus, and Grimya saw him raise one hand to his face in shock, heard the ghostly voice that echoed across the canyon.

"Anghara!"

Indigo shrieked, and with an appalling flash of prescience Grimya bunched her muscles and hurled herself forward in a desperate attempt to stop her friend. She was too late. Indigo rushed onto the bridge—and as her foot touched the first stone of the span, the bridge and Fenran vanished. For one terrible moment Grimya saw her teetering on the ledge, arms flailing wildly: then with a yell of terror Indigo pitched over the edge of the crevasse.

·CHAPTER·XV·

Indigo! Grimya's anguished mental cry broke from her throat as a high-pitched, despairing yelp, and her paws scrabbled on loose rock as she wriggled as close to the canyon's edge as she dared. *Indigo!* Grief swamped her; there could surely be no hope that her friend might have survived such a fall—

"Grimya . . ." The voice came weakly from just a little way below the edge of the drop, and the she-wolf started, every muscle tensing.

"I'm here, Grimya . . . beneath you. Be careful; the edge isn't stable. . . ."

Grimya looked over and saw her. She had slithered no more than ten feet down the slope of the canyon, and lay flat against the wall, feet precariously braced on a tiny lip of a ledge, both hands gripping protruding knobs of rock. Her face was smeared with dust and tears, and her teeth were clamped hard on her lower lip.

Indigo! Grimya's relief was short-lived. *Are you hurt?*

"No, I—don't think so. Just—shaken. And sorry, so very sorry—"

Sorry doesn't matter; what's done is done. Can you climb up?

"I don't know . . . it falls away sheer just below me, I think—no, don't try to look!" as Grimya peered out. "You might overbalance." Indigo drew two rapid breaths, licked a strand of hair from her mouth. "I *think* I can climb, but if I slip, there's nothing else to break my fall." She started to turn her head to look over her shoulder, then thought better of it. Remember the Southern Isles cliffs, she told herself. This is no worse; just higher.

Grimya watched in trepidation as Indigo took a firmer grip on her handholds and, cautiously, raised one foot until her toes scraped against a narrow crevice. She wedged her boot in the crack and, eyes shut and teeth clamped, raised her other foot from the ledge so that the crevice took her full weight. It didn't give way; she found another toehold, slightly higher; jammed her other foot into it, pushed. Hand over hand, with excruciating slowness, she levered herself up the slope, until at last Grimya was able to reach out, grip the shoulder of her coat between her teeth and help her over the edge to safety.

Indigo sprawled on the ledge, forehead pressed to the ground, lungs heaving with exertion and relief. Grimya fussed around her, licking and nuzzling, until she was able to raise her head. Her eyelashes were wet with fresh tears, and when she tried to speak she all but choked on the words.

"Grimya . . . Grimya, I'm so sorry. How could I have been such a *fool*?"

It doesn't matter! You are safe now; that's all that counts.

"But when I *saw* him, I thought—he looked so *real*, so *solid*—" She covered her face with her hands, unable to express her misery. "I didn't stop to think; but I should have known that if that monstrosity could trick me once, it could do so again."

I saw him, too, Grimya told her. *In your place, I would have made the same mistake. The illusion was very clever.*

Indigo wiped her cheeks and gazed across the black gash of the chasm. Nothing moved on the far side now, but the image of what she had seen was still agonizingly clear in her mind. Had it been no more than an illusion? She was well aware of Nemesis's skill and guile, and of her own weakness. But she couldn't help remembering the words of the Earth Mother's emissary; that Fenran was not truly dead, but was trapped in some eerie twilight between life and death, a prisoner in a world of demons.

A world akin to this . . .

She didn't want to ask herself the question that hammered in her brain; to give it any credence could lead her into new dangers far worse than the perils of the canyon. But the seeds had been sown, and they were rapidly and darkly taking root. It was possible, just possible, that the tormented figure she had seen was not a skillfully conjured mirage, but Fenran himself. And however cogently her wiser self might argue against it, a part of her that was too strong to ignore had grasped hold of that possibility and turned it into an insane hope. That part of her *believed*, and until the belief was dispelled beyond all doubt, she knew she would find no peace of mind.

Which might be precisely what Nemesis had intended.

She looked down into the canyon once more, then drew her feet back and stood upright. "There's no point in staying here any longer. We should go."

Grimya licked her own nose. *I would be happier to be away from this ledge. But I don't see how we can hope to continue our journey now. The chasm is impassable; there is nowhere else to go.*

"I'm not so sure." Something was nagging at the back of Indigo's mind, triggered by her unhappy thoughts about Fenran and about Nemesis's machinations. The demon had tried to kill her and had failed; it would not, she suspected, abandon its efforts, but would be planning another attempt on her life. Yet it must know that the same strategy would not work a second time. And that gave her a clue. . . .

She thought further about it as they made their careful way back along the cliffside path. Reaching safe ground, Grimya would have turned back into the valley, but hesitated when Indigo seemed reluctant to follow. Instead, the girl stood at the edge of the canyon, staring across the black gulf to where the track took up once more.

It is far too wide to jump. Grimya watched her friend anxiously, uncertain of her intentions. *Even the strongest wolf would fall to his death—don't think of it, Indigo. Please.*

Indigo came out of her reverie and looked at the she-wolf with a faint smile. "Don't fret, Grimya; I'm not about to do anything so foolish. But . . ."

But what?

Indigo pointed. "Look at the far side," she said. "The ledge path we saw there has vanished: it was as much a part of the illusion as the bridge. And that makes me wonder if . . ." Her voice trailed off thoughtfully and, to Grimya's horror she slid one foot forward, over the drop.

No! Don't—Then Grimya's yelp died stillborn as the air before Indigo vibrated, shimmered, solidified: and where an instant before there had been empty space, a bridge appeared across the great crevasse. Not an arch of stone this time, but a contraption of rope and planks, slung between wooden posts that had been hammered into cracks in the rock and now leaned at drunken angles.

Grimya's hackles rose and she snarled, *Another illusion!*

"I don't think so." Indigo took hold of one of the ropes and jerked hard on it. The bridge shook but did not dematerialize; she could feel the coarse solidity of the twisted rope strands in her fingers. "You see? It's as real as we are. And it was here all along—we simply couldn't see it!"

Grimya slunk forward mistrustfully, still half expecting this new manifestation to vanish before her eyes. She sniffed at the ropes, at the wooden posts. Real. There could be no doubt of it.

"The demon must know that we won't be deceived a second time by a bridge that vanishes when we try to cross it," Indigo said softly. "It will try again to kill us, but not yet."

Then it wants us to continue our search for the gateway?

"Perhaps. Or perhaps it can no longer prevent us." Indigo tested the bridge cautiously with one foot. Despite its flimsy appearance, it seemed capable of taking her weight. She thought of Fenran, then of Nemesis, and hatred flowered in her heart. She would *not* be mocked and tormented by that evil being; if this was a challenge, she was ready to face it.

"We *must* go on, Grimya. We know what lies behind us, and it offers us no hope. This is the only way."

Grimya moved to stand beside her, still eyeing the bridge uncertainly. Then she shook herself.

You are right. There is no other path we can follow if we hope to find the gateway from this place. But . . . let us go quickly. She looked up into Indigo's face. *Before my fear gets the better of me!*

The crossing was a nightmarish experience. Despite Grimya's anxiety—which Indigo privately shared—to reach the far side of the chasm as swiftly as possible, the rope-and-plank bridge swayed so violently at every step that they dared not progress at anything more than a stumbling and painfully slow pace. Clinging grimly to the ropes on either side of her, and trying not to think of the fate that would befall them should a single strand give way, Indigo kept her gaze steadfastly focused on Grimya staggering with splay-legged caution ahead of her, until at last, after what seemed an eternity, they finally jumped from the last rocking plank and onto solid ground.

Ahead of them the valley rose steeply into a defile that snaked away between two brooding peaks, its farther reaches lost in shadow. It didn't look prepossessing; the intense gloom could hide any number of horrors or perils, and there was no way to judge how far the dark cleft between the mountains might extend. Indigo looked up at the disturbing crimson sky and the monstrous black sun that hung there unmoving, and forced down the cold fear within her. To dissemble now would achieve nothing; they must face the defile, for there was not other way to go.

As much to reassure herself as the she-wolf, she reached down and patted Grimya's back. "Are you ready?"

Ready enough. Grimya's ears were flat to her head,

but she quelled her reluctance as, without a further word spoken, they moved into the pass.

Shadow like a vast, cold wing enveloped them. Indigo refused to look over her shoulder until she was sure the bridge must be out of sight; the temptation to turn and run back to what felt like comparative safety was already strong, and she feared her ability to resist it. She was aware, too, of the unknown dangers that could lie in wait for them, and her gaze flickered constantly this way and that, tensely alert for the smallest hint of trouble.

For some time they walked in silence broken only by her own footfalls and the quicker padding of Grimya's paws. The quiet was eerie and unnatural; it opened unhealthy gates into the imagination, and at last Indigo could bear it no longer. She had to speak—any word, however meaningless, was better than this enduring and awful emptiness—and began to say: "Grimya—"

The word was cut off by a vast and appalling voice that erupted into the vale from nowhere, a titanic hooting that smashed against their ears in an insane wall of sound. Indigo yelled in terror, clapping both hands to her head and reeling off the path to stagger against the sheer rock face; with vision blurred by tears of shock and pain she saw Grimya crouch, whirling like a maddened, cornered dog as she vainly sought the source of the hideous din.

The sound rang on and on, swelling and beating against Indigo's mind and body like a psychic tidal wave. Then suddenly the hooting shattered into a monstrous cascade of insane laughter that made her scream anew—though her voice was utterly lost in the gargantuan onslaught of noise—and stopped. Vast echoes shouted away and away over the mountains, receding and fading until the vale sank finally into crawling silence.

Very slowly, Indigo opened her eyes. She was on her knees, face pressed flat to the cliff, hands clutching at the unyielding stone as though in blind panic she'd been trying to claw her way through it to escape the horrific onslaught. Her fingernails were broken, and blood seeped from beneath them; she felt the sting of grazes on her cheeks, and her temple throbbed where she had collided with the rock. She couldn't believe it, couldn't assimilate—her body shook with a series of huge, painful shudders and she crawled back from the cliff, jaw working, gasping for breath.

Behind her, a thin whining intruded on the enormous gulf of silence. And there was Grimya, belly flat to the ground, teeth bared, shaking as though overcome with a terrible palsy. The she-wolf's eyes stared, unfocused; when Indigo crawled to her side and touched her, she started as though shot, and only when the girl slipped her arms round the densely furred neck and held her tightly did some measure of intelligence return to the wolf's look.

Wh . . . wh . . . Even telepathically, Grimya couldn't articulate the stunned question. *What was . . .*

"I don't know . . . may the Earth Mother help us, Grimya, I don't know!" A stone shifted under her foot and Indigo felt her skin tighten with momentary terror, as though the slightest untoward noise might trigger the return of the monstrous voice.

I have never heard anything so dreadful! Grimya was regaining some measure of self-control; she sat upright, shaking her head. *My ears . . . they hurt.* She blinked rapidly. *Do you think it was another of the demon's tricks?*

"I don't know: I only hope it was. If there's anything big enough to possess a voice like that inhabiting these mountains, I don't want to risk a closer encounter with it." Indigo got unsteadily to her feet, and her eyes narrowed as she stared along the gloomy track ahead. Nothing moved, nothing disturbed the quiet, and anger began to supersede the receding shock in her brain.

"I think that Nemesis is playing games with us," she said with soft venom. "Its first effort to kill us failed, so now it tries to frighten us, and make us easier prey for its second attempt."

I would rather believe that than believe some vast monster lies in wait for us. At least with the demon we know what we are facing, Grimya replied with some feeling. *We should go on, without any more delay. Show this creature that we are unafraid.*

She was right. Indigo brushed the pervasive red-brown dust from her clothing and licked dry lips. "Yes . . . but we must be doubly on our guard from now on."

The trail wound on between the peaks, climbing gradually but steadily higher as it penetrated deeper into the mountains. So far there had been no further illusions, no new sign of Nemesis's trickery, but Indigo was constantly alert for danger. Every now and then she looked up at the unnatural star flickering gloomily above them. Its position in the sky still hadn't changed, and uneasily she remembered how the black sun had sprung so instantaneously above the horizon to change night into day. It seemed as though the laws that governed time in her own world had run amok here, and she wondered how she and Grimya would fare if the star were to vanish as suddenly as it had risen and leave them in darkness. The thought made her quicken her pace, but only for a moment, as she realized that she was being foolish. They had no idea how far this trail extended or where it was leading them; if the capricious forces that governed this parody of nature chose to play a new joke on them now, they were powerless to avert it.

Grimya, she noticed, was beginning to flag. The she-wolf had fallen behind and her head hung low, tail dragging in the dust. Indigo stopped to allow her to catch up, then stroked her head.

"You're weary, I know," she said sympathetically. "But we must keep walking, Grimya. There's nothing for us here." She gazed at the trail winding on before them. "This path can't go on forever; we must surely come to the end soon."

Grimya's tongue lolled. *I can endure. But I would give much for some water to drink.*

For a few moments neither of them noticed the faint sound that followed on the heels of Grimya's last words. Distant, vague, it was a little like the gentle rustle of leaves in a light breeze—or, Indigo thought with a shock as she suddenly became aware of its presence and her mind abruptly attuned, like the muffled chatter of an underground stream.

Her fingers clenched in the wolf's fur and she said huskily, "Grimya—"

I hear it! The hair on Grimya's spine rose, bristling. The sound was growing louder by the moment, and more discernible. *Water! It sounds like water!*

And Grimya had at that very moment been complaining of thirst . . . Realization hit Indigo like a bolt, and at the same instant the distant noise swelled to a liquid roar—

"Grimya, get away from the path!" she yelled. "Climb the cliff, as high as you can! *Quickly*!"

They raced toward a place where a rock fall had formed a steep but scalable spur, and as they scrambled over the treacherous boulders it seemed that the entire cliff began to quake. The approaching roar dinned in their ears, louder, closer—Indigo slipped, grazing her hands and shins; Grimya grabbed her sleeve, frantically pulling her to her feet again. Then round the curve of the track ahead, moving with the speed of a riptide and deafening them with its titanic noise, a sheer wall of foaming, churning water came thundering through the canyon.

"*Grimya!*" Indigo clung to the wolf's neck, pressing herself flat against the cliff and struggling to keep her balance as the boulders beneath her feet rolled and shifted under the flashflood's onslaught. Flying spray smacked against her unprotected back with a force that all but knocked her from her precarious hold; as the canyon shook to the echoing racket, she saw the torrent as a blurred concussion of racing black water and fountaining white spume, waves and cross-currents leaping and smashing together in the wild chaos.

Suddenly a boulder under her left foot moved, dislodged as the thundering water pounded against the foot of the spur. With a groan and scrape of rock against rock that was drowned by the flood's din, it rolled from its place, taking others with it, and Indigo felt her balance going. She scrabbled frantically for purchase, her foot flailing at empty air—then, even as Grimya tried to turn and aid her, she slipped from her perch and went sliding back down the slope, tumbling helplessly toward the torrent—

To land, bruised but otherwise unhurt, on the dry, undisturbed track at the bottom of the cliff.

"Uhh." The wordless protest cut the appalling silence, and turned into a painful, ugly retching as Indigo rolled over, her stomach heaving. It was a blind reaction to terror and shock and confusion; she clutched at her gut, trying to drag air down into her lungs and bring her muscles under control, and when the spasms finally subsided she was on all fours, shaking.

Dust under her hands and knees. *Dust.* But . . .

Indigo! Claws scrabbled on rock and Grimya bounded toward her. *I thought you were—*

"I know." Her stomach tried to heave again; she put the back of one hand to her mouth, drawing breath between clenched teeth. The wolf nuzzled her face, and at last she was able to kneel upright. There was dust in her mouth; she wiped it again, spat. "It was another illusion . . ." And she thanked the Earth Mother for it; for had it been real, her broken body would now be tumbling down the canyon in that murderous current.

Grimya looked along the track and showed her teeth. *I spoke of being thirsty,* she said darkly. *And—*

"Don't." Indigo put out a hand to touch her warningly. "Don't say it, Grimya." Her self-control was returning, though the queasiness wouldn't leave her, and as she got slowly to her feet she could feel a fuse of rage burning inside her. "It seems that our demon friend has a sense of humor. You spoke of water, and water we had—but not as we might have anticipated. And before, when we heard that—that voice . . ."

The voice?

"Yes. You didn't know it, but at that very moment I was about to speak to you, say the first thing that came into my head, because I couldn't bear the silence any longer. I *wished* for something to break it." The fuse in her mind was burning still, fueled by hatred, by fury at being so carelessly mocked and tormented. "The demon still plays with our minds. But it hasn't the courage to show itself and face us directly." She swung around, turning her face to the canyon ahead of them. "Have you? *Have you*?"

Her shout echoed away: nothing answered. Uneasily, Grimya watched as she strode up the track, breaking into a run for several paces, then slowed and stopped.

"Where are you?" Indigo yelled. "Damn your filthy tricks, I'm not afraid of you! *Show yourself*!" She spun on her heel, fists clenched and raised as though to strike out at the smallest sign of movement. The canyon was utterly and indifferently still.

Grimya trotted to join her. *It's no use. It will not come to us, not like this.*

"Very well." Indigo's jaw was set in a harsh line. "Then I'll find another way. If it's so fond of granting us twisted wishes, let it grant this one! I wish—"

Be careful!

Indigo ignored her. The fuse had burned out, recklessness had overtaken fury and she no longer cared for the consequences of anything she might do. Raising her voice, she called loudly, "I wish this path to end! Do you hear me, you Nemesis, you evil child, you spawn of darkness? *I wish this path to end*!"

For a moment there was no sound, nothing but the eerie stillness. Then, seemingly close by yet echoing as though from a vast distance, something chuckled.

Grimya spun around, dropping to an aggressive crouch, and Indigo looked quickly behind her. The canyon was empty. No silver-eyed figure, no horrors, nothing. Only the memory of that eldritch, quicksilver laugh. As though from its lair—whatever and wherever that lair might be—Nemesis was answering her challenge with a challenge of its own. And just a short way before them the defile turned sharply around a massive rock buttress that hid the trail ahead from view. . . .

She smiled. It was a vicious, private smile, the smile of a predator scenting its quarry. "Grimya." Her voice was deceptively soft. "We must go on. It's just a little way now." And without waiting for an answer, she began to run toward the buttress and the turn in the track.

She heard the wolf running to catch up with her, but didn't slow or wait. The buttress was only yards ahead, the path steeper suddenly so that she plowed uphill, and her pulse was racing with more than physical effort. Then suddenly she was level with the buttress, turning, rounding the sharp bend—

Indigo stopped, and stared in chagrin at the vista that had opened out before her.

Her wish had been granted. The defile was at an end—and in one foolhardy moment it seemed that she had brought them to an absolute impasse. A steep-sided valley lay directly before them, enclosed by tall crags that reached impassively into the crimson sky. There was no trail leading away onto those slopes; their path simply curved away down into the vale. And the entire valley floor was covered by a vast, still, opaque and unguessably deep lake.

Grimya slithered to a halt by Indigo's side, panting. For some moments the she-wolf stared at the lake below them; then she raised her head to scan her friend's face. Indigo's expression was tight, withdrawn, bitter; no words were needed to tell Grimya that she was inwardly cursing her own foolishness.

The wolf lowered her head again, and her nose twitched, nostrils flaring wide. Suddenly she moved forward and slithered, with great caution, a little way down the slope toward the lake's surface.

"Grimya?" Indigo came out of her reverie, and her voice was sharp. "What are you doing? Be careful!"

Grimya hesitated, still sniffing. Then she turned tail and bounded back to the girl's side. There was a spark of excitement in her eyes, and she said:

It isn't water!

Indigo frowned, nonplussed. "What do you mean?"

Just what I say! I can't smell water, Moisture, yes, but not water. There's a difference. And no water that I have ever seen is white and cloudy like that. This is not a lake!

Acid? Indigo thought. She had seen the opaque, deadly liquids sometimes used by the apothecaries of her father's court, and she shuddered inwardly at the thought of what a lake of such stuff could do to flesh and bone. But surely Grimya's acute sense of smell could discern such a lethal cocktail? Moisture, she had said. Just moisture . . .

Look at the way it moves, Grimya said. *Not like water. More like fog.*

Fog! Irrational hope flared up as Indigo recalled the way the autumn mists lay pooled in the valleys of the Southern Isles, for all the world like huge, calm tracts of water. She looked quickly at Grimya. "There's only one way to be sure."

Yes. Grimya was already starting off down the slope again, moving in a careful, crabwise manner, and Indigo followed. The descent was rough enough to prevent sliding, and there was little loose rubble to make the going treacherous; a few inches from the still, white surface they halted, and Grimya leaned down to test the lake with her nose.

"Wait," Indigo cautioned. "Let me. If it's something deadly, my boot will give me some protection."

She stretched out one foot. Her boot vanished into the whiteness, which billowed and shifted sluggishly. There was no splash, only the silent movement of the cloudy mass.

"Mist." She tried to keep the excitement from her voice. "Not a liquid: mist. If it's breathable air, and not some poison—"

Grimya leaned down and sniffed. *We can breathe it.*

It is safe. She looked up. *But how far is it to the bottom?*

"We can only try to find out." Indigo probed with her foot, allowing herself to slide a little farther down the slope. "I can still feel solid rock. If we go carefully, we shouldn't come to any harm."

Gingerly they lowered themselves into the dense fog. It was a peculiar experience, like sinking slowly into a calm sea; as they inched their way down, the mist rose and lapped around their legs, their bodies, their chins, until finally they were immersed in a strange, muffled, white world. Droplets of moisture clung to their hair and to Indigo's clothes; within moments her garments were chill and clammy against her skin, but after the aridity of the canyon she welcomed the sensation. Grimya licked delightedly at the fog, soothing her parched throat; dimly seen through the drifting veils, she looked bizarre, her fur plastered to her skin, her tongue lapping and lapping.

The steep slope began to decrease, and suddenly Indigo felt something beneath her fingers that was not rock. She peered down, and made out a dense cushion of what looked like grass under her hands; clenching one fist, she tore a few blades free and examined them more closely. Grass, yes; or grasslike—but *blue.* She peered through the fog at the shadowy figure of Grimya.

"I think we're near the bottom." Her voice was oddly flat; the mist gave back no echoes. She could stand upright now, she realized, without fear of falling. Three more paces, and the slope flattened out to even ground carpeted with the same strange blue grass.

Grimya slithered down the last of the descent to join her, and together they gazed about them. The mist shifted in a slow parade of pale, writhing tendrils, creating shadows and phantoms; if any solid structures lay within the vale, they were hidden from view.

Where now? Grimya asked.

It hardly seemed to matter; chances were that, whichever direction they took, their route would meander. And that in itself could be a danger, for if they lost touch with the valley slopes, they might wander forever in this white world without finding a way out again.

Indigo turned to her left and pointed into the fog. "We'll go this way," she said, "but we'll keep to where the ground just begins to rise, so that if we want to climb out we can find the slope easily."

That is sensible. Grimya's tail wagged approvingly. *What do you think we might encounter here?*

"Who knows?" Indigo smiled grimly. "We must wait and see."

Indigo soon began to wonder if perhaps she was not awake, but asleep and dreaming. Time and dimensions had no discernible meaning in this eerie world of shifting whiteness; she and Grimya seemed to have been walking forever through unchanging veils of moist nothing, forging like drifting swimmers in a slow, endless current. The fog created strange phantasms, shapes that quivered on the edge of vision only to dissolve back into nothing; images that loomed formlessly, their scale and distance unguessable, then faded and became one with the uneasy gloom. Only the sensation of the ever-present moisture on her skin and the soft padding of Grimya's paws behind her held Indigo's mind to any semblance of reality. She couldn't tell how far they had come, or how far they must go before they had circumnavigated the entire valley.

And then, among the hallucinations and the mist-ghosts, a shape appeared that did not swirl back into the whiteness and vanish. A blur of dimmer solidity in the fog, motionless in their path—but how far ahead?

She couldn't tell—but it seemed, to her disoriented mind, to be waiting for them.

"Grimya . . ." She whispered the warning, and the sound was absorbed by the mist. Grimya did not answer.

"Grimya?" Indigo turned and looked back. There was no dark shape moving behind her, no sound of padding feet. Grimya was not there.

Her heart began to race unevenly. Where was Grimya? Moments ago—was it only moments, or had her disordered sense of time deceived her?—the she-wolf had been at her heels. Now she was gone, as though the mist had enfolded and dissolved her like one of its own phantoms.

"Grimya . . ."

A soft, malign chuckle made her whirl. The white fog before her agitated, the veils parted briefly, so that her vision was momentarily unobscured. And not five paces from her she saw the figure of a child, its silver hair shining softly, its silver eyes regarding her with cool and malevolent acknowledgment, and a small, cruel smile of greeting on its feline face.

·CHAPTER·XVI·

Nemesis said: "Welcome," and Indigo felt the twin sicknesses of loathing and fear rise within her as she realized that the demon's voice was identical to her own.

"Where is Grimya?" The words were a harsh snarl. "What have you done with her?"

Nemesis showed its sharp cat's teeth. "I have no interest in your beast-friend. She will doubtless return when she has a mind to." The smile widened. "You are the one of concern to me."

Indigo flexed her right hand, almost reaching for her knife before she remembered that it, together with her crossbow and harp, was a world away, beyond the boundaries of the sacred grove in the Horselands forest. Nemesis laughed.

"Weapons would be of little use to you here, Indigo."

"Maybe. But you still won't find me an easy victim to kill!"

"Kill?" The child raised pale eyebrows in mock chagrin. "Oh, no. You gave me life; our destinies are inextricably linked. I have no wish to do you harm."

"Liar! You've already tried to destroy me—"

"Not destroy." A snakelike tongue flickered momentarily. "Perhaps I frightened you a little, but you have come to no real mischief at my hands. I simply intended to show you something of what I can do." It paused, then chuckled again. "Or should I say, what *you* can do? It's all one, is it not?"

A nauseously hollow feeling pervaded Indigo's stomach as she saw what Nemesis was implying, and she retorted savagely, "Don't try to turn me to your twisted logic! You're nothing but offal, corruption, filth—"

"Harsh words, from my progenitor."

"Damn you!" She lunged forward, striking out, and her fist sank into a curtain of empty mist as Nemesis's form flickered and vanished. "*Damn* you!"

A mocking voice to her right said, "Have a care whom your curses fall upon, Indigo, lest you should damn yourself!"

She whirled. Four paces away, Nemesis stood smiling at her. She fought down an impulse to lunge for it again, and said through clenched teeth:

"What do you want from me?"

The snake's tongue flicked again. "Ask yourself that question. Ask your heart, ask your soul: what do *you* want, in your deepest dreams?" The demon raised one hand in a sweeping gesture, indicating that she should look to her left. "This, perhaps?"

Indigo turned her head, and a ghastly sound rattled in her throat. Wreathed in the fog, stooping and racked, a dark phantom amidst the white veils, was Fenran. He stood with one arm outstretched as though to ward off some invisible horror, and his mouth was open in a soundless cry, but he did not move. It was as though she glimpsed a single, frozen moment of his nightmare existence.

Indigo's lungs heaved, and she spat, *"Illusion!"*

"Yes," said Nemesis. "Illusion." The tortured figure vanished. "But it could be otherwise."

Ice-cold fingers clutched at her mind as she recalled what she had seen at the chasm, what she had hoped, what she had wanted to believe.

"The choice is yours alone," Nemesis added with soft amusement. "But my patience is not infinite." Its form wavered, so that for an instant she could see tendrils of mist through its translucent body. "And if you lose me now, you may not find me again." Silver eyes glinted ferally, briefly—and Nemesis disappeared.

"No!" Indigo's shout of protest fell away into empty fog. *"Come back!"*

Laughter like a shower of glass shards rang in the distance. "Find me, Indigo. For Fenran's sake, find me. If you can!"

She lurched forward into the fog, arms groping before her. "Damn you to hell! I command you, *return*!"

"Command yourself, my sister." Something shimmered in the whiteness ahead and Indigo stumbled after it. "Run!" All pretense of kindness was gone from the distant voice now; it was a vicious, mocking challenge. "Run!"

She ran, blinded by tears of rage. Nemesis's laughter led her on, one moment tantalizingly closer, the next receding, so that she forced herself to greater effort, her feet slipping on the alien, dew-soaked grass. As she ran she was swearing, cursing, sobbing, and so desperately intent on her fleeing quarry that she didn't hear the rush of something running to intercept her, didn't see the blur of a dark form streaking low to the ground across her path.

Indigo! Grimya came racing out of the fog, misjudged her distance, and they collided. Indigo lost her footing and went sprawling; when, dazed, she picked herself up, her eyes were glazed with misery and shock.

I lost you! Grimya was breathless. *The fog thickened suddenly, and you were nowhere to be seen. I searched and searched. . . . Indigo, what has happened to you?*

The cold, damp air was raw in her throat, and for a few seconds she couldn't speak. At last words came, haltingly, gaspingly.

"Nemesis—it was here, tormenting me! I saw . . ." She shook her head.

Has it hurt you?

"No . . . it doesn't want to kill me, Grimya. It wants—" And she broke off as from the shifting fog the crystalline laughter sounded again.

Grimya called out as Indigo sprang to her feet, but her cry went unheeded. Indigo was already running, plunging into the mist, and the she-wolf bounded after her, afraid of losing sight of her a second time. Zigzagging like a drunkard, Indigo raced over the grass—then with a cry of shock echoed by Grimya's startled yelp, she swerved aside when what had looked until that moment like a white blanket of mist revealed itself suddenly as a vast, solid wall blocking the way ahead of them. Indigo reeled back and all but overbalanced; Grimya skidded to a halt beside her, and they both stared at the smooth face of veined white marble that stretched into the fog as far as the eye could see in all directions.

Indigo reached out and touched the wall, not entirely convinced that it wouldn't melt away into the mist as so much else had done. But it was real—and its smoothness was too complete, too uniform, to be natural.

An unpleasantly familiar chuckle whispered through

the fog to her right, and she turned quickly, pacing along the wall. Ahead, something interrupted the marble's symmetry, and as she drew closer she saw that the wall was broken by an arch, twice her own height, set into the stonework. Beyond the arch—where, strangely, the mist didn't penetrate—was darkness.

She turned to look at Grimya, who had followed her. "I'm going in. You don't have to come with me, Grimya, but I must find Nemesis again."

Grimya snorted. *Do you think I would leave you to face whatever is in there alone?* She padded forward, peered into the gateway's black maw. *I scent nothing untoward. Shall we find out what the demon has in store?*

They stepped under the arch, and emerged from the mist so abruptly that for a moment Indigo was disoriented, feeling oddly vulnerable without the soft white fog to cloak her. Grimya shook herself, sending a fine spray of water showering everywhere, then padded a few paces forward. Indigo followed; her eyes strained into the gloom, but all she could make out were the faintly reflective marble walls of a corridor or tunnel stretching ahead. The floor, too, was of marble, and she could feel the chill of its smooth surface striking up through the soles of her boots. If this place had been created by demons, she thought, its solidity and form were reassuring nonetheless. She might have been walking in one of the gracious eastern palaces her mother had so often described to her, or . . .

The thought trailed off into an uneasy *frisson*, an abrupt realization that something about this corridor was vaguely familiar. She stopped, staring at the veined walls and racking her memory, but the link wouldn't come.

Indigo? Grimya was some way ahead of her and had

stopped to look back. She was in shadow, only her eyes shining. *There are steps here.*

Pushing the unanswered question aside, Indigo went to join her, and saw that the passage ended in a flight of stairs that turned obliquely downward. The sense of recognition came back, stronger this time, but again its nature eluded her when she tried to grasp it.

Should we follow the steps? Grimya asked.

"Yes . . . yes, I think we should." She took the lead this time, Grimya following and making heavy weather of the stairs' unfamiliar contours, and still the nagging thought was there at the back of her mind. She had walked this route before, or one so like it that the differences were almost imperceptible. But where? *Where?*

Then it came to her, and the revelation was so shocking that she stopped dead, an awful, strangled sound bubbling in her throat.

What is it? Grimya hastened to her side, peering down into the gloom. A short way below them the flight of stairs ended in a tall, narrow arch; beyond, a flicker of pale light showed faintly.

"I . . . can't." Indigo felt as though she were suffocating as she stared in dawning horror at the doorway. "It's . . . I *can't*!" She began to shiver uncontrollably.

There's light ahead. Grimya tried her best to be reassuring, but she was confused and troubled by Indigo's untoward behavior.

Oh, yes; there would be light right enough. The warm and welcoming light of the fire that burned in the great hearth of the room beyond the doorway. She knew it all—the corridor, these stairs, the arch, the hall—because it was as familiar to her as her own body. She had known it all her life, and the fact that the dimensions were slightly out of kilter, and that the granite had changed to marble, made not one whit of difference.

They were in Carn Caille.

She couldn't move. Grimya's whining and nuzzling provoked no reaction; only when the wolf thrust her cold nose, hard, into one of the girl's clenched fists did she finally jerk away with a convulsive movement.

What's wrong? Grimya asked anxiously. *I see nothing to fear!*

"Oh, but I do. . . ." The words grated between Indigo's teeth. Slowly, almost unaware of what she was doing, she took a step down and felt an uneven dip in the marble, a place where a piece of the stair had chipped away, so many years ago that the ragged edge was now worn smooth again. This would be the fifth step from the bottom . . . she looked, counted, bit her tongue as memory was confirmed. She had fallen on that stair once, when she was six years old, and Imyssa had comforted her and bathed the graze with one of her herbal nostrums. . . . The shivering broke into a racking spasm that jarred her spine, and she took another step. Grimya kept pace, worriedly looking up into her eyes and trying to glean her thoughts. But they were too turbulent, too uncontrolled. . . . Another step, another, and she was at the foot of the flight, facing the arched and open door.

This was what Nemesis had meant when it taunted her with her own longings. *Ask your heart, ask your soul: what do you want, in your deepest dreams?* She had known the answer then, but had refused to acknowledge or admit to it. Now it had risen from the realm of ghosts to confront her.

Indigo stumbled forward and clutched at the carved stonework that framed the archway. She couldn't run from this—there was nowhere for her to flee. She could only face it, and pray that her courage would not fail her.

She took a deep, deep breath, the cold air sawing in her throat, and stepped over the threshold.

Everything was as she knew it. There were the high windows, curtained against night. There were the long feasting tables, though they, like the walls, had been transformed into marble. There was the magnificent hearth, the fire blazing—but the flames were not the comforting orange-gold of true fire. Instead they burned a pale and nacreous blue, giving off no heat. Ghost-flames; an echo of reality in the empty hall.

She didn't want to turn her head to where she knew the royal dais must be, but a compulsion was on her to know all or nothing. And there was the high table, the king's huge carved chair; marble now, like the rest, its rich crimson cushions changed to a pale, icy blue-green.

All ghosts . . .

In the depths of the king's chair, a slender figure stirred.

Grimya growled, hackles bristling, and Indigo felt the wolf's fur brush warm against her leg as Nemesis rose with obscene grace to its feet. It held out a hand, a sardonic parody of royal greeting.

"Welcome home, Indigo."

Indigo hissed a curse and turned her head sharply aside, repelled and maddened by the sight of such a creature occupying the place—even a replica of the place—that had been her father's. Her fingers clenched in Grimya's fur; the wolf's presence gave her a thread of comfort, but it was a thin and insecure thread.

"This is not my home!" She snapped the words out with all the contempt she could muster, and Nemesis gave its soft chuckle.

"True. And Carn Caille—the *real* Carn Caille—is

barred to you. But it could be otherwise." The demon smiled, regarding her calculatingly. "If you wish it."

"I do not wish it!" Indigo's furious rebuttal was supported by a snarl from Grimya. Nemesis ignored the wolf and returned to the chair, tracing a pattern on the carved arms as it paced measuredly around the dais. Then it stopped, looked back at her, and the silver eyes flashed with dangerous confidence.

"Are you sure of that? You were happy in Carn Caille, after all. Most of your memories are fond ones, are they not?" And it snapped its fingers.

Indigo was utterly unprepared for what happened. She opened her mouth to curse Nemesis afresh—and her jaw locked in disbelieving horror as a figure stepped through the door, behind the dais, that her family alone had used. Auburn hair, graying but still abundant; an economy to his movement that belied his heavy build, the mark of the skilled and seasoned warrior; the robes; the studded belt; the ceremonial sword; the tear in his cloak that Imyssa had mended—

Indigo stumbled backward, almost falling over Grimya, and put a hand to her mouth as her voice rose in a wail.

"Father . . ."

Nemesis snapped its fingers again. And behind Kalig came Queen Imogen, serene, smiling, taking her husband's hand with graceful formality as they moved toward their places. And on her heels Kirra, hair rumpled, grinning as though at some private joke.

Her family. Her closest kin; her lost, dead loved ones. . . . Indigo tried to shout a denial of this hideous impossibility, but the only sound she could make was a thin, inarticulate cry of pain and distress. On her knees now, and unconscious of Grimya, who stood snarling and bristling with protective menace in front of her, she could only watch, transfixed, as Nemesis glided aside to allow the king and queen to take their places at the high table. Her mother's lips were moving, and her father laughed in reply; but no sound emanated from their mouths. And they acknowledged neither Nemesis nor their stunned and shuddering daughter, but sat in their chairs, and heaped invisible food onto invisible plates, and lifted invisible winecups to their lips. They were mummers, playing their roles in ghastly silence; ghosts who in death meaninglessly pantomimed the everyday pleasures they had pursued in life.

"Memories," Nemesis said cruelly. "Do they not remind you of the heritage that has been stolen from you?"

Indigo heard Grimya's mental voice as the voice of one trying to wake her from a nightmare, calling from the real world but unreachable, unconnected; only when the wolf hurled her warm, solid body against her did the words break through and take coherence in her mind.

Indigo, what is it? What do you see? Tell me!

"My family . . ." Her tongue was desiccated and shrunken in her mouth, and she raised one trembling hand, pointing at the high table. "They're here, in this hall—*my family*!"

Grimya looked, and saw only Nemesis and the empty chairs. The demon smiled at her confusion.

"Your beast-friend lacks our subtlety, Indigo." It took a pace forward and Grimya dropped to a crouch, baring her fangs threateningly. Nemesis ignored her, but the wolf's intervention broke Indigo's paralysis.

"They're dead." She got to her feet, advanced one pace, two, toward Nemesis. Behind the demon, at the high table, Kalig and Imogen and Kirra continued their silent, empty masquerade; she couldn't bear to look at them. "Dead," she repeated. "You can't bring them back. You can't make me *believe* that you can bring them back!''

''Indeed.'' Nemesis acknowledged the truth of that with a sly inclination of its head. ''I'm not such a fool as to attempt to deny that. But while your family may be beyond my ability to restore, there is another whom you loved; and he still lives, in his own fashion. *He* is the crux of the bargain I would make with you.''

What little color remained in Indigo's face drained away; her skin was suddenly as gray as a winter sky. ''Bargain . . . ?'' *No,* something within her screamed. *Don't listen; don't let the words be so much as spoken—*

Nemesis smiled, an obscenity in the innocent child's face. ''Let me show you what I have to offer.'' It raised one hand, made a careless gesture, and the shades of Kalig, Imogen and Kirra froze. Another gesture, and the figures dissolved like smoke blowing on a light breeze. Indigo stared, numb, at the empty places, and Nemesis held out its hand toward the door behind the dais.

He staggered onto the platform as though pushed by invisible hands and stood swaying, dazed, gripping the edge of the high table for support. Indigo tried to give voice to the violent rejection that shrieked in her brain, but her vocal cords were frozen, locked. She could only stare at his sweat-dampened black hair, the bones of his face stark in his skull, the gray eyes unfocused and wild with the memory of images she couldn't comprehend. He wore the bloodstained clothes in which she had seen him fall to the demon in the courtyard of Carn Caille. And still, horribly, hideously, he bled. . . .

Grimya raised her head and uttered a long-drawn, terrible howl. The sound snapped Indigo from her shocked hiatus, and, her voice breaking, she cried out.

"Fenran . . . oh, my love!"

Painfully, Fenran raised his head. Their gazes met, and intelligence flooded into his eyes as though someone had struck him full in the face. He lurched against the table, stumbled, almost fell to his knees. *"Anghara!"*

She took a trembling pace toward him, stopped as she realized she didn't dare approach him lest he too should dissolve into nothing and be lost to her. "Fenran, what have they done to you?" Shaking, she turned on the smiling demon. *"What have you done?"*

"You know your lover's fate." Nemesis's eyes were malevolent. "And he will continue to suffer as he suffers now, unless you choose to free him."

Indigo began to back away from the dais. "He isn't real," she hissed, knowing even as she spoke that she didn't believe her own words. "You're trying to deceive me; he's no more real than my father, my mother, my—"

"He is as real as you." Nemesis cut across her protest with cruel indifference. "See for yourself. Touch him."

"I . . ."

"Touch him, Indigo."

She was terrified of rising to the challenge, but an inner compulsion made her walk slowly forward and mount the dais. As though caught in a terrible dream, she saw Fenran raise his head. Her eyes took in every detail of his ravaged face: the sweat, the strain, the cracked and papery texture of his skin, the sunken cheeks and eye-sockets. They had broken him, in body if not in spirit, and the terrible look in his eyes that mingled hope with fear and an inability to believe was almost more than she could bear.

Her hand trembled, palsied, as she reached out toward him. Weakly Fenran raised one arm, tried to whisper her name: his fingers caught hers and she shut her eyes with a moan of distress as she felt his feeble, shuddering grip.

"Fenran—" She started forward to embrace him, but Nemesis rapped out, "Enough!" A cold fork of light flashed like earthbound lightning across the hall, crackling between Indigo and Fenran, and a terrific force threw the girl off-balance. She pitched backward from the dais and heard Fenran's cry of angry protest echoed by Grimya's snarl as she fell heavily to the floor. The wolf ran to aid her; cursing, sobbing, she struggled to her feet and turned on the demon.

"Damn you! *Let me go to him!*"

Nemesis gazed down at her, its silver eyes coldly calculating. "You are satisfied, then, that he is not simply another illusion?"

"Yes!" she fired back with bitter venom. "I am satisfied of that!"

"Then would you not free him from his torment?" Nemesis gestured to where Fenran had slumped back into the chair, now barely conscious, it seemed. "Look at your lover. Has he not suffered enough? Don't you want him by your side again?"

Indigo, don't listen to the demon, don't listen! It might have been Grimya calling to her, it might have been her own inner self; she didn't know, didn't care. Again her eyes drank in Fenran's figure. She couldn't turn her back on him. She *couldn't.*

She said, her voice barely audible, "What is your price for Fenran's release?"

Grimya snarled, and Fenran's head came up. Nemesis smiled, its small, feral teeth gleaming in the unnatural firelight.

"My price is simple, Indigo. I want you to yield to me, merge with me, so that we may live as one entity again.'' It paused, then added softly: ''Is that so much to pay for your lover's life?''

Indigo looked at Fenran, her face agonized, and the warnings of the Earth Mother's emissary rang anew in her mind. *Your salvation or your doom.* To do what Nemesis wanted of her would be to bow to the evil within herself, and open the floodgates to the demons she had unleashed from the Tower of Regrets. Their monstrous influence would spread through the world with nothing to stand against it, and her quest would be ashes even before it had begun. She would betray the Earth Mother's trust.

But there was another trust, another duty. Her love, her tortured love, at the mercy of all the horrors of this world. To turn her back on him, even for the greater good, was surely another kind of evil. She couldn't do it. She was too human, too fallible—

Your salvation or your doom . . .

Her jaw worked spasmodically and she tried to deny what she already knew to be the truth. ''You're lying.'' Her voice was shrill. ''You haven't the power to restore Fenran to me—''

''But I have. And I will do it gladly.'' Nemesis's voice dropped to a soft, persuasive whisper. ''Think, Indigo—think of Carn Caille, your home. You could return there with Fenran and take your rightful place on the throne, to continue Kalig's line. *Think* of it. To live out your days in peace, free from torment, free from travail, free from the snares of a cruel destiny.'' The demon paused, then added with infinite gentleness, ''Isn't that what you want, in your heart of hearts?''

''No!'' Fenran's voice cut through the hall suddenly and he pulled himself upright, hands pressed down on the table and white with the effort of supporting his body. "Anghara, don't listen! The demon lies—it's trying to trap you!"

Furious, Nemesis turned on him. *"Be silent!"* It made a sharp, sweeping gesture, and Fenran screamed, staggering back from the table as though from a massive physical blow. He fell against the chair, collapsed onto it and sprawled, shuddering.

"Don't touch him!" Indigo yelled. "Don't *dare* to touch him!"

Nemesis pivoted on one heel and stared down at her from the dais. All pretense of amity was suddenly gone from its expression; its eyes were cruel, calculating, baleful.

"That was nothing to the agonies he has already undergone," it said dispassionately. "And his torment has only just begun. Our kind are skilled and subtle in the art of inflicting suffering." It took a step toward her. "I have given you a simple choice. Take what I offer you—or condemn your lover to our mercy!"

"*No*, Anghara!" Fenran's protest was pain-racked but savage. "I won't let you do it!"

Nemesis whirled again to silence him, but Indigo cried desperately, *"Don't!"*

The demon paused, looked at her challengingly. "Well, Indigo?"

She couldn't abandon him. She loved him too much to let him go on suffering. Damn the emissary and its warnings, damn her quest, damn the world—Fenran was all that mattered!

Your salvation or your doom . . .

"Release him," she said harshly. "Release him, and I'll pay your price."

"Anghara, you can't!" White-faced, ravaged, Fenran was on his feet again, though he barely had the strength to stand.

She met his wild gaze, and tears blinded her eyes.

"I can, Fenran—and if it's the only way to save you, I will!"

"*No!* You know what it means—you'll condemn the whole world to hell! *You can't sacrifice the future of the Earth!*"

"I don't *care* about the future! The Earth Mother has asked too much of me!"

"And what of what *I* ask of you?"

Her face froze. "You . . . ?"

"Yes. *I* ask you not to do it, Anghara. Not for your sake alone, but for mine." Fenran wiped sweat from his eyes with an unsteady hand. "If you give way to this monstrosity, you destroy any future we might have—"

"Be silent!" Nemesis turned on him, raising a hand to strike.

"Damn you, I will *not*!" Fenran fired back through clenched teeth. "Anghara, *listen* to me! I don't want to live in a world condemned to ruin!"

Nemesis hissed like a maddened snake. Light flared shockingly through the hall, and Fenran screamed as a bolt of energy struck him and sent him flying backward. He and the chair crashed to the floor of the dais and Nemesis darted forward, face twisted with rage and malice. The demon's hand rose again—

"No!" Indigo shrieked.

Nemesis stopped. For an appalling few seconds the tableau before Indigo's eyes was stilled and rigid, Fenran cowering by the overturned chair, the demon poised to deliver a second bolt of agony. Then, very slowly, Nemesis turned to stare at the shuddering girl, and she recoiled from the sheer malevolence in its silver eyes. The serpent's tongue flickered, and Nemesis hissed with deadly deliberation:

"My patience is exhausted."

Indigo felt as though her mind were breaking apart.

She was human, only human. Prey to human weaknesses, driven by human emotions. She couldn't withstand such a test as this; the strength wasn't in her. She was too fallible. And she loved Fenran too much.

She took a step forward, stumbled on legs that were unwilling to support her, and her voice pleaded.

"Let it be done." She saw but didn't register the light of triumph that flared into life behind the cold, silver mask of the demon's eyes. "I accept your price—let it be done!" And she staggered forward to take Nemesis's outstretched hand.

·CHAPTER·XVII·

The child's fingers reached toward her, the child's face smiled with the cruel joy of victory. Indigo stretched out her arm—and from nowhere a voice erupted in her head, a wordless, howling cry of enraged and desperate denial. A dark form seemed to explode from the gloom behind her, and Grimya leaped between her and the demon, twisting her powerful body in midair to send Indigo crashing to the floor of the hall.

"Grimya!" She had forgotten the she-wolf's existence amid the turmoil of her encounter; now they rolled together in a furious, fighting tangle, Indigo flailing, spitting, screaming curses at the creature who battled to keep her from her goal.

I will not let you do it! Grimya's voice seared through her. *The demon has stolen your reason and made you weak! Indigo, listen to me—*

"No!" She battered the blur of brindled gray before

her with clenched fists. "Leave me *alone*, you have no *right*—"

I have the right! I am your friend!

"Damn your friendship, a thousand curses on you and all your kind!" Indigo shrieked. With all the strength she could muster she flung the wolf away from her, but Grimya sprang up again before she could leap to her feet, barring her path to the watching demon. They both froze, crouching, facing each other in a silence that was suddenly deadly.

Indigo. She could sense the churning emotions underlying the wolf's voice in her mind. *This must not be.*

Indigo's lungs heaved. "Get out of my way!"

I will not. I will stop you, Indigo. I will stop you if I have to kill you.

She sneered, an ugly rictus. "I said, get—"

Grimya snarled. Her hackles were raised and her eyes glittered crimson; suddenly she was no longer a trusted friend but a predator, an attacker. Her hindquarters quivered with suppressed power and her fangs were white ivory in the uneasy light.

Don't test me, Indigo. Don't make me do this.

Something deep within Indigo was crying, crying, but it was too weak and too far away for her to grasp and hold. She bared her own teeth, aware that sanity was slipping from her, took a step forward—

Grimya leaped like a coiled spring suddenly and violently released. Indigo glimpsed the bunched, muscular body, heard the whistle of displaced air, felt the surging slash of fangs clashing together inches from her throat as she went sprawling backward. Her spine hit the marble floor with a crack that jarred her to the marrow, and she found herself lying spread-eagled beneath the growling, slavering she-wolf. Hot breath fanned her face; she stared into Grimya's cavernous jaws . . .

Fight me! Grimya snarled. *If you want your mate, your Fenran, fight me! Or are you like all the other humans—just a weakling who hides behind empty words?*

Indigo felt renewed rage bubbling and roiling up inside her, but this time it was a tidal wave, a tornado, a cataclysm of fury. Her mouth opened to voice a savage stream of fresh curses—and she gave vent to an animal snarl.

Survival. She felt the power in her jaws, the strength in her shoulders; felt the warm density of the fur that covered her quivering body. *Wolf.* She laid her ears flat, felt the floor's cold marble surface beneath her raking claws. *Wolf.* Her lips drew back, exposing canines like white knives in her skull. *Wolf.* Grimya, her sister, her own, crimson-eyed and feral, standing over her as she shed the cloak of humanity. She didn't want to fight Grimya—

And the last of her confusion shattered as she saw the world, the hall, the silver-haired form of Nemesis, through Grimya's eyes, and realized what the she-wolf had done. The demon had snared her in a web of her own emotions. And Grimya had known that there was only one way to tear that web apart and free her from her own weakness. *Wolf*—her mind and her blood sang with the sensations of a new, unshackled awareness—*Wolf*—

The chilling, duetting howl of two denizens of the forest night rose to the shadow-drenched ceiling of the hall. They sprang to their feet as one, and as one turned to the dais, and to the figure of the evil child that now was backing away from them in alarm.

"Indigo!" There was anger in Nemesis's voice, but

it was fast giving way to fear. "Indigo, hear me! Think of Fenran! Think of what we will do—"

Grimya howled again, drowning the demon's cry. As it stumbled backward, Indigo saw it as a foul skeleton of a figure, clothed with writhing maggots, only the silver eyes still burning in its misshapen skull. Corruption, decay, darkness—freed now from the chains of humanity, she saw with the clearer, simpler consciousness of the animal she had become, and she saw how close Nemesis had come to leading her into a deadly betrayal. Fenran had been right . . .

Fenran, my love, forgive me! It was an echo of the human Indigo, and when she turned her crimson gaze to where he crouched, stunned, beside the overturned chair, the sensation seared her soul. But the ties that had almost led them both to damnation were broken, for she was no longer human. And wolf-Indigo lusted for revenge.

"*Nemesis!*" She spoke the word in her mind, and her throat gave voice to a feral snarl. The alarm in the eyes of the maggot-creature on the dais changed suddenly to frustrated fury; as the two wolves dropped low to the ground and began to slink forward, Nemesis opened its mouth—and its jaws gaped wide, wider, stretching impossibly as the demon began to alter its shape. Its body writhed sinuously, its skin took on a nacreous sheen, fangs dripped venom in the cavernous mouth—and a gigantic serpent reared high above their heads, hissing with a sound like thunder.

The wolf that was Indigo yelped and cringed back, but Grimya's voice called out, *Illusion! Illusion!* And suddenly she saw through the disguise, as Grimya had done; saw the reality of the demon-form beneath. Her yelp changed to a howl, and together they sprang, muscles powering them from the floor and straight at the swaying snake. There was a shrieking whistle, a flash of light, and the serpent-form collapsed under the wolves' onslaught, coiling and thrashing and changing as they tore into it. A twisted, silver-eyed face reared before Indigo's vision; she snapped, felt her jaws crush bone, then snarled in fury as her quarry dissolved into a ball of light that streaked between her and Grimya even as they twisted to catch it. The brilliant comet flashed toward the great hearth, and the cold flames of the fire erupted suddenly into a towering column that coalesced into the form of a burning, silver snow-bear, five times the size of Indigo and Grimya. Eyes like embers glared insensately down; the jaws opened to reveal hellfires within the vast mouth, and the appalling phantom began to pace slowly, deliberately, toward them.

An innate and primal lupine terror warred with her own rage for control of Indigo's instincts. Humans and wolves alike feared these great kings of the tundra, and with good reason; one blow from a massive paw could disembowel or break the neck of the most skilled hunter. And this horror was twice the size of any snow-bear ever born.

But it was illusion, illusion. She chanted Grimya's litany over and again in her mind, and as the two wolves circled to flank the monster, her gaze never wavered from the huge, menacingly swinging head. Adrenaline coursed through her, making her quiver with anticipation; the phantom bear opened its mouth, roared—

And Grimya cried: *Now!*

They leaped in unison, and a terrible cacophony of snarling, roaring and yelping dinned through the hall as they attacked Nemesis with all their strength. The demon flailed and struck, but its bear-form was too insubstantial to inflict harm on them; it had relied on intimidation, and the ploy had failed. Indigo reveled in her newfound power as her blood raced with wild sensations: the joy of the hunt, the frenzy of the kill, the savage taste of impending victory; and underlying them all, and driving her on to new heights of ferocity, the human hatred for the demon which had so nearly sealed her doom.

The thing that was Nemesis roared again, and the bear-shape flickered into the form of a dragon that clashed its silver-scaled wings and breathed cold fire. Grimya's teeth sank into a wing-pinion and she dragged the monstrosity off-balance as Indigo sprang for its serpentine neck. She was snarling and shrieking with a bloodlust that turned to thwarted rage when the dragon suddenly became an eagle, arrowing up toward the ceiling. Desperately she bunched her muscles, leaped, and her snapping jaws clamped on the eagle's tail. Bird and wolf crashed to the floor together, and the eagle became a ghastly chimera of a beast, jackal and ape and toad, six-legged, winged, gape-mouthed and hairless. Indigo's human self would have recoiled from the obscene thing in revulsion; wolf-Indigo set off with a yipping snarl in pursuit as the chimera flapped and shambled, squealing, across the hall. As it ran, its body changed again and again, as though Nemesis had lost control of its shape-shifting powers: animals, birds, fish, reptiles, and other things hideously unrecognizable, vied for brief and horrible manifestation in its form.

And then the demon could flee no further. It was cornered, the two wolves advancing menacingly on it—light flared, and suddenly the chimera was gone, and in its place the child with the malevolent silver eyes crouched, arms outspread, against the marble wall.

Loathing fired through Indigo and her entire body began to shake. *"Kill it!"* Her voice was a guttural and vengeful explosion. *"Kill it!"*

Nemesis laughed. "You cannot kill me. We are one and the same."

"Never!"

The silver eyes glittered savagely. "Tear me apart, and I will return to you in another guise! You will never be free of me, Indigo!"

Indigo's control snapped. With a howl of insane rage she launched herself at Nemesis, snarling, tearing, rending, fangs ripping at the writhing child's body, scrabbling claws gouging flesh from bone. All self-control was gone; she didn't hear Grimya calling out to her to stop, and only when a heavy body cannoned into her, and teeth seized the scruff of her neck to pull her away from her victim, did some semblance of reason surface through the chaotic turmoil of raw emotion in her mind.

Indigo, stop! Grimya cried. *The demon has gone!*

She sprawled on the floor of the hall, panting as her vision slowly cleared. And there between her front paws was the shift that had been the demon-child's only garment, a limp, torn rag. Nemesis had vanished.

"No-o!" Frustration and anguish mingled with fury in Indigo's protesting howl, and the howl coalesced into a recognizably human cry. The hall spun about her; she twisted her body around, found her coordination gone, fell back. And a hand—a human hand—clawed at empty air as she screamed:

"Nemesis! *Nemesis!*"

From the hearth, dark and empty now, came the echoing sigh of soft laughter. Convulsively Indigo began to struggle to her feet, but Grimya intervened.

It's no use, the she-wolf said. *The demon has eluded us.*

Indigo couldn't balance; her consciousness was still rocking dizzyingly between the human and the lupine. She fell back, hunched and shivering on the floor, gritting her teeth against the bitter anger and disappointment of defeat.

We tried, Grimya said mournfully. *We did our best, but it wasn't enough. I am sorry.*

"I wish—" Indigo began savagely, then shook her head. "No. It doesn't matter now." She raised her head, pushing sweat-damp hair from her eyes, then stopped, staring in shock as her eyes focused on the far end of the hall.

"Fenran!" The word choked off into a gasp. She had imagined that he, too, would be gone; that Nemesis would have snatched him away. But no: he was on his feet, weakly but determinedly struggling around the table on the dais. What he had seen, whether he had witnessed her transformation, she didn't know; his eyes were wide, feverish, and he seemed to be in the grip of deep shock. But he ws trying to come to her.

"Fenran!" She scrambled upright, fighting disorientation, and began to run toward him.

She was halfway down the length of the hall when the first of the block trees smashed up through the marble floor to block her path. Grotesque, distorted branches, clothed in thorns the length of her arm, clashed and twisted in a hideous parody of sentience, and she swerved aside, yelling in shock and chagrin. A second tree exploded into grisly life beside the first even as she turned to duck around the vicious thorns; another beyond it, another—and horror swamped Indigo as she grasped what was happening.

Frantically she flung herself at the barrier. Thorns tore at her clothes, her skin, tangled in her hair; she beat and pulled at the warped branches, screaming Fenran's name; saw him try to jump from the dais to come to her, saw more of the dreadful trees rear up before and behind him, trapping him in a deadly, tightening circle—

"No! Ah, *no*!" Fenran twisted about as he realized the danger, but he was too late. Black branches uncoiled like snakes to wrap about his arms, his legs; he thrashed, the thorns ripping into him while the ghastly, living thicket rose higher, denser, to engulf him.

Indigo was screaming on a wild, insensate note, her eyes mad as she struggled vainly to smash her way through the barrier to reach him—until suddenly the tangle of branches beneath her flailing hands shivered, warped, lost its solidity. For one frozen and eternal moment an image of Fenran was imprinted on her mind, helpless and immobile among the thorns, his stark white face shockingly contrasted with the trees' black web, his mouth open and distorted in a soundless cry of agony. Then the entire image shuddered before her—and the thicket, and Fenran with it, dissolved into a silent, shimmering mirage and was gone.

Indigo stood rigid in the middle of the empty hall, staring in numb disbelief at the dais, the table, the unoccupied chairs. So near, so close—and he had been snatched from her, dragged back into the hideous astral world of his torment, where she had no hope of following and finding him again. She had almost reached him. But almost was not enough: he was gone, and she had failed him.

Grimya crept to her side, but the moment she felt the she-wolf's gentle touch Indigo jerked violently away, stumbling toward the dais. She climbed up, stood staring at the table, the chairs, and for a crazed moment wanted to kick them over, fling them about, gouge and crack and break them in her blind misery. But there was no point, her saner self argued; no point. What could she gain from venting her bitterness on inanimate objects? It wouldn't bring Fenran back.

Indigo? Grimya had followed her, and her hesitant inquiry was full of pity. She looked up anxiously into her friend's face and saw that Indigo's eyes were tight-shut and she was biting her lower lip against the slow tears that forced themselves out between her lashes and trickled down her cheeks. *Indigo, if I can—*

Indigo cut her off with an ugly sob, and covered her face with both hands. She sank onto the nearest of the chairs and slumped forward, head buried in her clasped arms while her body racked and shuddered with her silent, agonized weeping.

There was nothing, Grimya knew, that she could do to help. Time seemed to stand still in the deserted hall; there was only the stillness and the gloom and the broken, shivering form of her friend crying as though her soul would shatter under the weight of her grief. Grimya lay down at Indigo's feet, chin on her front paws; dismally she wished that she had some skill, some magic, that would bring comfort or hope. But wishing was useless. The storm within Indigo must pass in its own way and its own time.

And eventually a moment came when the shuddering sobs began to subside. Grimya watched, anxious; and at last Indigo raised her head.

Her face was white and ravaged, and the lines of strain etched her skin like acid. But her eyes were filled with the terrible calm of a pain that could and must be borne. Grimya rose. She was reluctant to speak, yet longed to communicate the pity she felt, for what little it might be worth. Tentatively she uttered a soft sound in her throat, and Indigo looked down at her.

"Grimya . . ." One hand touched the top of the wolf's head, stroked a silky ear. "I . . ."

Don't feel you must say what is in your heart, Grimya replied. *I understand. And words are not enough.*

The girl nodded. There *were* no words to express the emotions that moved like a slow, powerful tide within her; what she felt was too close, and cut too deep. She could only grieve, silently, privately, without hope of relief.

We should leave this place, the she-wolf continued gently. *There is nothing more for either of us here.*

"Leave . . ." Indigo looked around the hall, though it was some moments before her mind could take in what she saw. Her gaze lingered on the great hearth with its empty seats, on the high, curtained windows, on the contours of rafters and walls. Familiar; so familiar—but it wasn't truly Carn Caille. And at the far end of the hall, in a corner, lay something that sardonically confirmed the illusion; something that looked like a crumpled gray shawl discarded on the floor . . .

Yes: it was time to go. But not by the way they had come; she didn't want to walk between the tall windows and past the great hearth and among the ranks of the ghosts held in her own memory. She turned. At their backs was the small door, the replica of the private royal entrance to the great hall at Carn Caille. What lay behind it in this unhuman realm she didn't know. But whatever it might conceal, she must face it. Her path lay onward, not back.

Grimya stayed close beside her as she walked to the low door and laid her hand on it. Even the latch was marble, though it worked well enough. She began to lift it, then looked back over her shoulder one last time. To Grimya, it seemed that she was looking beyond the physical dimensions of the hall, perhaps even beyond this world, seeing something—or someone—invisible to other eyes but her own.

"Goodbye, love." She spoke so quietly that the words were barely audible. "I'll find you again, no matter what I must do. As the Earth Mother is my witness, I'll find you." And she turned her back on the empty hall, and opened the door.

Soft flakes of whiteness met their eyes, falling quietly and steadily against a backdrop of velvet dark. Indigo felt the icy, tingling breath of moist air on her cheeks, tasted the bittersweet cold of deep night, saw the gleam of interlacing branches, leafless and dimly phosphorescent, ahead. And in the distance, among the trees, someone was waiting.

Grimya said, her voice an odd blend of uncertainty and awe: *Who is . . . ?* But Indigo knew, and was already moving forward, stepping through the door and into the night-black land beyond. She felt her feet sink into the snow's white softness, felt the prickling of the cold flakes as they brushed her skin, her hair, her hands; heard the deep, deep silence of the winter like a faraway singing in her ears.

The figure did not come to meet her, but waited where the latticework of young trees began. Its cloak now was of fur, tawny-pale as the coat of a great mountain cat. But the rich brown hair was unchanged, and the golden eyes, and the sad, enigmatic smile.

"Indigo, my child," the Earth Mother's emissary said gently. "I have been waiting for your return."

·CHAPTER·XVIII·

For a silent, enduring moment Indigo stared numbly at the bright being's serene and beautiful face. And slowly, so slowly that it was like awakening from a long fever, understanding dawned in her mind. The trees, this land, the scent and touch of the quietly falling snow—they had stepped back through the gate of the demon world and had returned to the realm of Earth.

She felt something warm press against her leg and knew that Grimya had stepped forward to join her. She was shivering, but not with cold; Indigo reached down to lay a hand on her head, wanting to reassure her but unable to find words that were adequate.

"Grimya." The milky golden eyes gazed down on the she-wolf and were suddenly filled with warmth and kindness. "There is nothing for you to fear."

Grimya's shivering stopped and she uttered a faint whimper. "I . . ." The guttural, painful voice broke from her throat as, still confused and overawed, she strained to speak. "Please, I . . ."

"Be calm, little sister." The emissary held out a hand, and slowly, compelled by something beyond her control, Grimya went forward. The hand stroked her head, and a long shudder ran through the wolf's body.

"You have found a true and loyal friend, Indigo," the emissary said.

Soberly, Indigo nodded. "Were it not for Grimya, I would have fallen to Nemesis's influence," she said. "She—"

"I know what she did." There was kindness for her, too, in the being's smile, and Indigo's heart quickened. "And I know that it takes courage to admit to your own near failure."

"Near?" Indigo hunched her shoulders, her voice suddenly sharp. "No. The truth is, I *did* fail. I betrayed your trust—the Earth Mother's trust." She looked up, her eyes challenging the emissary to deny it. "In that mockery of Carn Caille I would have killed Grimya, if I could, to win Fenran back. Only when she goaded me into seeing through a wolf's eyes did I have the strength to fight my demon. I was tested, and I failed."

"You tested yourself, Indigo. And ultimately, you triumphed. Your presence here is proof enough, is it not?"

Indigo didn't reply, but looked about her. At her back, shining faintly in the diffused light from the sky far above, was the rock face with its natural cleft where Nemesis had masqueraded as the grove-sprite. The tiny waterfall was frozen now into a motionless cascade of icicles, the pool below a black mirror of ice: she remembered how she had been tricked, how the demonic gateway had opened to drag her into the world of the black sun. She remembered the chasm, the illusions, Nemesis's mockery. And Fenran. Above all, Fenran.

"The price of success was high," the emissary said gently, knowing her thoughts. "But perhaps you can find solace in the thought that you have lessened your love's torment a little."

"Lessened . . . ?"

The being nodded. "With every defeat they suffer, the demons' power is fractionally weakened. You have granted Fenran some small surcease, at least."

Indigo frowned, struggling to come to terms with the thought. Some small surcease? It was nothing to what she could have brought him. But she knew in her heart—though it was chill comfort—that to buy Fenran's freedom as she had so nearly done would have been the most bitter victory of all.

She looked again at the frozen pool, and said: "I came here to seek a kind of wisdom. It seems I found only the depths of my own folly."

"No," said the emissary. "I think not." And when she returned its gaze, uncomprehending, it added: "The knowledge which you sought to find in this grove was already within you. Think back on the trial you underwent in that world, think on what you did; then look into your own mind. What do you see?"

For an instant she was back in that semblance of Carn Caille, steeped again in sensations of the alien, animal consciousness that had given her the strength to turn against her demon. And as the memory coalesced, she felt the singing surge rise anew in her blood, in her bones, felt the change beginning within her—

Wolf—

Alarmed, she tried to take a grip on herself—and to her astonishment felt the sensations bow to her mind's control. They slid from her, faded away, and she stared, shocked, at the emissary. The bright being smiled.

"The power is yours to command, Indigo."

"Grimya—" Still not quite able to believe, to assimilate, Indigo turned to her friend.

It is true, Grimya said, and Indigo could hear her silent, psychic voice as clearly as if the she-wolf had spoken aloud. *You have awoken. I can see it, in your mind.*

The emissary smiled down at the wolf. "Grimya is wiser than she knows." Then its eyes met Indigo's again. "You have earned the reward of your newfound skills, child. And in consequence, the Earth Mother bids me grant you another boon that may aid you in the times ahead." It held out a graceful hand. "Come; follow me." And it turned and moved away through the trees.

Grimya stayed close by Indigo's side as the bright being led them among the crowding branches. Their breath misted and mingled on the frosty air; snow flurried down to obscure the two sets of footprints behind them. Grimya gazed around, her eyes wide and wondering, and Indigo read the uneasy thoughts half formed in the she-wolf's mind. *Winter.* When they entered the demon-world, spring had been burgeoning; now the year had advanced through the ripeness of summer into hoar-month or beyond. She remembered the emissary telling her, at their first meeting, that the currents of time flowed on strange and different courses in the worlds beyond the Earth; and gently, silently, she tried to convey to Grimya that there was no need for doubt or alarm.

They reached a place where the trees thinned a little, and the bright being stopped. Gazing about her, Indigo believed that this was the very spot from which she had walked out alone to seek the magic of the grove; though the onset of winter had changed it almost beyond recognition, she felt an echo of familiarity.

The emissary waited until they all stood together, then gestured toward the ground. And there, lying unsullied and undamaged on the carpet of snow, were Indigo's harp, bow and knife. The girl's eyes widened.

"They were kept safe for you," the emissary said. "That much I could do."

She dropped to her knees, heedless of the wet snow, and gathered the precious belongings into her arms as she stammered out heartfelt thanks. Then she paused, and stood up.

"How long has it been?" The question was hesitant; and suddenly she regretted asking it, lest the answer might not be bearable.

"The seasons have turned full circle once, and moved on again to winter."

A year and a half . . . Indigo thought of the Southern Isles and felt a dull stab of pain. She had lived through no more than a few days since leaving her homeland; yet within the walls of Carn Caille they had celebrated two springs, two harvests, two winter feasts. She thought of old friends, and wondered how many more of those she had known were now gone forever.

"There is peace in your land," the emissary told her gently. "And many who still think fondly in their prayers of the house of Kalig."

Indigo blinked away tears that were freezing on her lashes. "One day," she whispered, "I will return." She looked at the emissary, and there was a faint, defiant edge to her voice. "I *will*."

The being stepped toward her and laid its hands on her shoulders, looking deep into her eyes. "The Earth Mother shares your hope," it said gravely. "Whatever lies ahead of you, never forget that."

"No. I . . . I won't forget it."

The emissary withdrew its hands. "And now the time has come for us to go our separate ways. But before we part, I have gifts for both of you. Indigo—this boon is yours by right of earning, to aid you on your journey." It extended one hand toward her, and Indigo saw, lying in its palm, a small brown pebble veined with patterns of green and gold, Hesitantly she reached out and took the gift; it felt strangely warm, and as she looked more closely she glimpsed a pin-point of golden light that seemed to move within the stone like a tiny, captive firefly.

"This is your lodestone, Indigo," the bright being said. "It will guide you faithfully in your search for the evils you are pledged to destroy. You need only to hold the stone in your palm, and the light within it will show you the road you should take. It will never fail you."

Indigo's fingers closed over the pebble; it seemed to pulse in her hand, as though a tiny heart beat in its depths, and the sensation was reassuring in a way she couldn't define. She looked up. "Thank you," she said softly.

"It is given gladly. And now, Grimya." The being leaned down to stroke the she-wolf, who had watched the exchange with a faintly wistful look in her eyes. "Little sister, you have a warm and loyal heart worthy of your kind. Yet you are afflicted, and your affliction has made you an outcast. Would you be free of that stigma, Grimya? Free to join your own, to live among kindred and friends in the forest and no longer be lonely?"

Grimya looked up at the serene face, and her muzzle quivered. "To be . . . not *different*?"

"Yes. To be a true wolf like other wolves. That is the gift I offer you."

Grimya hesitated, and her eyes met Indigo's. Their expression was strange, unreadable. Then she said: "N-*no*!"

"Grimya—" Indigo began, but Grimya interrupted before she could say any more.

"I—have n-never been a wolf like other wolves. I don't . . . think I could learn to be one now. And I . . . I do not want to leave my friend!"

Indigo turned away in sudden distress as she realized that, from the moment the emissary had spoken, she had known what Grimya would say. And she was torn in two by the knowledge that to part from the she-wolf, with whom she had shared so much tribulation, would be a wrench very hard to bear; yet that for Grimya's own sake she could not, *must* not, let it be otherwise.

She said, her voice unsteady: "Grimya, you must try to understand. We *have* to go our separate ways: for you to stay with me would be wrong."

"No," Grimya reiterated stubbornly. "I am your fr-*iend*."

Desperate because Grimya's feeling so closely mirrored her own, Indigo turned in appeal to the emissary. "Please, make her understand! I couldn't ask such a thing of her; it wouldn't be fair to her. She has done nothing to deserve my burden—I won't let her share it!"

"The choice is hers to make," the emissary said gently.

"But she doesn't know what she'll be facing!"

"She does."

Indigo shook her head in denial. "What manner of life can she look forward to if she journeys with me? When she grows old and enfeebled whilst I am still bound to travel on—what will become of her then?"

Grimya said: "I—do not care!"

"Wait." The bright being held up a hand and looked at the she-wolf. "If Grimya does not want the gift I have already offered, then I am empowered to grant another. Grimya, is it truly your desire to journey on with Indigo, and help her in her quest?"

"Yes!" Grimya panted.

"Whatever the dangers you might encounter?"

"Danger does not matter."

The emissary continued to gaze at her for a few moments. Then it nodded and said: "Yes. I see you speak the truth, little sister." It turned to the girl. "Indigo, it is Grimya's will to go with you, and so you are free to accept or reject her companionship according only to the dictates of your own desires. If you accept, I may grant her that same immortality that you have gained, if she wishes it—though she must understand, as you do, that such a gift can be as much a curse as a blessing." The being paused. "*Do* you understand that, Grimya?"

"I do. And I . . . accept it gladly."

"So be it." The emissary's face was grave. "Well, Indigo? What will your choice be?"

Indigo looked at Grimya. The she-wolf's eyes were shining with excitement tempered by apprehension, and suddenly the girl knew that she could no longer pretend to feelings that were untrue to her inner self. Whatever the future might hold, a true friend and companion was more to be treasured than any gold. And loneliness was the darkest privation of all. . . .

She said, a catch in her voice: "Is it truly what you want, Grimya?"

Grimya's tongue lolled. "You—know it is."

"Then . . . yes." She couldn't say more; the words wouldn't come. "Yes . . ."

Slowly, as though she still couldn't quite muster the courage to give way to her pleasure, Grimya's tail began to wag. The emissary smiled down at her.

"Good fortune attend you, little sister." The golden gaze lifted to settle on Indigo. "And to you, my child;

good fortune. We shall be watching you, and we will aid you when we can."

She raised a hand, wanting to speak, to touch, to make some gesture that would express, however inadequately, what she felt. But as she reached out, a golden aura appeared around the being's tall figure. The air shimmered—and the emissary was gone.

For a long time Indigo stood motionless, aware only of the steadily falling snow, the quiet creak of branches in the night air. Then, treading delicately through the deep white carpet, Grimya approached and laid her head against the girl's clasped hands. They looked at each other, violet eyes and golden brown sharing an unspoken understanding. Then Grimya gave a small, eager wriggle, turned and trotted to the edge of the clearing. Muzzle twitching, she sniffed at the air, then looked back over her shoulder.

I have always liked the snow, she said.

A slight, involuntary smile came to Indigo's lips.

The hunting will be good, Grimya added, and her tail beat against a sapling tree, dislodging a shower of snow from the branches onto her back. She shook herself. *We shall eat well tomorrow!*

Touched by her friend's innocent enthusiasm, Indigo laughed. It was no more than a chuckle, but it went a small way toward easing the constricting knot inside her. She looked at the lodestone, still lying in her palm and pulsing warmly, steadily. The tiny light glimmered back at her in the dark, hovering at one edge of the pebble. North. Away from the Horselands, on into the strange and unknown lands of the great western continent. And despite her sadness, a sensation that might have been distant kin to Grimya's excitement stirred within Indigo.

With a care that verged on reverence, she slipped the precious lodestone into her belt-pouch. Then she gathered up her harp in its bag, slung it together with her crossbow over one shoulder and thrust her knife into its sheath at her waist. She didn't look back toward the silent grove; as Grimya set off eagerly into the forest, Indigo hesitated only a moment before moving off in the she-wolf's wake, leaving the clearing to stillness and the softly drifting snow.

·CARN CAILLE·

When the physician came soon after dawn with the news that the old bard had died as the sun's first rays touched the morning sky, King Ryen of the Southern Isles nodded quietly, and said that he wished to be alone for an hour before Cushmagar's successor was brought to him.

After the physician had left, Ryen walked slowly and thoughtfully down the corridor to the small hall in the southern wing of Carn Caille, in which his less formal audiences and meetings were conducted. This was his favorite room—as, he understood, it had been his predecessor's—and when he arrived, he sat down on a seat by one of the windows, from where he could gaze out at the bright winter day.

Cushmagar gone. It was hard to believe; the bard had seemed to him as much a part of Carn Caille as the very stones of its foundations. Impossible to think that his rich voice and magnificent music would never grace another feast. And sad to realize that the birth-song for Ryen's son or daughter, the eagerly awaited heir to his kingdom, must now be composed and sung by another.

Ryen sighed, and rose to his feet to pace across the sunlit room. He shouldn't feel such sadness; it was selfish of him to dwell on his loss rather than rejoice for Cushmagar's gain. The bard had been old and blind, and since last winter barely able to walk. He knew his tenure had been overlong, and had gone to the Earth Mother gladly and with relief that his duties were finally at an end. And though Imyssa might think otherwise, there were no untoward omens in the fact that Cushmagar's passing had fallen almost to the day on the second anniversary of Ryen's own elevation to the throne of the Southern Isles.

He smiled when he thought of Imyssa. She would be with Sheana now, as she had been for two days since her scrying had told her that the queen's child was almost due to be born. Ryen hoped—as did they all—that the new heir's arrival would finally heal Imyssa's enduring grief for the old royal family. Had Kalig had a brother or sister, even a cousin, to take the throne after his untimely death, the old nurse might have taken comfort from the thought that his beloved line was not entirely gone; as it was, she had found it hard to accept the presence of an elected outsider in his place. But, slowly, she was coming round. And when the child was born, she would nurse it as she had nursed Kalig's own children; perhaps then she would find her old contentment once more.

And perhaps she would at last lay aside her unfounded and eerie conviction that, somewhere, one of her lost ones lived on. . . .

Noises in the courtyard broke in on Ryen's reverie, and he shook his head to clear it, realizing that he had been lapsing into unhealthy morbidity. Returning to the window, he looked down and saw that a party of young men on horseback was setting out from the fortress. No dogs accompanied them, and they carried few weapons; the king smiled and relaxed as he realized that they simply planned to exercise their horses, and were not going hunting without inviting him. The favorite ride at this time of year, when the hills and forests were all but impassable, was the tundra to the south of Carn Caille, where it was still possible to venture for a mile or more before the snow and ice forced even the most surefooted horse to turn back. And some of the younger nobles would doubtless want to see for themselves—at least from a distance—the remains of the strange, ruined tower out on the tundra plain. Ryen had never caught more than a glimpse of the place; as yet, he had had no time for much in the way of leisure: but when the spring spate was over he planned to join one of the expedition parties, to assuage his curiosity. Nobody knew the tower's purpose, if it had one; some of the older folk, Imyssa included, muttered that it was an evil place and best shunned, but beyond that its presence was a mystery. There had been some talk of a story concerning the tower that Cushmagar had been wont to tell in the old days, but the bard had never mentioned it, and Ryen doubted that the tale existed, or if it did, that Cushmagar would have remembered it.

The noisy riding party had disappeared through the great gates of the fortress, and the courtyard was quiet again. Ryen rubbed his hands together, realizing that he was cold. He must order a fire lit in here; a poor liege he'd be if he greeted his new bard—who was, after all, one of the most influential and highly respected members of his court—in a room that felt as though a glacier had marched through it. A fire, and mead, and cakes. It was no less than Cushmagar would have wanted for his successor.

He turned toward the door, intending to go in search of his steward, then paused and looked back at the stone fireplace and the painting which hung above the mantel. Kalig and his family gazed back at him, motionless yet uncannily lifelike in their frame with its indigo draping. He wished he had known them: Kalig and Imogen, Prince Kirra and Princess Anghara. To die so suddenly, leaving only a memory and a portrait . . . it seemed wrong; unjust.

Ryen shivered suddenly and involuntarily; as though, to coin a sailor's expression, the sea had washed over his grave. He should order the mourning drapery taken down once his child was born; it would be more fitting with new life in Carn Caille, and one could not mourn forever. A further tragedy that Breym, the artist responsible for this likeness, had been among the fever's many victims. A similar portrait of his own family would have graced this hall well.

He looked away from the painting at last and walked slowly out of the hall. As the door closed behind him a breath of chill air stirred the drapery around the portrait, and the east wind, sighing through a loose pane in one of the windows, briefly mimicked the distant sound of a girl's bright laughter.